ROBIN'S EGGS

by David M. Hanner

ROBIN'S EGGS

by David M. Hanner

Published By
Positive Imaging, LLC
bill@positive-imaging.com
http://positive-imaging.com

ISBN 9781944071837

Contents

1

Encounter With Leslie

"Will not work for love or money, but gladly accepting beer and cigarettes (Honk If You Think Love Stinks!!)" proclaimed the cardboard sign. The bearded man in a mini-skirt stood proudly and defiantly at the corner of the clogged intersection. Perched on the curb's edge, he stared over the captive cars like a singer on a stage, gazing past his audience to a lover long gone and far, far away.

Edie was hopelessly lost and running late, not a good combination for her first day on the job. "Excuse me, sir," she called out to the bum, cracking the window just a little, "would you happen to know where Pemberton Avenue is?"

"Lady, what the hell are you doing on the drag, why didn't you take Lamar?" he asked in a surprisingly polished baritone voice, lending a dramatic contrast to the unexpected attire.

"Well then, which way to Lamar?" Edie asked, as the light turned green. "I'm new to town and I was informed the university was close to the Pemberton area," she lamely added, trying to ignore the blaring horns of the cars trapped behind her. But rather than point out the stupidity of not having specific directions to a place she'd never been to before, the stringy-haired hobo pointed to the 7-11's parking lot.

"Pull over there, for all is not lost, I shall correct thy course." Edie felt more than a little apprehensive, considering his unusual sense of style. But there were people and students everywhere on Guadalupe, the main drag running through the University of Texas; it wasn't like it was mid-night in a deserted alley in Liverpool. She quickly estimated the odds and decided the possible decapitation and subsequent dismemberment from a deranged street person fell within acceptable bounds, at least on this particular day, and therefore was a risk worth taking.

"I could always go to the pay phone and just call," she consoled herself, if the street person started behaving erratically, and then silently castigated herself for automatically categorizing him as a mental case. She of all people, and especially when one considered that her entire family was in the medical profession. "A state of homelessness shouldn't be used as a leading indicator of mental health," her father used to say. Edie turned into the parking lot and cautiously rolled down her window, but still not all the way, as he shuffled up to the car.

"What's the address?" He said and with the efficiency of a "traffic bobby" from back home in England began giving directions; concise, detailed instructions that just might allow her to make her appointment on time .

"Wait, let me write that last bit down, about which turn I take after Shoal Creek," Edie said, fumbling in her purse for a pen. She dug out an old bic lighter (God, she'd stopped smoking three months ago, when was the last time she cleaned out her purse?), then a ball point emerged. The bum patiently repeated the directions exactly as he had before, promising that Pemberton Avenue was only a few minutes away.

"Thank you so much, you've saved me from certain disaster," Edie said, relieved her savior wasn't as strange as he (or she) first appeared.

"Hey, give me a dollar" he said, holding out a gloved and sequined-adorned hand. She dug through her purse.

"I'm sorry, I don't have a one" she said, genuinely sorry.

"Spare change?" he asked and Edie looked in her wallets change pouch.

"I'm terribly sorry, all I have is a twenty, and I need that for lunch" she said.

"Well hell, at least give me a cigarette" the cross-dressing hippy said, spying the lighter still clutched in her hand.

"Oh, I really do apologize. I stopped smoking a couple of months ago." Edie shrugged her shoulders meekly, "I am truly very, very sorry."

"No need to apologize" he said magnanimously, pushing up his sagging halter-top, "I do stupid shit like that all the time."

Edie turned around and eased back up to the drag, waiting for a clear spot for her to reenter the flow of traffic. The panhandler in purple walked past on his way back to his corner. "Thanks again," she said, and then couldn't help herself. "You seem so intelligent and poised to…" She trailed off, now not sure there was a polite way to put it.

"UT School of Business, 1994" he-she proudly stated, "but in answer to your question, "What's a smart guy like me doing out here in a dress, flying a sign and hitting people up for spare change?" Let me say in my defense that the current school of thought in the advertising industry, my major, has wholeheartedly rejected my core thesis and deemed my sophisticated marketing techniques unpalatable in today's paradigm." "And that means?" Edie asked, not exactly following. He held up his ragged piece of cardboard, cut out of an Old Milwaukee 12-pack box, pointing to the Love Stinks portion.

"They kept saying truth in advertising just doesn't sell."

"Well, maybe they all just thought that it's more of a commitment than some people realize," Edie said, shifting into first, "I think that love can be like a fairy tale, but still you have to work at it–I mean, even fairy's magic has a price you must pay."

"Wow," the transsexual looked at her appreciatively. "I think that's gotta be one of the most romantic things I've ever heard. But that gig bit the dust a long time ago, I'm not gonna look back. Besides, people depend on me now, this is where I'm supposed to be."

"What do you mean, like, for directions?" Edie asked.

"Hell no!" he exclaimed. "Right now I'm out here enlightening this sullen mass of humanity and for what–to score a few bucks off the temporary alleviation of their misery?" He spat derisively in the general direction of his trapped audience.

"These same people, in the same cars, they go by me everyday–they're the real victims. There's your street people, they're the one's that are truly screwed. Here they are, on their way to their soul-crushing cubicles, and sometimes it's like when they go by me they see through the Matrix or something, like I'm representing, y'know?" He paused to raise his sign at a honking cab. "Yeah, that's what I'm talking about, brother, you feel me?" he yelled and pointed at the cabdriver. "Do ya feel me, buddy?"

"Word up, Leslie, I'm with you all the way, brother!" the driver shouted back, "Fuck love! I'm done, dude, I ain't gonna get suckered anymore, no way!"

"Yeah, at least not until quitting time, huh?" Leslie hollered back, "Then it's any port in a storm and it's a storm every night, right?" The cabbie honked in reply, rejoining the downtrodden stream of cubicle-crushed fools. The transient readjusted his mini-skirt and returned to his lost lamb.

"So it's as if I've been typecast, kind of like I've been sent here for a reason, just put out here to push this truth angle. I guess some higher power decided that all of these losers needed a minor prophet, y'know; a little personal Jesus to get them through another pointless day." Leslie stooped to pick up a crushed cigarette butt, and after a brief inspection, tucked it into a little red handbag. "And besides, what you're talking about wasn't what I was referring to anyway."

"What was your point, then?" Edie asked, a little perplexed by the modern day sage.

"All I'm saying is love stinks, lady," replied the mini-skirted messiah, "You don't believe me, just take a good whiff sometime. Then come back and tell me what you think.

Edie pulled out into the traffic, taking extra precaution as she drove towards 22nd Street, still adjusting to the Mini-Cooper her friend Amy had leased for her the week before she arrived.

"I thought having an English car might make it easier on you as you get a feel for the city" Amy had said.

"Does the leasing company have one with the steering wheel on the right side?" Edie had asked.

"What do you mean, it is on the righ–oh, I guess it's not right–or correct either, at least not from your neck of the woods, is it?" Edie had simply nodded in reply. There were times it just didn't pay to take the chance of more possible linguistic confusion from the sometimes dingy Texan. She suddenly slammed on the little red-with-white-racing stripes car's brakes as a large SUV cut right in front of her, turning into a Taco Bell.

"Asshole!" she thought, but didn't yell it out as her father would have done, not with her being a guest and all in this beautiful Texas town. Edie opted for "Hey, they're called turn signals! Try using them sometime!"

"Does anyone in Texas ever use their turn signals?" she'd inquired to her former nursing school roommate from England yesterday.

"I know everyone uses their hazard lights in a funeral procession." Amy replied, not helping but convinced she had.

2

The Interview

Actually, the fact that she was from England was what had gotten Edie the interview. The temporary medical staffing service had called and left a message the very same day she'd submitted her resume, asking that "the nurse from Oxford to please give them a call for immediate placement." They'd offered no further explanation when she'd called back, just giving her an address and a 9:00 clock appointment for the next day.

Edie turned right at 22nd and drove away from the university towards Lamar. The buildings west of campus, a mixture of frat houses and apartments, eventually gave way to older, well-built homes, many in the craftsmen style, with large porches and stone or brick based tapered columns. Crossing Lamar, Edie checked the time on the cars stereo, which was playing an old Ice Cube rap song. "Yeah…today was a good day, didn't even have to use my AK." Good, it wasn't as late as she'd thought; she was going to make it on time after all, maybe even a few minutes early. Edie started to sing along. It was a beautiful spring morning in Austin, Texas, "a better Berkeley" a writer had once called this old hippy college town turned major hi-tech research and development hub. She felt an uplifting wave of excitement as she began another chapter in her life, as if she was on the verge of a great adventure, her senses tingling in anticipation of wondrous things to come.

The Pemberton Heights neighborhood was old Austin-home to doctors, attorneys, and a smattering of state legislators, (Austin was the state capitol of Texas). It fluctuated between large mansions with manicured lawns and the occasional gated estate, many of which were hidden from view by ancient live oaks and ivy-covered stone walls. Edie took note of the passing house numbers. She passed 2205, 2207 and then pulled over to the curb. She was going to 2215, but took a quick minute to compose herself and check her makeup. Her nephew used to laugh at this ritual, one she habitually performed before meeting someone new.

"I just like to make a good first impression" she'd insisted-but Robin always referred to it as "Better look out, Aunt Edie's putting on her game face!", like when they'd had those insufferable meetings with all the attorneys probating her brother and sister-in-law's wills.

She smiled wistfully, remembering him meeting her at the airport in Zaire City, almost two years to the day. He had been so brave even in spite of the terrible tragedy he had just suffered. How could a thirteen-year old boy deal with the death of both parents and just calmly stand there, so alone and yet seemingly unafraid? Somehow he'd mustered enough inner courage to meet her at the airport, barking in Swahili at the porters, whisking her through customs without the usual extortion exacted by the local corrupt officials. She wondered, did his being a child prodigy help him assimilate and process grief easier than others? Or did it just mask the pain more believably?

Edie tore herself from her musings with a shudder, and then double-checked the time on the radio. 8:55, a perfect five minutes early, thanks to the help of the urbane hippy. "I should've taken the time to break the twenty" she thought, and made a little promise to herself that if she ever saw him again, that's what she'd do. One quick brush of hand at a stray wisp of reddish-gold curl, and Edie put the "Mini" in gear, pulling on down past flowering mountain laurels and blooming red oaks to the large estate at 2215.

Edie pressed the intercom button's keypad on the left side of the wide entrance. She hoped the uneasy sensation of everything being backwards in all things automotive would soon dissipate. The system was set in a small limestone post that matched the ornate stone columns supporting the tall wrought-iron security gates.

Edie leaned out the car's window, craning her neck for a closer look at her destination. A professionally maintained lawn of St. Augistine was flanked by hedges and native perennials that in turn trimmed the black asphalt drive winding back to the estate. It was an old, three-story square box-like structure that struck a familiar chord–where had she seen this style before? It suddenly came into focus as Edie remembered a ski trip to Germany years ago. It was a design referred to as German "smear-stone", a stone veneer that had white stucco broomed over the rough-faced blocks of limestone, giving an undulating, softened texture to the massive abode. She remembered Amy saying that Texas had experienced a large influx of German immigration back in the 1800's, with many traces still remaining out in the hill country, just west of the Colorado River that cut through the center of downtown Austin. It was a sturdy and warm look, not frilly or highly stylized, with large green shutters and gabled porch eaves supported by huge, white Doric columns. Edie relaxed a bit, its studied unpretentiousness calming her slightly jumpy nerves.

"Dr. Hollings residence, may I help you?" crackled the intercom, startling her so suddenly that she smacked her head into the top of the Mini's doorjamb.

"Ow! Damn it!" she exclaimed, then, "Oops, sorry about that, I'm the nurse from Girlings Healthcare, I'm sorry, it's just that I bumped my head on the door of this car, I'm still getting used to it, it's new and…"

"Yes, yes, Miss Langston, 9:00 o'clock, it's quite alright. I'll buzz you in. As you come up the drive you'll see the carriage house on the left. Park by the black Tahoe parked off to the side and I'll meet you there," The woman's voice thankfully had cut Edie off, saving her from further embarrassment. The gates were already swinging open. She drove up the drive slowly, taking in the scattered bunches of native plants tastefully sprinkled in flowerbeds among the perfect lawn. Lantanas and salvias were a recurring theme, with muhley grass and turkscap tucked back in the shade of the huge live oaks, whose thick lower branches gracefully dipped to within inches of the ground, gracing the landscape with an aura of a time gone by.

Edie parked by a stone path that started at the edge of the separated garage and curved up to a side porch of the house. The small mounds of decomposed granite beds of vinca and bachelor buttons were interspersed with purple plumbago and a variety of succulents, creating a unique xeriscaped effect that was neither lush nor harsh. A middle-aged woman wearing a nurse's smock with a stethoscope hanging out of a side pocket was coming down the walk.

"Oh, what a cute little car!" the plump, matronly nurse exclaimed. "You must be Edie. Hi, I'm Sarah Hardee, Dr. Hollings head nurse." She motioned to the house. "Let's go in and get comfortable. We'll get a little information about you and see if you're up for something a little different than the usual run-of-the-mill assignment."

Edie followed the short, pleasant woman down the smooth stone path past more gardens of flowering yucca, yellowbells, and spineless cactus that bordered the walk on each side, enclosed in low, rustic boulders. "What a perfect place for lunch break" she thought, passing underneath a trellis of honeysuckle and jasmine. She could see a large patio in back of the estate, garnished with roses that were arranged in formal English garden style. It was an incredibly idyllic spot, and Edie indulged herself in a small fantasy of lolling in a hammock with a short romance novel and a long glass of iced tea. She made a vow to be extra polite and eager, if for no other reason than to have the opportunity to familiarize herself with these gardens and their spectacular varieties of Southwestern plants, so different from merry old England.

There was a handicap ramp leading up to the small patio with what appeared to be a wider than average door, at least for a side entrance. Sarah pushed a button on the side jamb and the automatic, commercial-sized door swung out to reveal an office or den area. Bookcases filled one complete wall and half of another, with framed photos and what looked to be degrees from several dozen universities on the wall above the half, more diplomas than any one person could accumulate in two lifetimes, it seemed. There was a mahogany desk that had been lowered off to one side of the den, but with no chair behind it. She was surprised to see what looked to be a small broadcasting studio, complete with spotlights and video equipment in one corner, a boom microphone hovering overhead. Other than that the room was open, the only exception to the spacious floor plan being a couple of comfortable-looking leather chairs.

"Come on out here- this is my office and reception area" Sarah said. "Or rather ours, if everything works out to everyone's satisfaction," she added quickly with a smile. They were now in the next room, which in earlier times must have been the formal sitting room or parlor.

The "parlor" was just off the front entry, separated by open French doors. Looking through the opened doors Edie saw the main stairs, with an antique chandelier bathing the hardwood steps with soft, sparkling light. Past that she could see another set of matching doors that opened into the formal dining room filled with antique furniture that seemed to have remained in the original era of the homes construction.

Her (or their) office area, on the other hand, was not only firmly entrenched in the twenty-first century; it also could have passed for a state of the art emergency room. In front was an office desk that looked through large bay windows out onto the exquisite front lawn, while the back three-quarters of the parlor looked like a showcase of every device and accessory that a modern medical ward could desire. Behind that was a large open closet full of supplies and a locked drug cabinet. It was by far the most impressive setup Edie had ever seen outside of a hospital surgery unit.

"I always get a kick out of a fellow nurse's reaction to all this" Sarah said, laughing, "I need to start getting photos of that "deer in headlights look" and give'em to y'all for Christmas presents." Her southern drawl snapped Edie back to the real world.

"Oh, my" she exclaimed, "did you call for a nurse or a neurosurgeon?"

Sarah walked over and shut the French doors and pointed Edie to a chair. Giving her a hokey conspiratorial grin, Sarah glanced through the doorway that led to the almost as strange office and sat down at the receptionist desk.

"No, we already have a doctor, and these are his toys, not mine" she said, "Let me explain this unique position to you. It may be your dream job or it may not." Edie nodded, sensing that Sarah was expecting her to listen attentively and not talk. Sarah started speaking quickly and with practiced poise.

"I'm going to assume that you've never heard of Dr. Stephan Hollings or his work, but in the world of theoretical physics he's a demi-god, quite literally of rock star status. As such he's much in demand as a public speaker, and he's often called upon to be the final authority on the newest findings of other scientists. Every research scientist, observatory, or institution of higher learning would kill for his blessing on their publications, theories, or respective projects. He's just released his 4th book on the workings of the universe and gets 300 or so letters and e-mails a day." Sarah took a breath.

"Stephan also has Lou Gehrig's disease, and it has progressed to the extent that he is confined to a wheelchair. Our staff is committed to keep what one former president referred to as a "national treasure" alive and in as excellent health as humanly possible." She raised her eyebrows. "It requires one to at times appear in public, there's occasional international travel and of course the rather mundane task of checking blood pressure, keeping charts, and administering medication. Last and not least, is to deal with Dr. Steck, Stephan's childhood friend, personal physician and business manager. This can be challenging at times, but since you're an RN I would hazard you've had sufficient exposure to arrogance and mind-games. But if that part of the medical profession, remaining professional when you get treated by a superior in less than ideal courtesy, just happens to be one of your weak spots, speak up now or forever hold your peace."

"Now" Sarah held Edie with piercing green eyes, not waiting for Edie to reply, "It's very important for you to be honest with me, and to yourself as well. This job requires a little showmanship, lots of important people around, us humble nurses have to check our egos at the door- all in the name of science, of course," she ended on a lighter note. "So tell me, Miss Langston, a little about yourself and why you'd be interested, or better yet, why Dr. Hollings would benefit from your talents and abilities in this demanding yet rewarding position."

Edie took a minute to take in the unusual surroundings, letting all that Sarah had said sink in.

"Well, first of all, I may not be your ideal candidate" she began, "but boorish doctors are quite common in England, and also in Germany and Sweden as well. I would be rather surprised if it were any different here, I suppose. The travel sounds quite exciting and I've done enough to not be ignorant of its rigors. But as far as the show business part you referred to, I'm afraid I'm neither an entertainer or a master of ceremonies, so that's where I'm not so certain that you couldn't find someone more polished than me. Also, to be totally honest, I've found that most men of importance can be extremely difficult to accommodate on a daily basis, almost impossible at times."

Sarah smiled, a little thinly. "So you travel well, can handle obnoxious doctors, but don't provide critical medical care to jerks, did I get that right?" She seemed bemused. Edie felt embarrassed, then slightly angry–she had been asked to be honest, after all.

"You asked me for an honest answer and that's exactly how I feel. I can put up with short-tempered doctors primarily because my father is a doctor and I know the pressure they are constantly under. They are that way because they have to be that way, simple as that. But if a guys a jerk, then he's just a jerk, or horse's ass, or whatever." Edie plowed on. "So if this Dr. Hollings is an arrogant egomaniac just because he's been born with a big brain and feels the need to lord it over everyone on a daily basis, then I'm not interested. As a matter of fact, the more I think about it the less appealing it sounds so if you'll excuse me..."

"Miss Langston," Sarah cut in laughing, "You can stop right there. First of all, you're hired. Secondly–" Sarah held up her hand as Edie rose to leave, "If you'll turn to your immediate left,

I'd like to introduce you to Dr. Stephan B. Hollings, your new jerk of a boss." Sarah burst out laughing at Edie's second "deer in headlights look" as a man in a wheelchair rolled right up next to her left arm. "I gotta start bringing my camera," she cried, "I just missed another one!"

Dr. Stephan Hollings watched Edie's set jaw drop while her face simultaneously turned beet-red. Her hands flew up to her mouth and her eyes were wide in shock. "Sarah should've gotten a shot of that, those red cheeks really bring out the highlights in her hair," he mused, "Maybe someone should tell her she should try a little more rouge sometimes."

A small eternity later Edie recovered her voice; her composure, however, was still nowhere to be found.

"Oh, my god, I'm so sorry- I-I- didn't mean to call you an ass- I do apologize…"

"Don't dig yourself in any deeper, Edie" Sarah gaily broke in, "You'll just encourage him. And I'm sorry, but when I saw Stephan come in the room behind you I just had to let you finish that magnificent diatribe on modern day alpha males. Whaddya think, Stephan, have you heard enough or would you like my two cents worth on the subject as well?"

The physicist was now tapping on a keypad located on the armrest of his motorized chair. Edie now noticed how Dr. Hollings head was braced with an attachment from his chair so it wouldn't slump over too far and how advanced his debilitation was. A wave of pity swept over her for this poor man. How sad that his vocal chords were no longer functioning. There was an awkward silence, punctuated only by the tiny tapping noises from his slow moving fingers.

"Hello-Edie" suddenly emanated from a speaker on the wheelchair, with the "Edie" sounding like a metallic "E" and "D" put together by one of those automated phone systems. "I'm-Stephan-Hollings" he said with a pronounced space in between each word. "I'm-told-you're-from-England." He continued, "I-hope-you-can-tell-me-about-it-sometime. I'll-be spending-a-few-months-at-Oxford-soon. I-was-told-you-know-it-well". This whole time the sentences were slowly crawling out, with long gaps in between the arduous tapping. Edie watched his eyes flicker from a video screen positioned on a metal rod-like arm that held it just above his lap up to hers. Even though only his fingers and eyes were in motion she sensed the Herculean effort he was making. She stared into his soft blue eyes, transfixed.

"Hey, Edie, I think the good doctor just asked you a question, albeit in statement form." Sarah cut in, "Look, what it all boils down to is that he's been requested to participate in this formation of an international council on particle research and development that will be head-quartered at Oxford. I was thinking Dr. Hollings would benefit from some local advice about the town and the university so as not to be at any more of a disadvantage than Mother Nature has already provided. Believe it or not, theoretical physics is a combination of power politics and cutthroat competition. Some of these guys will do anything to gain an edge–it's dog-eat-dog, full-contact science with no knockdown rules."

Edie was slightly taken aback by the fact that she appeared to be wanted solely because she had worked at Oxford, but was realistic enough to see it was a sensible concept. Still she had to say it–"So I guess I'm lucky the council wasn't in Mexico City, or you'd have hired your landscaper instead." Her attempt at humor had more effect than she wanted–Sarah visibly winced and the Dr. started tapping immediately.

"Well let me be perfectly clear, Edie" Sarah quickly interjected, "This was my idea, not Stephan's. I just had seen too many instances where his alleged colleagues took advantage. I'll admit your background was a factor, but Stephan has the final say and his criteria may not rate it all that important." Edie was touched by Sarah's jumping to his defense, but before she could attempt to take back her ill-chosen words, the metallic voice spoke.

"We're-not-hiring-you-for-that. We're-hiring-you-because-your-name-can-be-spelled-with-just-two-keystrokes.E.- D. The-other-applicant-was-named-Alexandriana. Ha-ha-ha."

Edie stayed for a couple hours with Sarah, filled out paperwork, listening to her describe a typical day ("but there's always something going on, so the only real constant is just be ready for anything"), and came back the next morning at 8:00 a.m. sharp. She punched in her access code and parked in the same spot, but next to a black Mercedes instead of the Tahoe Sarah drove. Edie wasn't surprised; Sarah had said that she wouldn't be in until 10:00. All that Edie had to do until she got there was answer the phone as the night nurse and her aide bathed, dressed, and fed Dr. Hollings. Her nursing skills were going to be seldom in need until midday meds, and today not even that, as Sarah was scheduled to go with Drs. Hollings and Steck to the Texas capitol for a news conference with a couple of U.S. senators that served on a committee overseeing scientific research funding.

Sarah had said that the new administration was battling Congressional leaders in appropriations over the funding of a select few projects that involved Dr. Hollings latest paper on dark matter. She also said that Dr. Hollings had mixed feelings about anything to do with what could be used in a military manner, but that Dr. Steck was always pushing for any exposure and funding, no matter where it came from. Sarah went on to say that Dr. Hollings had been lucky to have such a longtime and devoted cheerleader, as long as it didn't kill him in the process with all its never-ending demands. She'd made abundantly it clear that if she had her way the constant stress of these endless sessions with the media and big money-interests would take more of a back seat to his health and physical well-being.

Edie came in the front door as Sarah had instructed and went to the reception desk. The night nurse was in Dr. Hollings office, talking to a man dressed in an expensive suit. He was listening impatiently, fiddling with his Blackberry. Suddenly it chirped and the man abruptly turned his back on the nurse, right in mid-sentence.

"Hello, Senator Billachek! Welcome back to Austin! Thanks for returning my call. Hey listen, I've just had an idea on how we can get you some great press during our photo shoot after the news conference. How about I bring what I've got over to the hotel right now and lay it out for you over breakfast. If you think it's a go I'll swing back over here to Dr. Hollings and brief him in the limo on the way over to the capitol. That work for you? Great, I'll be right there. No, no, I'm leaving right this second, no trouble at all. See you shortly, Senator." He clicked off, grabbed his briefcase off the desk and started out the side door, leaving the nurse without as much as a goodbye. She put her hands on her hips and just shook her head, then turned towards the reception area. She stared seeing the unfamiliar face, then realizing Edie must be the new hire, warmly smiled.

"Hi, I'm Cindy–you must be Edie. Welcome to another day of Dr. Steck's mad plan to take over the world, one politician at a time."

Edie laughed. "Sarah said sometimes days start to get hectic early. I see what she meant now."

Cindy walked through the reception area into the main hall. "I'll bring Dr. Hollings out and get him set up in his office. He might ask you for help reading his mail or to check his e-mail, but he's really nice and polite. You'll get to where you'll like helping him, its interesting stuff from all over the world that comes in. Other than that he and Dr. Steck are leaving at 10:00, so there's a limo service you'll need to let in. They usually get here about 5 or 10 minutes early. Any questions?" she finished, then gave Edie another cheerful smile. "Good, just make yourself at home. I'll go get Stephan." Cindy went down the hall towards the back humming some hip-hop song about "today's gonna be a great day, today's gonna be a great, great day…" Edie recognized it but forgot who the band was.

She must be getting old, she thought, the music was always the first thing to go. What would be next, her knees, or was that just in sports? Either way, she was still thirty-four and still just as single. Oh, well, maybe she'd meet the right one in Austin. It seemed fateful enough that she was here. It certainly hadn't been planned–two years ago, one eternity ago, her life turned upside down and backwards–Edie fought another sudden, unexplainable urge to cry, and tried using the mantra Robin had told her he always used.

"Don't think, just step forward, just go. Don't think, just keep moving, just go."

Well, if he could pick up the pieces and keep on, then so could she. It was he who lost both parents at the age of thirteen, not her, and it was Robin who got up the day after the funerals and went right back to his research and his animals. He'd simply stated that he was less alone there, and if and when he needed to talk he'd let someone know. He'd become a walking cliché of one "losing oneself in ones work".

3

The Primate Center

Edie called at least once a week to the primate center now that she was here in America. Her brother's best friend Ed was director of the facility, and he and his wife practically adopted Robin overnight after Bob and Anna were killed in an ambush, caught up in the wrong place in the wrong tribal war. They were both shot and Bob beheaded, just 30 kilometers from the Center by bushmen believing they were government officials helping a rival tribe obtain arms and ammunition.

The fact that one of the worlds most sophisticated bio-tech research facilities was located in a remote corner of Africa known more for its primitive tribes and diverse species of flora and fauna was not lost on Edie. She had commented on the seeming incongruency of the matter to Robin soon after her arrival in Alibibi, the town (if it could be called that) closest to the Life Science Primate Research Center of Africa complex. Robin had explained that bio-technology was advancing at an exponential rate and how India and China were pouring billions into the Center's medical research worldwide, thereby circumventing such annoyances as international regulation agencies and costly clinical trials that took years, if not decades, for approval. Too many good drugs and medical advances had simply run out of funding or had lost commercial appeal before gaining approval for the market. Leah, Robin's surrogate mother at the center, had chimed in, "Medical research has been so over-regulated that it has forced us into using black market tactics that border on illegality. It's wouldn't be an exaggeration to say that the situation has disintegrated into a kind of Wild West mentality. In other words, we're primarily here in Alibibi to avoid prying eyes, not because of it's proximity to the various indigenous species. It works for us, it works for China, and it makes everyone's work here more tangible. We are inventing tomorrow today, literally right here, right now–we see our ideas spring from concept to reality in months, not years. How could anything else be more fun?"

Not to mention lucrative. Edie had no idea until she and her nephew were read his parent's will that Bob and Anna were multi-millionaires from several licensing fees of devices developed as a result of their research. Robin would never want for anything for the rest of his life. Yet all he wanted was to get back to the Center and go back to work on what had been his parents' latest project.

Edie had learned when Robin was only 5 years old and Bob and Anna were in Switzerland that he had shown intelligence far exceeding his age group. Next came the news that he had been placed in an accelerated program which immediately deemed him a prodigy. Of course, when your father was a neurosurgeon/research scientist and your mother held advanced degrees in electronics engineering and robotics it only stood to reason Robin would posses at the very least a sharp mind. But when she learned that he had quietly been accepted to a medical school in Brazil (at the age of ten!) that had trained several young "exceptionally advanced intellects" (according to what she found out on Academia Medicina Brazil's website) she was astonished. The subject had never come up when Bob and Edie talked over the phone, usually on holidays and the occasional birthday. The simple fact was that while she was pursuing her own career, working at Oxford and taking classes in nursing, Bob and Anna were globetrotting research scientists, very seldom in any one country for more than a year. Sometimes it seemed life refused to ever allow time for living, never willing to relinquish its treacherous grasp on the here and now, at least not without a fierce battle.

The one Christmas they had flown back to Oxford the subject of Robin being whisked through college and med school came up only once, and Anna was content to make it short. "Robin is still just an ordinary kid, and if he's a little quicker study we're certainly not going to force him to die on the vine over archaic academic protocols. If he's happy, great, but we are determined to treat his gift as a natural thing and not let it get turned into a freak show like has been done to others." Bob added that several TV and newspapers had tried to get an interview with "the real-live Dougie Howser", but had eventually given up. The two (and Robin) seemed more interested in the snow falling outside than discussing their lives in Brazil.

The only noticeable display of Robin's incredible acumen came when Edie took him to the airport to pick up Aunt Blythe two days before Christmas. Bob and Anna purposely set this up so that while Edie and Robin were at the airport they could sneak off to do Christmas shopping for Robin. Edie went to the airport early on a pretense of possible heavy traffic just to give Bob and Anna a good two hours to shop. It was only as Edie and Robin were in the airport and walking towards Aunt Blythe's terminal did she notice Robin cocking his head occasionally and pausing. The first couple of times she dismissed it as maybe he was trying to listen to the different Christmas music that was playing from all the shops they were passing. But Robin didn't seem to slow when there was music–only when there were foreign travelers close, or passing by, did he turn and perk up his ears. Finally, after a group of chattering Asian businessmen caused Robin to stop, dead in his tracks, to observe their rapid-fire exchange did Edie say something. "I guess it must be exciting to see all these different people from all over the world after being stuck in Brazil, hearing nothing but Spanish all the time. I'd love to know what those guys were all worked up about. I bet it can be tough living in a country where you can't even understand what anyone's saying half the time, isn't it?"

Robin looked at Edie quizzically, then said, "Well, first of all we speak Portuguese, not Spanish back in Sao Paulo, but that's a common misconception. Those men were from Hong Kong, here for a software sales conference sponsored by Sun Microsystems. They were making plans for tonight, but I couldn't quite get the last bit. Aunt Edie, what's a 'titty bar'?"

After Edie regained her composure and hem-hawed around the subject of gentlemen's clubs (rather poorly), she found out that Robin was a linguistic prodigy as well, speaking 9 languages and numerous dialects ("my hobby", he'd explained). She'd also found out that he was now studying neurosurgery and helping out on his father's current project, but that his true love was electronics systems and design. They had sat munching popcorn at the terminal while he spontaneously gave an impromptu lecture on the future of electronics and bio-technology. Edie was spellbound–she could barely keep up, even with her advanced medical training, and was at times keenly aware that Robin would carefully phrase his wording to "dumb it down" for her. She said after his discourse that she just couldn't believe he was so smart and that he was a doctor at the age of twelve. He immediately changed the subject and when Edie brought it up again, Robin sighed tiredly, like an old man.

"Look, Aunt Edie," he finally said, "I'm the son of two of the most brilliant people on the planet. Is it really that amazing that their offspring inherited some of those traits? If my father was 6'9" and he married a woman 6'4", would me playing in the NBA as a 7-footer make me a phenomenal athlete or merely an easily projected statistical result?" Robin smiled at her pained expression as she realized the trap she'd fallen into–stereotyping her own flesh and blood.

"The way I see it, everything I am intellectually is nothing more than the predictable probability of 2 remarkable parents." He looked past all the scurrying travelers, hustling and bustling to destinations unknown. "It's only what I do, if I could somehow change the world with some great discovery or miraculous breakthrough, that I'll ever be able to prove I'm anything more than just another kid genius. I mean, what's that worth, really? I bet all the plastic surgeons in Hollywood were considered minor prodigies, too. So until I actually accomplish something worthwhile, if ever, just remember this–there have been a lot of people 7 feet tall in this world that never made it to the NBA."

4

Caring For Doctor Hollings

The sound of Cindy's voice coming down the hall roughly dragged Edie back into the here and now. "The new nurse, Edie, is here, Stephan, and Dr. Steck just left but will be back shortly. I've told Edie you may want her to read you your mail; I've got your computer setup to your e-mail already. I just assumed you'd putter around until the limo gets here, not really enough time to do any heavy lifting. Unless you have different plans, which all you have to do is let us know, sir, otherwise I'll be heading out as soon as I get you settled at your desk."

Edie noticed Dr. Hollings started typing halfway through her briefing. Cindy saw his fingers laboriously moving as she was finishing what she was saying, then stopped as his words came haltingly out of the chair's speaker. "I'd like for E. D.-to-read-me-the-mail-Cindy. Please-open-the-curtains-we'll-stay-here-by-the-phone-for-her."

It took over a minute for him to have put those few words together. What a terrible burden for such a seemingly polite and kind person, she thought, not to mention how long did it take him to craft an equation or write an article? Days, weeks, maybe even months? It must be pure hell.

Cindy parked Stephan by her desk and opened the curtains on the bow windows overlooking the front lawn. Sunlight flooded the room and Edie saw two squirrels playing tag, chasing each other around and around the trunk of a large live oak. The grass was wet from the sprinklers whipping around in a staccato pattern. She noticed a blue jay buzzing a couple of grackles taking a bath in a low spot where runoff water had ponded. She glanced over at Dr. Hollings and saw his eyes also flitting across the green expanse. Edie could see with his limited mobility in his neck that even his eyes had to work twice as hard as anyone else's–so, so, sad. Cindy came back from Dr. Hollings office with a handful of unopened letters. She dropped them on Edie's desk and produced a letter opener from her front blouse pocket.

"OK, Edie, here's the drill. You pick up an envelope, read who it's from and show Dr. Hollings the front of the letter. If he wants you to open and read it out loud he says OK. Or if he says no go on to the next." Cindy paused. "Just so you know we try to make the most from as little verbiage as possible from Stephan. I guess you've already seen how much effort he has to exert just to get a few words out." Edie nodded.

"Oh Edie, before I go, one other thing. Dr. Hollings also likes to just listen to someone else talk at times without him having to hold up his end of the conversation. We've got a simple system. Stephan will say "Just talk to me about" and then he'll add things, like your day, or your family, or where you're from. He calls it his therapy" she laughed. "I call it a break from Dr. Steck, who can't seem to talk about anything but the next committee meeting or what some theoretician in Oslo just published and how Stephan can prove it's wrong and get his picture on the cover of Nature again." Cindy saw Edie's eyebrows furrow in concern that she would take a swipe at Dr. Steck in front of Dr. Hollings. Cindy grinned mischievously.

"Don't worry, Dr. Hollings has highly developed humor quotient to go with his I.Q. Even Stephan gets a dig in now and then." She patted Dr. Hollings on the arm. "And with that I bid thee adieu. See you tonight, Dr. Hollings. Ya'll have a great day." Cindy grabbed her things off the sideboard in the entryway and was out the front door, closing it with a wave and a smile.

Edie picked up the first letter. "Pierre Jalouse, Academy of Science, Paris, France."

"No."

"Ralph Sanders, Washington Observatory, Eureka, Washington."

"OK." Edie read the letter about how there was an upcoming stellar event that could prove or disprove Barrington of the

Royal Observatory in England's claim that star UB-936 was a neutron star by utilizing radial spectrometry at precisely the point where suspected comet DYE-48 passed in front of the red-shift…" and so on until she had trouble on the 3rd page and ended up just holding it up for Stephan to see the accompanying graph. Then on to the next letter and for next 20 minutes or so it was "No" or "OK" and an occasional "Stop-read-that-again-please." Once Edie had to show Dr. Hollings a difficult to read equation about meteorites.

Just as she going to suggest a short break Dr. Hollings suddenly said, "Tell-me-about…your-family." It sounded a little funny–Edie realized that he must have pre-programmed phrases in the computer connected to his keypad that operated his "voice", because the "Talk-to-me-about…" came out as one sentence with a gap and then the added "your-family", like a fill-in-the-blanks. Edie wondered how many other shortcuts had been programmed to shave off a few precious keystrokes, just to ease his constant struggle to churn out the simplest of sentences.

So Edie told him about growing up in England as a doctor's daughter, going to nursing school and working at Oxford after graduation, about Aunt Blythe's bad hip…

"You–were–an–only–child?" he asked and Edie said no, she had a brother who became a doctor as well, then a research scientist, but tragically died in Africa.

"Africa?"

"Yes, Africa." And perhaps because of her earlier thoughts which didn't surface that often or because of the beauty of the day, or maybe just because she had someone who would listen Edie told the story of Bob and Anna Langston and how their son, her nephew, was still there. At some point she had started crying, not much, just a few tears that slowly puddled on her day calendar as she gazed out the big window onto the pristine lawn, and when she reached the end where she'd left Robin in Africa, she was at the end of her tears too, painfully aware she'd just totally opened up to a relative stranger. Edie found a tissue and turned to Dr. Hollings, who was also looking out the window with a funny look in his eyes.

"I'm sorry, I didn't mean to throw all that on you" she said, sniffling and daubing her eyes. "It's just that I was thinking earlier of how it was 2 years ago this month and it just all came out." Dr. Hollings was tapping as she was talking and now, "Why -did -your -nephew -stay -in -Africa?"

"Oh," said Edie, brightening as she thought of her nephew's work with animals, "Robin's staying with my brother Bob's best friend. Ed and Ed's wife Leah, they wanted to adopt him, but Robin says he's too old. Robin's very smart but plays it down like he's just an ordinary kid, not someone who's…" Edie froze in mid-sentence. She swiveled in her chair to grab Stephan's arm, tears forgotten. "Dr. Hollings, you absolutely must talk to my nephew. I think Robin can help!"

Dr. Hollings had half-turned his motorized chair to put Edie in his field of vision. She was rifling through her purse and talking excitedly half to herself, and half to him, he assumed. One minute there had been tears streaming down her face (and it was good she stopped when she did, he was on the verge of joining her) and the next she was acting like she'd won the lottery. She was very attractive, in a natural way, with curly red hair and soft round features that accentuated expressive, light green-brown eyes.

"Ah-ha!" Edie exclaimed, "Found it!" She had a business card in her hand. "I've got Robin's number at home in my Rolodex but I knew it was in here somewhere." She laid the card down and picked up the phone on the desk to dial, then stopped.

"No, we need it on speakerphone." Edie said, punching the button. She was just starting to dial when she heard the side door open. Distracted, she misdialed the number and had to hang up the phone. Looking up, she saw the man in the Armani business suit come in. He strode up to Edie's desk, looked right past her as if she didn't exist and started talking to Dr. Hollings.

"Stephan, I have wonderful news. I just came back from Senator Billichek's hotel and I've come up with how to get that grant request from the National Institute of Science pushed through right away! See, with Billichek on the appropriations committee, I've gotten him to agree to modify his speech today so it will put heat on the NIS to jump on board or risk being portrayed as a bunch of partisans playing pork-barrel politics, which we all know they are, but they sure as hell don't need the rest of the world to know. I'll give you the rundown on the way over but right now I have to call Edwards at NIS and give him a heads-up. Boy oh boy, I'm going to love watching him try to weasel out of this one this time!" He stomped back into Dr. Hollings office and sitting on the lowered desk started punching numbers on his Blackberry.

Edie looked at Stephan and said "That's Dr. Steck?" to which the reply was "Yes." Edie shrugged and went back to dialing the phone to the Primate Center. While it was ringing through to Africa Edie began to explain, noticing that Dr. Steck had walked back in the room, muttering "Pick up, Ted, you bastard, pickup!"

"Robin, my nephew, has been working with chimps and has actually had some success with getting them to communicate. It's really remarkable and I couldn't help but think surely he could help you…"

"Good evening, Primate Lab, can I help you?" interrupted Edie's excited explanation. "Oh, hello, this is Edie Langston calling from Austin, Texas. I need to speak with Robin Langston, my nephew, please."

"OK, Edie from Texas, that's the U.S., correct?"

"Yes," Edie replied, "Robin's usually in Lab 3-C about this time, could you check, please?"

"Yes, ma'am, I know the maintenance man just went down to fix a leaky toilet in 3-C, so I assume someone had to let him in. Let me buzz you down there." Edie was placed on hold and noticed Dr. Steck watching with an annoyed look on his face.

"Too bad," she thought, "You can't be the center of attention all the time."

"As I was saying, Robin has gotten a chimp to communicate and it just occurred to me that this technology should be perfect to help you. It would get you away from that awful machine you are using. It must be terrible to have to be so constrained and painfully slow."

"Excuse me, nurse, I don't know who you think you are, but I personally designed Stephan's communication device with the help of an organization you might have heard of. It's called NASA," interjected a now visibly agitated Dr. Steck. "Who are you, and how does upsetting Dr. Hollings with your nephew's lame science fair experiment fit into your job description?" His face was a little flushed and his voice had risen in volume with each word he was biting off.

"I-I'm Edie Langston, the new nurse and..."

"Whassup," the speakerphone crackled to life, "Whaddya want?"

"Oh, is this Fred?" Edie breathed a sigh of relief. "Fred, its Edie, is Robin around?"

"Call back in ten minutes" came the brusque reply.

"Could you go get him, Fred? I have a Dr. Hollings here that needs to speak with him right away."

"Oh... a doctor, huh? Well, now, that makes everything different. Just tell the Dr. that Fred said to Call—Back—In—Ten—Minutes." Dr. Steck pushed his way past Edie and snatched the phone out of her hand.

"Now you see here, Fred the Janitor, this is Dr. Dick Steck and the doctor you just insulted is the greatest physicist on the planet. So why don't you just put down your plunger and go do as you're told!" Edie's jaw dropped at Steck's imperious tone.

"Now you listen up, Dr. Dip Stick" drawled the voice over the line, "Me and you are fixing to get all cattywompus and then you ain't ever gonna talk to Robin, how do you like that?"

"Fred!" Edie jumped in over the speakerphone, "Please, just go get Robin, it's very important, tell him it's Edie!" Just then the buzzer went off on her desk–the limo had arrived. Edie looked frantically for the intercom while Dr. Steck turned to Dr. Hollings.

"Stephan, I recommend you fire this incompetent woman, or let me do it. This is what we get for hiring temps!"

"Oh, so now you like picking on women," the gravelly voice snarled, "You must be some piece of work, Dr. Dip Shit."

"My name is Dr. Dick Steck, YOU IGNORANT BABOON!" Steck roared, "And if you were standing here I'd strangle you to within an inch of your miserable life!" Edie had found the gate's control box and let the limo in. A low, guttural sound came over the phone.

"Oh, you're gonna pay for that, bucko" the eerily low and menacing voice said, "You are gonna pay." With that the line went dead. Dr. Steck wheeled around and grabbed Dr. Hollings wheelchair's handlebars.

"Come, Stephan, we're going to be late for the Senators and I've still got to brief you on the NIS." Dr. Steck's knuckles were white, clenched with rage on the handles. He pushed Dr. Hollings towards the side exit, through the automatic door. Two men from the limo service took Dr. Hollings down the ramp and towards the long, sleek car. Dr. Steck came back for his briefcase that was on the office desk. Helplessly, Edie stood there, wringing her hands.

"I'm sorry about Fred" she said, "let me explain…"

"Explain!" Steck yelled, "Let me explain something to you! Your services are no longer required! The last thing I needed today was some flighty nurse trying to con one of the greatest minds on the planet into buying into some punk kid's science project about a monkey that's learned how to do sign language that's probably fake anyway! Tell that to Fred the Janitor!" Dr. Steck stormed out the door.

Edie's head was swimming with emotion and guilt. She had never meant to cause harm. She wished she'd never made that call, and why did it have to be Fred who had answered the phone? Wait! Why was she the guilty party? It was Steck who wouldn't let her explain, it was his fault for being such a controlling ass and in such a damned hurry! Edie held her head high, drew herself up to her full 5'1" height, and marched out the side door of the house past the trellis and down the stone path to the drive. The black limo had just turned around and was starting towards the gates. She saw through the open window in the back that Steck was leaning over Dr. Hollings, showing him some papers that he was holding in one hand while talking on the cell phone he held in the other. Edie reared back and sucked in a huge gulp of air.

"Hey, Dr. Dip Shit!" she screamed at the top of her lungs, "My nephew's name is Dr. Robin Langston, neurosurgeon and head scientist at The Life Science Primate Research Center, with a billion dollar annual operating budget!" Edie cupped her hands around her mouth, "And you weren't talking to Fred the Janitor, you pompous bastard! You were talking to Fred—the—Fucking—Chimp!!!"

Trembling, Edie watched the limo accelerating towards the tall iron gates. Her adrenalin still coursing through her veins, she spun on her heels to go grab her purse and leave before Dr. Steck could call the police and have her forcibly removed. Even though she was still shocked at her sudden outburst, Edie was filled with righteous indignation.

She had taken no more than a step, however, when the unmistakable sound of screeching tires stopped her dead in her tracks. Edie whipped around in time to see the smoking tires of the limo as it slid to a stop at the gates. The red brake lights framing the trunk turned to white as it shifted into reverse–with a lurch the wheels spun backwards, searching for traction. Now the large vehicle was backing rapidly up the drive, and in the back of her mind it registered that the driver had the skills of a Hollywood stunt driver.

Edie felt her heart rise into her throat as anger turned to dread, with more than just a touch of fear. She didn't know which way to run and in the end just stood there, frozen, as the limo slammed to a sharp stop with the rear end mere inches away from her feet. The back window was up but rolling down. She saw Stephan's head pitched over towards Steck. Edie heard Dr. Steck talking very fast and sounding all the world like a scolded schoolboy. Edie heard snippets such as "I-I didn't know" and "but Stephan, the Senators…" and intermittently Dr. Hollings mechanical voice saying over and over again

OUT!" "OUT!" Edie realized the system had a volume control and it was LOUD. Then doors started slamming–the driver and his assistant were double-timing it to the back of the car–and Dr. Steck was briskly walking towards her with a strange look on his face. The hand that didn't have the briefcase in it was holding the chirping Blackberry, which for the moment had lost its magical powers over the suddenly nervous physician.

"Uh, Miss Langston," Steck's voice had a slight waver to it, "could Stephan perhaps have a minute of your time?" Edie stared in amazement at the suddenly unctuous jerk. Speechless she turned to where the two men had adroitly removed the doctor, wheelchair and all, from the limo and onto the pavement. He was tapping something while the assistants pushed him up to her. His head rolled over to make eye contact.

"E.-D.-do-you-think-it's-been-ten-minutes-yet?"

5

Doctor Hollings Meets Robin

They were all back in the house, in the office. Dr. Hollings said something to Steck and the assistant and Edie watched as they started setting up the stage lights and moving cameras around, plugging in cables to some sort of electronic device that in turn was wired to his desktop. Dr. Hollings drove himself over to Edie.

"Call-your-nephew-tell-him-I-want-a-video-conference-over-the-Web. Him-and-Fred." Edie saw him smile, an endearing lop-sided grin. "Now." Edie started to say that she didn't know how to set that up and caught herself. It was her job to call and tell Robin what Dr. Hollings wanted, nothing more. Like her father was fond of saying,

"Don't worry about the horses, Edie, just load the wagon."

She went to the nurse's office and called Africa. Thankfully it was Robin that picked up the phone in Lab 3-C.

"Hey, Aunt Edie" sang Robin's cheerful voice, "Fred told me you called. What's up?"

"Well, Robin, I'm here at Dr. Stephan Hollings house and I mentioned your work with Fred to him, and Dr. Hollings was hoping to have a video-chat with you if possible."

"Did you say Dr. Hollings?" Robin's voice sounded surprised. "Dr. Stephan B. Hollings, the physicist?"

"Well, yes" Edie replied, "have you heard of him?"

"Heck yeah, I've heard of him, he's like the superstar of particle physics! Really, he wants to talk to me?" Robin cried, "Oh, wait a sec, he's got Lou Gehrigs' disease, where he uses this computer interface to move around and talk or something, right? Hey, I could probably help with that. Is that what he wants to talk to me about?"

"Well, yeah, Robin, Dr. Hollings would like to talk to you and hopefully a little with Fred if that's OK."

"Sure," Robin said, "Hey, could you get his autograph for me? Oh, wait, I forgot, my bad. So when does he want to do this?"

"Right now, if you know how to do it, Robin," Edie said, "I'm just the messenger."

"Of course I do, Aunt Edie" Robin said, "I need his e-mail address and what platform he uses. I've hot V-chat, Windows vid-chat, get me that and we're good to go." Edie turned to Dr. Hollings, who had silently rolled up at some point during the conversation and explained the situation–she'd deliberately left the speakerphone off this time. He pressed a button on his keypad and Steck appeared and then went and got the assistant. The young man in turn took the phone from Edie and started relaying the info to Africa. He wrote down Robins URL and some other techie stuff Edie didn't understand and then hung up. The intern, as it turned out, was a grad student majoring in computer science. He looked at Edie and said with a grin,

"How old is your nephew? He sounds like a kid, but talks like he's some kind of rocket scientist or something. He was losing me there for a second!"

Edie smiled. "He gets that a lot."

Andy, the techie, went back to the doctor's office with Edie in tow. He explained that Dr. Hollings often utilized the Web's video-conferencing capabilities conducting lectures to advanced physics classes world-wide. He pointed to the honorary degrees on the wall,

"He's probably never even set foot on some of those campuses but his contributions to the next generation of Einstein's and Oppenheimer's are incalculable." Then he went on to the mini-studio–"I call it our little $200,000 web-cam," Andy smiled, "We've even recorded some documentary material here that's network quality."

Sometime later another tech guy showed up as Andy was typing in commands at Dr. Hollings computer. He introduced himself as Hajj and set up the lights for the cameras and brought in a couple of low-slung leather armchairs that he set on either side of the chair Andy was using while sitting in at the keyboard. He then asked for Edie to sit in one then the other to adjust the lights surrounding the desk.

"Why these other chairs?" Edie asked.

"Doctor's orders," Hajj replied with a shrug. He then started messing with the huge flat-screen monitor on the desk, easily twice the size of a regular screen. After he was finished, Andy ran a test and Edie all of a sudden was on the screen, for the all world looking like she was on a studio set about to deliver the local news. She became very aware that what make-up she had started out with this morning was in dire need of a touch-up after the crying bout earlier. She excused herself with ill-disguised embarrassment and went in search of a restroom.

She went out to the main hall and headed on back, checking doors for the lavatory–it came up on the second try. She washed up, redid her face (with a little more effort than usual, did she really look that frumpy or was it true about TV and the 10 lbs.?), and teased her curls out. Edie headed out the door and almost collided with Dr. Hollings wheelchair coming down the hall, Dr. Steck pushing from behind. Steck smiled a little anxiously.

"Ms. Langston, would you please join Stephan and me in his office, please? I'm sure you would like to say 'Hi' to your neph–uh, Dr. Langston while the cameras are rolling." Edie did a double-take hearing Robin referred to as "Dr.Langston".

"That's what we call my father," she replied, "I'm pretty sure Robin's more comfortable with just 'Robin.' Dr. Steck gave a strained but polite smile.

"As you wish, Ms. Langston." With that she followed them into the office turned TV studio.

Andy had moved the chair he had behind the desk over to the control board Edie had seen earlier, and Hajj was fiddling with the boom mike. Andy instinctively took over–Edie could see this was practiced routine between he, Hajj, Steck, and Stephan–everyone moving into their places, Hajj calling out last second sound-checks while Stephan was being pushed between the two armchairs by Dr. Steck, who then sat in one to Dr. Hollings left.

Andy said, "OK, we're going on in 10 seconds. Ms Langston, your chair, please," and before Edie could protest he started counting down, "seven, six, five..., and we're live!"

Edie sat down just as a live shot of Lab 3-C's day room came on the huge display screen. She recognized immediately that they were being fed a view from Robin's computer at his desk-behind it was the TV and a couple of old couches, with a crate for a coffee table. The TV was on with an old Batman DVD in, the one with Danny Devito as the Penguin. Edie wondered where Robin was and then she saw the door that was past the sofas open–she recalled it led to the inner open-air commons that were located in the middle of the hexagonal compound.

In sauntered Robin, who turned back around in the doorway and cried out, "Come on, Fred, Edie's going to be on the computer and wants to say 'Hi". He listened for a second, then said, "OK, but hurry up" and came over and plopped down in an old battered chair that spun around as he sat.

"Hey, Aunt Edie, wow! You look great! Man, that's some kind of setup you guys got, is that a studio you're in?"

Edie laughed, "No, but it feels like it. Robin, I'd like you to meet Dr. Stephan Hollings. Dr. Hollings, Dr. Robin Langston." Edie threw in the formality at the last second, realizing it might be important to not make Robin feel slighted. She was wrong.

"Just Robin is what I'm used to," Robin said easily.

"And this is Dr. Richard Steck," Edie continued, "He's Dr. Hollings personal physician." Robin nodded in acknowledgement. "I hope I didn't give Dr. Hollings false hope here, but I told him you might be able to help him with some of the wonderful things your group has developed with primates like Fred."

"Maybe, maybe not," Robin said, "Hey, before we get down and dirty with all the technical jargon, you said you guys wanted to say 'Hi' to Fred?"

"Yes-Robin," Dr. Hollings said, "and-please-call-me Stephan."

"Well, OK, Steve-O," Robin said, obviously pleased, "let me go see if I can pry ole lover-boy away from his new girlfriend." Robin jumped up and trotted to the door. Opening it, he yelled, "Hey, Fred, enough already, Edie's got some friends she wants you to meet. Come on in!" Robin turned and loped back. "He's coming. He's just got a little attitude going today. I don't know, something got him going earlier and he's all bulled up like a pit bull on steroids or something."

Edie heard a chirping and saw Steck's hand go for his Blackberry on the desk.

"Ah, excuse me for one minute," he said walking into the other room. Edie liked his newfound manners–she wondered what exactly Stephan had said. But she didn't have time to dwell on that because behind Robin the door to the commons opened and in scampered Fred. He grabbed a barstool against a wall and dragged it over to the computer desk. He jumped up in it and it twirled around a couple of turns. He looked at the screen and had a sudden look of concern appear on his primitive face. He seemed to be staring at Dr. Hollings.

"Fred, you remember Aunt Edie, and this is Stephan, her friend. He had something bad happen and now he can't do all the things he used to, but maybe we can help him out, like with his voice and stuff. Whaddya think?"

"Well yeah, we gotta do something," Fred rasped, "What was it, elephant or rhino? I saw it on TV yesterday, about that guy that the elephant trampled–was that the same one? Man, something's gotta be done about that! Heck yeah, I'll help." Edie realized that Fred had seen a man in a wheelchair who had been trampled and was now assuming that was what had happened to Stephan. She thought it very touching, in a humorous way. She saw Dr. Steck return to his chair, eyes glued on the talking chimp.

"No, Fred, Steve wants us to help him talk. You know, like we did for you," Robin said laughingly, "We'll worry about the elephant later."

"What do you mean, he can't talk at all?" Fred asked. "Man that elephants gotta go, dude. Hey, Steve, don't you worry, man, Robin can get you fixed up."

"Thank-you-Fred," Dr. Hollings said, and Fred's mouth dropped open.

"Holy shit, someone put a hex on you with some witch doctor? You sound like a robot! Hey, Steve, don't sweat it, bud, after Robin gets you put back together right, you and me, we'll go for a little payback, alright? Man I hate elephants. All chimps hate elephants, almost as much as baboons. You ever want to piss a chimp off, just call him a baboon, then you got a big problem. Chimps don't forget about stuff like that, no sir."

Robin was laughing good-naturedly, "Hey, Fred, I gotta talk to Stephan about the things we did to get you talking, so you start working on a plan to take out that elephant and I'll handle the rest, OK?" Fred jumped down and in one leap was on one of the couches.

"Alright, I ain't gonna forget. That dude's toast!" Saying that Fred grabbed the remote and turned up the volume to the TV.

"Say, Doc, can you give me an assessment of Stephan's functional ability? You know, just a basic summary of what we've got to work with here?" Robin asked Steck. Edie suppressed a smile at Robin's informal use of Dr. Steck's title.

"Of course, Dr. Langst–er, Robin," Steck said, obviously not entirely pleased with the informality. "Stephan has advanced Lou Gehrigs disease. He can no longer talk due to his weakened state–his condition has progressed to where Stephan can only use his mouth to eat, no vocal chord function. He can move his hands and fingers well enough to type on a computer interface so he can communicate," Steck paused, "which was designed by me in conjunction with a group of NASA scientists, not witch doctors," he pointedly remarked in Fred's direction. Fred didn't show a reaction, obviously not listening, more concerned with Batman and Robin's current predicament in Gotham City's harbor by the evil Penguin.

"He can move his head and wriggle his toes slightly," Steck continued, " For now Stephan's condition has stabilized with the cocktail of drugs we've hit upon, but even that may not last forever." His voice actually cracked a little with these last few words–Edie was surprised yet pleased to see Dr. Steck did seem to care about Stephan as a person, not just a powerful tool to achieve political power. "So I don't see how what you've accomplished there with Fred could possibly be applied to Stephan's situation," Dr. Steck concluded, then hastily, "Not that what you've done is anything less than remarkable, Dr. Langston." Old habits, thought Edie, die hard, at Steck's return to the proper professional address.

"Well, let's not be too hasty, shall we, Dr. Steck," Robin answered with a totally different tone in his voice–Edie saw Fred whip around from his seat on the couch at the mention of "Dr. Steck." Uh-oh, she thought, from the look on the primates face, there was no doubt Fred remembered the name. Fred slowly, and with exaggerated movements got up and climbed onto the back of the couch, never taking his eyes off Steck. Edie was suddenly very thankful they were 3000 miles apart from the large chimp, recalling the incident a few years ago in Southern California that ended with a woman having her face ripped off by a "pet chimp", blinded and maimed for life.

Robin started giving a short lecture on vocalization techniques to Dr. Steck and Edie could tell Robin was purposely establishing his authority and superior knowledge of the matter by his using the formal "Dr. Steck" as would a professor formally addressing a college freshman with "Mr." He quickly lost her and from a quick sideways glance Edie noticed Steck wasn't far behind.

"...And therefore what the end result of cavitation versus resonation, well–here let me show you something," Robin said, " Fred, can you join us for a minute?" No sooner had the words left Robin's mouth than Fred violently launched himself into the air. He landed drop-dead perfect onto the rickety barstool a dozen feet away- right next to Robin who took little notice of this amazing feat.

"Fred has several implants to make speech possible, one of which is here," Robin pointed to the side of Fred's neck, "this one picks up electro-chemical signals from the brain to the nerve bundle that controls the vocal chords, which in chimps is somewhat crude, comparatively speaking. All primates are similar; our ancestors were probably pretty much the same as well." Fred never took his eyes off Steck, looking like a boxer staring down his opponent.

"OK, Fred," Robin instructed, "Say something, a word or two, it doesn't matter what." Fred smiled, like an executioner welcoming a condemned man to the gallows.

"Hello. Dip. Shit."

"Thank you, Fred, for that uh, unusual choice of words," Robin said, "Now what had to have happened, what sequence of events transpired from a thought being formed in the cortex of the brain to the vocalization of that thought in a standardized form recognizable by others?" Robin asked, as he produced a white-board from his desk and began to sketch a side-ways drawing of a human head and neck. "So we tried to digitize the electrical pulses from the nerve bundle that leads to the vocal chords and build a database of words that could be recognized, but we soon realized we were only getting part of the information we needed. Someone came up with the notion of a feedback loop through the auditory nerve system, to refine and prompt the brain's nimbus for tone and inflection." Robin had sketched as he talked, the lines from the nimbus to the nerve bundle ending at the voice box, and a line from there to the ear and back to the nimbus.

"All of a sudden, the quality and quantity of the data jumped off the charts. But we were still light years away from what you see here today." He erased all the connecting lines, leaving just the head and neck outline intact.

"However, the center here is funded by venture capital that has an equity stake in all of this and I can't disclose anymore details over the net. If you're still interested I'm afraid you have to go through the vetting process and visit us here at the Center." Robin sat the marker board down and Edie saw Fred pick it up as soon as Robin turned back to face the screen. Fred swiveled his chair around, putting his back to the web-cam and started drawing.

"That's probably more trouble than it's worth, I'd think," Steck said, "I mean, Dr. Hollings is a busy man and his work can't be interrupted vainly searching for a solution to a problem that frankly is very different from that of uh, your monkeys.

Stephan doesn't have muscular control nor is he some lab animal for experimental research. Irregardless, Dr. Hollings time is much too valuable to "fritter away" over any pie-in-the-sky ideas you might have."

Dr. Hollings broke his long silence. "Robin-can-you-fix-me?" his metallic voice asked. Edie glanced over towards Stephan and she would later swear that she saw fire in his eyes. And she could tell even from three thousand miles away that Robin had taken Dr. Steck's words as a poorly disguised insult. She saw his mental tachometer shift a little into the red zone. It wasn't anything specific, yet he'd taken the slight as a challenge, she could just feel it. Robin leaned back and folded his arms across his chest and gave them a cool analytical stare.

"Yeah, I can fix you, Steve," he said, "I just don't know how yet."

"Now, young man–" Steck began, but before he could go any further, Dr. Hollings cut him off.

"Then-let's-fritter-away-Robin," he said.

Steck started to protest and then realized the less said right now, the better, and let it drop. He'd already been called on the carpet once, and settled back with a disappointed sigh of resignation to watch a perfectly good day of political schmoozing get shot straight to hell.

"How-soon-could-I-come?" Dr. Hollings asked.

"Actually, the sooner, the better," Robin replied, "the team that worked with me on Fred's project is still here working up the clinical trials for patent submissions. If we could switch them over to your project, it would save from having to train new personnel. We can let another group take over the trials, and have the "dream team" hit the ground running on yours. As for me, all I've been doing is monitoring "Project Penguin", and that's been leaving me with more free time than I like. Heck, I'm more than ready for something new."

"Project Penguin?" Edie asked, "What's that?"

"That's what we call Fred's vocal simulator," Robin said, "Fred picked the name–it's because he loves the Penguin on the Batman movies. That's also why I programmed his voice to sound like Burgess Meredith, the original Penguin." Fred looked up from his sketching, smiling wickedly, then went back to his artwork.

"Hey, Steve," Robin exclaimed, "That's something you get to do. You can come up with a project name for the team to use." Immediately Dr. Hollings began typing a response. Half a minute later came his reply.

"Robin-you-can-call-me-Batman."

Robin broke out in a huge grin and swiveled to face Fred.

"Hey, Penguin," he cried, "Better look out, here comes Batman and Robin, the boy wonder!"

Preliminary plans were made for Dr. Hollings trip to Africa amidst the diminishing protestations of Steck.

"We have guest quarters here at the compound," Robin said, "Just let us know who's coming with you and we'll have everything set up." Dr. Hollings began typing. "Just-us-three," he said. Edie turned to look at him surprised.

"How do I fit in?" she asked, amazed. The answer came back quickly. "Even-Batman-needs-his-good-luck-charm," Stephan said.

"Awesome!" Robin cried, "Maybe we can fit in a week-end trip to Spain, or when we're finished, even a week or two in Oxford, Aunt Edie!" Edie was still in shock, speechless at the kindness of Dr. Hollings.

She finally managed to get out a "T-Thank you, that would be lovely."

"Oh my God," she thought, "how can this be happening, I just got here! Nothing like this ever happens to me, never!"

"Hey Fred, you hear that?" Robin said over his shoulder to the chimp that was still hunched over the dry-erase board. "Steve, Aunt Edie, and Dr. Steck are coming to see us! Won't that be great?!" Fred spun around in his chair and casually stood the erasable board up on the desk but angled away from Robin. The neck and head now had a name. At the top it said "Dip Shit" in bold letters. And the lines depicting the neural pathways had been replaced with a hangman's noose around the neck.

"Why, I think that's great," Fred said, "You could say it just makes—my—day," in an admirable imitation of Clint Eastwood, hoarse and malevolent.

"Great!" Robin sang, "Now everyone's happy!" And everyone was, except for Dr. Richard Steck, who now saw weeks, if not months, of careful political maneuvering going down the drain, and a date with a deranged chimp in Africa to boot.

6

About The Primate Center

Eight days later Edie, Dr. Hollings, and Steck landed at Zaire International Airport. Robin met them on the tarmac in a shuttle bus with a handicapped lift installed, pulling right up to the stairway of their chartered jet. Bypassing customs they were driven to the other end of the airport where a large 8-seat Cessna awaited. Two seats had been removed for Dr. Hollings wheelchair and soon they were airborne again. Robin gave them a short lecture on the Congo, and its potential in bio-technical research. He subtly alluded to the Center's sway with the governing bodies, noting that cutting through unnecessary red tape such as customs and little oversight of their research methods were contributing factors that had came into play during the location selection process.

"What you see down there," Robin said, pointing below to solid jungle, as far as the eye could see," is a thousand square miles of mostly unexplored rainforest, home to thousands of unknown species of plants and hundreds of animals. This is our lab, which in conjunction with our other sister locations, provide some of the most advanced scientific and medical research and development on the planet. We have other centers in New Zealand, Brazil, Indonesia, and three oceanic labs as well. We're a private consortium with an annual operating budget the size of a third-world nation's GNP." Robin smiled. "And yet we strive to stay out of the public eye. We shamelessly bribe local officials, and probably have financed at least one 'coup-de-etat' since I've been here–all for the preservation of flora and fauna." He paused for effect.

"We are a profit-driven organization with legitimate agendas for social responsibility. The Centers official view is that the world is in the midst of a mass extinction, not by comet or another ice age, but by man. It's estimated 50 species of plant or animal goes extinct every week in the Amazon Basin alone. We take a realistic approach by buying up large tracts of jungle, collecting and cataloguing, discovering a few medical breakthroughs in the process. Our goal is to do the unthinkable–make preservation financially attractive. Anybody have any questions?" he asked.

"I have one" Edie said, "Do your people go out there collecting on their own, or do the locals bring items to the Center? I mean, it looks very dangerous, uh–you know wild tigers and such," she ended, rather poorly, not pointing out the obvious–that both Robin's parents had been killed in the bush.

"It has been a process that has evolved by trial and error," Robin stated. "We now have a system in place that minimizes both the natural danger to our teams and to the habitat. We still have an occasional tragedy–but then few things worth doing are risk-free, are they? What's a little danger when one day you can tell your grandkids about the species that you, the first civilized person, found and perhaps saved from extinction? Some even have their names in the Latin classification!"

"Well, surely you have the local governments' army or police to protect them in the jungle?" Dr. Steck asked, "Didn't you infer they were at your beck and call?"

"Beck and call for overlooking minor regulatory violations with the mandatory small contribution is one thing," Robin said, "But yeah, we tried using nearby military and the local police, but got poor results. If a researcher picked up an interesting rock in the field, a few days later the surrounding area would be decimated by the neighboring tribes hearing rumors that we had found diamonds. Dig up a plant from the bank of a stream, the next thing we knew the same stream would be dammed up and destroyed by word getting around that we had struck gold." Robin shrugged. "We were doing more damage than good. There is so much poverty, greed, and corruption at every level, you couldn't blame anyone. We just had to stop using them."

"But if you said you still have teams out in the bush, and you can't use the army or police, what do you use?" asked Edie, "Surely they aren't left to fend for themselves, are they?"

"Oh, no" Robin replied; "Now we use mercenaries."

A vast clearing soon came into view, and Robin pointed to the small town, a couple of kilometers away.

"That's Alibindi. Over there's the airstrip." Robin gestured, "And that Pentagon looking building with eight sides instead of five is the Center." Robin rubbed his hands together and arched his eyebrows, affecting the sinister grin of a mad scientist. He looked at Stephan wolfishly. "We can rebuild him, make him stronger, faster, than ever before!" He laughed wickedly. Dr. Hollings had a comeback ready.

"Just- get-me-talking-and-the-next-galaxy-discovered-will-be-the-Robin-Way."

"Wow, could you really do that?" Robin exclaimed, "Shoot, I'll make you sing like Pavarotti!" He turned to Edie.

"Hey, Aunt Edie, a nerd with a sense of humor, you better make your move, don't let this one get away!" Robin laughed like it was the funniest thing he'd ever heard, slapping Dr. Hollings on the thigh and giving him an exaggerated man-to-man wink. Luckily the pilot came on and began announcing their landing procedures. Edie uttered a small prayer of thanks to the gods that be, as everyone busied themselves with buckling up, not noticing that she was dying from embarrassment.

What looked to be a decent-sized structure from the air upon closer inspection was huge, more like a military base than a lab, Dr. Steck thought. Two 12-foot high fences with razor wire and gates with armed sentries gave him second thoughts about agreeing to what he considered a very expensive wild-goose chase. The gates swung open without hesitation as they pulled up in the dusty Land Rover. No one demanded for them to halt and give the secret password, so perhaps it wouldn't be as regimented as it seemed, even for a man who liked a certain level of protocol.

They proceeded to Section C's guest quarters, Robin explaining that there were eight sections A through H, for each corresponding slice of the hexagonal pie. Edie was provided a suite the size of a small apartment, with Steck and Hollings given an even larger 2-bedroom version that came with a study.

Robin showed them his living quarters right down the hall, "You need anything, you come on down and get me. The rooms you've been given were designed to function exactly like rooms at a 5-star hotel, they were built for VIP's and visiting emissaries so there's room service, wake-up calls, whatever." Refrigerators were stocked as well as the bar and kitchen.

"Order special requests ASAP, because it takes several days to truck in peanut M & M's from Zaire City, I can attest to that" Robin said. He walked them back to their respective rooms, Edie saying she needed to freshen up and Dr. Hollings looking fatigued after a taxing day. Edie closed her door and Steck wheeled Stephan to their home away from home.

Robin followed the doctors in and after Dr. Hollings was situated, he turned to Dr. Steck and said, "Hey, Dr. Steck, could I show you the medical emergency system I had installed?" Dr. Steck followed Robin into the living room where there was a pull box and intercom like a fire alarm, mounted in the wall.

"Simple enough," Robin said, "this is hard-wired straight to medical which is 24-7 here. I'll introduce you to the staff later if you like, they've already gotten copies of the medical records for Stephan that you e-mailed me."

"Thank you," Dr. Steck replied, "you've been very thoughtful."

"No problem," Robin said, "but while we've got a minute, can I ask you something? Is there something that might possibly have happened between you and Fred that day I missed the phone call from Texas?" Robin quickly went on. "Don't take this wrong, but every time your name has come up this week it always seemed Fred had to throw in some snide comment. Did you and he have words or anything else happen you can think of?"

Caught off guard, Steck was momentarily at a loss for words and finally reluctantly conceded, "Well, there was a small misunderstanding for a very short time where I mistakenly referred to him as the janitor," and Steck went on to explain how it all had started with the receptionist saying that the maintenance man was working in 3-C and how Robin could see that given Fred's uncultured, raspy voice how such a regrettable case of mistaken identity could have happened. How degrading, Steck thought, to be cornered into making an apology for insulting a damned monkey!

"Oh, great," Robin said, "I knew I was making something out of nothing. There for a while I though you guys had really had a go at each other, the way he's been acting. I mean, at least you didn't provoke him, like call him a baboon or something. Then we'd have a different case altogether. Well, I'm glad that's all settled so we can get down to business. Aren't you, Doc?"

Steck winced. "Indeed, Dr. Langston, indeed."

7

The Rocks

Later that night Robin lay in bed, thinking about the day. He wanted to tell Dr. Hollings about those rocks that had turned a square kilometer of their 'lab' into a 'diamond rush'. He rolled two marble-sized pieces around in his hand. What sort of rock is magnetic but only to other rocks of the same kind, not metal? He recalled the day they came into his possession. A team member on a foraging mission had stumbled upon them while eating lunch in a small clearing. The intern had noticed several small mounds of round rocks, clumped together in piles. Taking the toe of her boot she had nudged a small mound, wondering if it was the product of some small burrowing animal. The stones all moved, but they had shifted as one, staying linked together. The student then gave the misshapen mass a little kick like one would use to clear away an overly attentive puppy–to her surprise the stones broke apart, but the ones remaining closest to each other rolled back towards one another, and reattached themselves.

Pulling out her steel machete, she went to pick them up, wondering what would magnetite ore be doing out here in this form. Only the stones wouldn't stick to the blade. She tried several times before putting down her sandwich and picking them up. Sure enough, all the stones in that little pile would stick to each other but not to metal. The young woman tried with her folding army shovel as well to make sure. Same thing, with that pile and the other clumps she found scattered about. Not knowing what to make of this, the scientist-in-training called the team leader, a thirty year old biologist from Sweden, over to her find. Soon they were joined by the rest of the team, along with the local guides and militia. The natives were not quite sure what to make of all the excitement over some ordinary looking rocks, but later back at their village someone pointed out diamonds don't look like diamonds coming out of a mine; they looked like plain rocks, too.

But Robin did get three dozen or so before the area was ravaged, and while they weren't diamonds, they were scientifically even rarer. They actually were part of the implants used in Fred's vocalization simulator for they worked just the same as other magnets, but with vastly improved sensitivity because of their immunity to any distortion from all things metal. The components, the component housings, connecting leads- all had metallic parts. Even though these were tiny, when normal magnets were used there was a significant loss of range and clarity, thereby losing much of the subtle inflections of human speech. Robin likened it to AM versus FM radio. Which brought his mind back to Stephan Hollings, or the 'Batman Project.' Robin closed his eyes and started running simulations of different applications through his minds eye. He drifted off to sleep, the two small rocks stuck to the side of his head.

The next day began in earnest, with Robin having rigged up some prototypes of experimental components. He began probing Stephan's neck and spinal cord and ear canals, asking the physicist to try to say a word such as apple or flower. The various apparatus' Robin kept switching out were all different in appearance. One resembled that halo-and-screws with a collar object that whiplash patients sometimes wear, another looked like a space helmet but no visor. There was one that was similar to the headset NFL coaches were always wearing, with the big earmuff connected by a wide band across the top of the head. In place of the little mouth mike were two similar looking devices, one on each side of Stephan's chin that ended down onto his neck, close to his Adam's apple. Robin spent a lot of time with those. All the devices were connected by cables to different computers and these were in turn were routed to a glassed-in room. That was where another scientist named Sarim Fuchi sat with earphones on, monitoring a large board with all sorts of digitized info scrolling across, the red and blue and green lights dancing across his face and the sound-proofed walls.

It looked similar to a DJ booth of a recording studio, Edie thought. Robin kept making adjustments and asking Dr. Hollings to try to say specific words–he had on a blue-tooth headphone as did Sarim. The Dr. would try, Sarim would say something in the booth and slide a lever, twist a knob, or type in a command, then Robin would make tiny adjustments to his devices and start the process all over again. This went on for most of the morning, with several breaks for Dr. Hollings, which Robin and Sarim used to analyze the data they had collected and strategize for their next session.

Edie decided to take a stroll in the inner atrium after Dr. Steck came in to observe, sometime around midmorning. He had a laptop and a satellite phone with him and Edie wondered if he ever stopped schmoozing up the politicians and big money interests. Perhaps she could go find Fred and he could give her a tour of the place. Maybe he could show her where the fitness center was, she thought, remembering her moment of fame turned to shame when she saw herself on screen last week. There's a good way to fill in her free time here, Edie thought, shed some winter fat. Buoyed by new goal, she set off in search of someone who could help her find her way, forgetting all about Fred.

Back at the lab, Robin greeted the two engineers that had entered the sound booth with Sarim, Ian and Zenoida. Zenoida was from Mexico City, a software engineer. She loved Robin's habit of suddenly lapsing into Spanish in the middle of the sometimes very technical-design-consults-turned-battlefield. He was the one who gave her the infamous nickname "Technical Ecstasy," in honor of her obsession with the coding of any program, no matter how insignificant the perceived flaw was. Now whenever she raised her voice at any one in on the joke the other party would sooner or later say something like, "OK,OK, take it easy there, T.E.," and then quickly beat a retreat before she unleashed whatever she had available to throw.

Ian Bowden was 'King Geek' of hardware (also pegged by Robin), but wore the title with pride, actually going by KG, or KGB. He was the final authority on all hardware and electronics, his only contemporary being Robin. K.G. conceded Robin's edge in the creative design department, but as Robin succinctly put it, "If K.G. can't get it to work then you've got a software problem."

Robin noticed that everyone was on their best behavior in front of their esteemed guest. "If I got my face splashed all over Nature and Science," he mused, "I guess I'd have to get used to normally poised and aloof scientists fawning over me like a bunch of little girls at a Jonas Brothers concert, too." Now he understood why Newsweek had described Dr. Hollings as having a 'rock star' following in the scientific community. "Oh, well, maybe by tomorrow everyone will be back to their opinionated, bitchy selves," he thought. "All we'll need is a little rough sledding to get the team back into fighting form."

"Hey, Steve, when are you going to give me and Sarim a lunch break?" he asked as noontime rolled around, "First day and you're already taking over!" Robin turned to Dr. Steck. "How about we all meet at 3-C around 2-ish?" he said, "I think we've got enough preliminary data to get these schoolgirls started on their homework. That okay with you, Stephan?" Robin had been watching Stephan closely, and had been keeping an excuse ready for the first sign of fatigue, keenly aware of his guest's limited endurance.

"OK-Robin-what-fine-people-you-have-here. I-want-to-thank-all-of-you-for-your-patience", he said, having typed that up earlier, storing it for replay. But to his newest fans it sounded totally spontaneous and fell like heavenly praise on their ears. After Steck and Dr. Hollings left the audio lab, Robin and his partially assembled team had an impromptu bull session, mulling over his medical charts and printouts of the data that Robin and Sarim had gathered this morning. First impressions were sometimes powerful harbingers, Robin knew, catching connections out of thin air before their rational, analytical training took over. But for now it was a free-for-all, stream-ofconsciousness session where there was no such thing as a bad idea or stupid suggestion.

That's why only these three, of the twenty-five or so members that would ultimately comprise the team for "Project Batman", were here on this first day. They were the most creative, each in their own way, and anyone else in the room could upset that delicate and magical balance from whence Robin had seen miracles spring up out of nothing more that an off-the-cuff remark. He didn't know if any of them had noticed he had purposely arranged for only them to be here at the first strategy meeting, but he sure wasn't pointing it out. Neither did Robin mention they were being recorded either, but he meant to jump in up to his neck and didn't want to slow himself down with taking notes, trying to retain every little gem that might fall out of someone's mouth. At this stage of the game they were all equals, and Robin had every intention of getting his licks in, too.

"Nice to incorporate some motor functions" Sarim was saying. "Most definitely more processing power."

"Bigger and better" Ian muttered–he had a notepad and was outlining a schematic absentmindedly, more doodling than a blueprint of anything.

"If he thinks as quickly as I think he does the code has got to be a lot more 'elegant' than what Fred's using," mused Zenoida, sipping on strong coffee imported from Brazil. Robin knew that 'elegance' was a software engineering term, meaning software that was as short in bytes as possible, thereby achieving more with less code. Elegant code was more efficient, faster, and contained far fewer bugs–he remembered attending a lecture once given by one of the pioneers of C-Lang, Thad Smith, who had, as a young prodigy, helped NASA standardize software procedures back in the moon days. He described millions of lines of computer code that wasn't linked in any logical form to each other, just endless loops and loops of command lines, often repeating previously typed instructions.

"That was the original birthplace of the term 'spaghetti code'" Dr. Smith had said, "Just imagine a big bowl of strings of code all looped and tangled together. The real miracle that happened on man's first trip to the moon," he dryly observed, "was that we made it there, much less back, without a major computer crash, not of equipment, but of simple typed instructions. Many programmers privately agreed it was a suicide mission, our computer language skills weren't developed as far along as the equipment. And there wasn't any way to debug the code if that would have happened, debuggers hadn't been invented yet. We would have had to have start all over, rewriting entire programs from scratch. Which would have taken days, and in some cases weeks, with the end result being catastrophic, of course." He smiled to the crowd. "Elegance is the beauty of simplicity, the art of saying the most with the least. Consider e=mc2, quite possibly the most powerful scientific statement ever made. Now that's elegance."

Sarim and Ian were discussing the added pressure of doing restoration work on a 'national treasure'.

"I don't remember, was it Clinton who said that?" and Zenoida saying

"Yeah, like, you'll just be messing with perhaps the greatest mind of the 21st century, no pressure there", Ian replied, and they all laughed a little wryly over that. Then it struck Robin, as he chuckled along with the rest, and then it hit him like a ton of bricks.

"Hey, guys," he said, "did it occur to anyone yet that while we're in here brainstorming, fifty yards away is someone whose brain should be in here storming with us so-called geniuses?" They all stopped whatever they were doing and looked at Robin, then each other, as it dawned on the group.

"It's times like this," Robin said, "I'm reminded that sometimes our great minds don't seem to be so great."

"Thank you, Captain Obvious," Zenoida chided, "I'm sure one of us would have snapped to the fact sooner than later."

"Yeah," K.G. laughed, "but boy, do I feel stupid right now!"

"I don't" said Sarim, "that's what these little get togethers are all about, right, to develop a plan of attack?"

"You bet," Robin chimed in, "that and to give our egos a good old fashioned dose of humility!"

8

An Addition To The Team

So at 2:00 p.m. Dr. Stephan Hollings was asked to join the team as a card-carrying creative engineer. He was to have access to any and all material and data, and upon hearing this Stephan displayed one of his lop-sided grins.

"Thank-you," he typed, "I'm-flattered."

Robin had brought four more team members to the meeting and he had printed up the morning's preliminary data, Dr. Hollings medical history, and a few bullet points from their "jam session" earlier. All told there were eleven, with Edie and Dr. Steck present, quietly sitting off to the side of the long conference table. Robin gave his thoughts, which he emphasized were "very rough and extremely negotiable," of what the final product might consist of, and then laid out some very broad performance specifications that he and the other three senior members of "Project Batman" had agreed on as a good starting spot. From there a division of tasks were assigned within each subgroup with the understanding that some were much more difficult than others.

"As soon as we can get some hardware up and running good enough to start slapping some basic code in, we'll reassess our priorities and modify our resources accordingly" Robin said, "So if someone starts feeling overwhelmed, he or she is to report immediately and directly to me. In order for this project to succeed–and we don't have an unlimited window on this one–we can't let any critical steps fall behind over pride or plain-old stubbornness." Robin grinned. "Not that I would ever have committed such errors in judgment, of course." The group all had a good laugh at that, as Robin was famous for taking on any challenge he faced with a warrior-like zeal that at times had been known to approach insanity.

"OK, let's hear opening remarks, starting with…Ian," Robin said, "Let's get this party started!"

A lively discussion ensued between hardware, software, and medical teams. Edie was soon out of her league. She heard a door open and saw Fred lope in unnoticed from outside, as everyone else was either talking, scribbling notes on legal pads or tapping away at laptops. There was a lot of academic and technical data being put up on a large flat-screen monitor that anyone could post whatever it was they pulled up off the internet or from the Centers network's database library.

Ian had brought a mannequin's upper torso and head that was mounted on a roll-around set of wheels with a tray containing markers, post-its, thumbtacks, and a bunch of small electronic components and devices. He had a little tool box with pliers, scissors, and other assorted tools, mounted on to the mannequin as well. Periodically, he'd put a tack or a mark or some device on the dummy, then someone else would say something, and he'd shrug and take it off or move it a little. At times he'd add another piece and the discussion would start up all over again, the team debating its merits.

Dr. Steck wasn't entirely pleased about Stephan's admittance to the group. He had spent the last hour locating a computer lab that could suffice for a studio away from home until some of the equipment arrived from Austin. He wasn't going to lose the momentum he had achieved in Washington in the last six months if he had a say in it. As long as he could get Stephan on Web-chats four or five times a week to the powers that be, he could handle the rest over e-mails and his Blackberry.

Speaking of which, he should call Texas and check on that shipment of video equipment right now. There was more technical issues than medical at this point, nothing he was needed for. He stood up and started punching in the number to Austin in the satellite phone, walking out into the hall.

Two maintenance men were running wiring down the hall, with their drills and sawzalls cutting through the conduit, grating on his teeth. Steck ducked into the audio-lab where the sound engineers had been earlier.

"Hello, Hollings foundation" Sarah answered, "how can I help you?"

"Sarah, this is Dr. Steck," he said, and then was interrupted by the door opening. One of the new team members came in the door with a push cart.

"Hi, Dr. Steck, sorry but they need some of the test equipment next door." Steck merely grunted his annoyance and turned to leave, then spotted the sound-proof booth where Sarim had been earlier.

"Hold on a second, Sarah," he said, and turned to the young man.

"Is there anything you shall require from the sound booth?" Steck glared at the intern, "or shall I find a broom closet somewhere, instead?"

The unfazed Aussie flashed Steck a big grin. "No worries, mate, it's all yours" and went back to rummaging through desk drawers with cheerful abandon. Steck went into the booth and closed the door, instantly being rewarded with silence.

"All right, Sarah" he said, "Now get the shipping order from Fed-Ex for the video equipment. I want to know what's been shipped and when it's due in Zaire City." The Aussie scientist waved good-bye to Steck, who acted like he didn't see him and turned his back to the glass wall.

"Jesus," thought the young man, "I've got a masters in robotics and that guy treats me like his garbage man. What a jerk!" He started out the door, but it opened just as his pushcart was drawing near.

"Hey, thanks, mate!" he said, "It's good to see someone sporting some decent manners." The Aussie tossed his head back towards Steck as he passed through the held door. "Some blokes could use a lesson or two about the importance of being a bit more civil, eh," the young man said as the door swung shut.

"Well, then, let's give the bloke a little lesson in the do's and don'ts of common courtesy," said the large primate in a prim British accent, "And let's start with the don'ts."

Back in the lab Robin was breaking up a small quarrel between Ian and Zenoida.

"Hey, slow your roll, there, T.E." Robin said, and ducked under the table as the inevitable object, this time her laser pointer, sailed over his head. He laughed along with everyone else, and then added, "Actually, Zenoida's probably right, Ian, remember the first time we tried that with Fred? Hey, where is Fred, I saw him a minute ago?"

"He just walked out," Edie said, "You want me to go see if I can find him, Robin?"

"Thanks, Aunt Edie, I just want to be sure everyone gets a good visual on this one. This is a prime example of the kind of problems we'll dealing with" Robin replied, "Plus that will give me time to hide Zenoida's favorite weapon!" He turned back to the group. "Now, if you'll remember..." Edie heard him start up as she headed for the door to go look for Fred.

"Okay, Sarah, I want you to e-mail that copy to me... Yes, as an attachment, how else would you do it," Steck said, with a touch of sarcasm. "Then call FedEx and have them pick up these following items. Number one..." Behind him the door to the booth opened. "Hold on, Sarah" Dr. Steck bit off and raising his voice, said over his shoulder, "Whatever you've forgotten, you've had your chance, now you can just wait!" He turned back to the list he was holding under the corner light. "Number one..." and Steck felt a heavy hand clamp down on his shoulder.

Before he could react, a raspy voice sounding eerily like Clint Eastwood's Dirty Harry said, "I haven't forgotten anything, punk. And I have been waiting–it's my turn now."

Edie looked at the two maintenance men and asked if they had seen Fred. The one on a ladder said, "Yeah, I saw him go down the hall, I dunno, five minutes ago." She saw Randy coming up the hall with some more electronics.

"Hey, Randy, have you seen Fred? Robin wants him to come to 3-C for some small demonstration."

"He's in the audio lab, Miss Edie; I was just down there a couple of minutes ago," the good-natured kid from Australia said. She walked into the unlit, darkened room.

"Fred! Hey Fred, are you in here? We need you for a second!" Not hearing a reply Edie turned to leave when she caught movement out of the corner of her eye.

She turned towards the sound-proof glass of the sound booth and gasped in horror–Fred was attacking Dr. Steck! The large chimp had Steck in a head-lock over the sound board. Fred was standing on a chair, bouncing up and down with Steck's head under one arm, the blue, green, and red lights bouncing off Dr. Steck's bald head, and in Fred's other hand was–"Oh, my god, Steck wears a hairpiece!" Edie realized, running towards the door and flinging it open.

Fred was chanting, "I will never stick my nose up, not at anyone ever again, unless it's up a baboon's butt, and who knows where that's been! Say it! I will never…" and Steck said it, muffled but audible enough to understand, "I will never stick my nose up, not at anyone ever again, unless it's up a baboon's butt, who knows where that's been!"

"Unless I want to eat this hair-thingy on You-tube!" Fred screamed in his ear.

Unless I want to eat my toupee on You-Tube!" yelled Dr. Steck, from under Fred's hairy armpit. Fred pulled the doctor up straight, and then slapped the hair-piece haphazardly on Steck's head.

"There you go. Now we're even. I say we keep this between you and me, Doc. No need for everyone to know you like wearing a dead rat on your head." Fred came strolling out of the booth.

"Oh, by the way, I recorded that. You better not erase it." He looked back at the doctor menacingly–"Unless you want to do another take." He turned to Edie. "Old monkey rhyme my first girlfriend taught me, reworked it a little bit for ol' doc there. Tell Robin I'll be right there."

Fred went over to the sink in the small bathroom and started to wash his hands. Edie closed the booth's door, a little shaken, but relieved Dr. Steck was alright. He had brushed by her, making a beeline for the audio lab's exit, and disappeared out into the corridor. She took a deep breath, thankful that Fred hadn't been going "rouge" on them, and then let it out as she started back to the lab. Just as she reached for 3-C's doorknob a hairy black hand shot out and grabbed it.

"Allow me, madam," Fred said, opening the door with a flourish. On the other side was Randy, coming out from the noisy dayroom.

"Well, bloody nice to see a bloke with some manners, eh, missy?" he said, "I was just coming to see what the devil Fred was up to. Has he been giving you a hard time, letting go of the Doc just to pay us a visit, then?"

"Oh, I was finally able to pry them apart, Randy," Edie smiled. "It just took a few minutes, that's all."

9

Working On Doctor Hollings

The next few days went by quickly, the hum of activity constantly shifting from fabrication to assembly, to design changes, and back again. Robin would periodically leave to go check on a couple of techs that he said were working on "another little project I've got going on". He'd return to monitor the steadily growing team's progress, usually within the hour, and with gusto jumped right back in wherever he'd left off. There were at least twenty different people working in five different locations everyday. There were also visits from the occasional senior scientist. "Hard-core eggheads with serious nerd issues", Robin had called them, in reference to their dropping by on a daily basis, "ostensibly for consults, but really just nosing around and sucking up to our celebrity savant."

Dr. Hollings hadn't offered any advice but had made every meeting and seemed to give an excellent grasp of what was going on. There had been several minor setbacks, but so far every problem that had popped up had been resolved before stalling the entire team out. Robin was pleased with the absence of major obstacles at this point–but he knew that one was probably lurking somewhere down the road. Ian called them ghosts in the machine, something he'd picked up from some old rock song. Robin had said that the very thought of little poltergeists living in the inner workings of machinery gave him chills down his spine.

"It just makes too much sense," K.G.B. had insisted, "It explains a lot of things. Like why your car will start every time for that dentist appointment, but on a cold winter morning, a Monday morning, oh hell no–and there you are, late for work.

Man, I'm telling you, they're there alright, and they sure know when to crash a party! They only manifest themselves when it can hurt the most." Robin ventured that he hoped there would be no need for exorcisms on "Project Batman", but Ian had assured him he was "an expert at eviction of mechanized apparitions."

"Hello-Robin," Dr. Hollings said. "Anything-especially-exciting-on-for-today?" Robin swung around in his chair. "Hey, Steve! Let's see, Ian's fab team is re-casting the #4 component housing to accommodate the new configurations, assembly's working on wiring harnesses for the audio loop sensor, testing is burning in yesterday's finished components. Zenoida's got a couple of meetings today with a bio-tech software dude flying in from our New Guinea Center. He's probably going to leave smarter than he came, but we'll just have to take our chances on that. I'm a natural-born sucker for all the free advice I can get, you never know, we might get lucky," Robin went from the flowchart to his day-runner, humming to himself. He brightened up considerably and hit a key on his keyboard.

"Well, since this is the first morning where everyone has something going on and no one has decided to manufacture a crisis yet, there's something I've got I'd like you to take a look at. Let's roll, bucko." Robin said. He shut down his laptop, having just sent an e-mail to the teams letting them know to call him on his cell if he was needed, otherwise he was taking two hours personal. The five different teams were all to Robin's left as they exited 3-C, but he turned right, toward the living quarters.

Right before Robin came to his own apartment, he took a right into a small alcove, pushing a button on the door. He waited until someone came to the door and let them in.

"Hey Duc, Inga around?" Robin asked the small Asian, "or you stuck here by yourself?"

"She went for lox and bagels," said Duc, wiping his hands with a towel. "I can call her and tell her to bring more for our honored guest," he added, "You must be Dr. Hollings. I'm Duc Ngyuen, professional geologist and amateur astronomer. Pleased to finally meet you."

"Thank-you," said Hollings, "Do-you-have-a-telescope-here?" he tapped out while Robin and Duc wheeled him on into the work area of the small lab.

"I do, but there's the Center's fifty-incher fifteen minutes outside Zaire City, up on Mount Sybali if you want to go sometime. We'd have to take the chopper, but the light pollution is almost nil, it's worth the trip. Just let me know a day ahead of time, I'll set it up. I'm sure the staff would be thrilled!"

"Yes-maybe-later-when-we're-not-so-busy" Stephan typed.

"Okay then! Well I'll shut up about that for now," Duc said, grinning like he'd won the lottery, "What's up, Robin, you ready for some samples?"

"More like a tour and a briefing for Steve about what you and Inga are working on is what I had in mind," Robin said, "Bring him up to speed on what we've got, what we know, and what we don't know."

The buzzer sounded and Duc went to let Inga in. Duc said a few low words and they heard a woman's voice draw a sharp gasp. A moment later a tall, blond woman with a beaming face came in the room holding a bakery bag. Inga almost started to put her hand out but quickly took it up and smoothed her hair, nimbly avoiding an embarrassment.

"How wonderful to meet you!" she purred with a touch of German accent. "Back in Germany you are very well known, back there we treat top scientists like America does baseball players."

"It's-lovely-there-I-know" Dr. Hollings responded politely.

"Hey, Inga," Robin said, "Did you happen to get an extra bagel me and Stephan can split while Duc here gives his wildly entertaining monologue on the magnets who don't know they're magnets?"

"Sure, you can both have one," Inga said, "Look, Robin, I've got some data to compile while Duc gives Dr. Hollings an idea of what we're doing, is that OK?"

"Sure," Robin said, "But I'll come get you before the fat lady sings."

"What?" Inga asked, then, "You with the funny sayings. Ok, liebschen."

Duc had taken the liberty of opening up the bagels, and now was munching on one of the four he'd prepared as he returned to the group. He finished gulping it down, then while wiping his hands on a napkin, asked what the doctor knew about the Robin's Eggs.

"Only about how we had to stop using locals because of the diamond rush episode." Robin said, grabbing a pastry for Dr. Hollings. "Take it from there, Duc."

Duc switched on a monitor mounted on the wall, clicked on a program on his laptop, and a second later there was a pile of small stones displayed. He told about the discovery and how the natives had razed the area for a thousand square meters, digging for diamonds, all over about five kilos of marble to golf ball sized stones that the Center's researchers had gathered. The researchers (and Robin) had choppered to the site a week after the initial find and encountered total destruction. They'd never even landed, Robin rationale being the less made of the find the better. All that destruction and nothing to show for it, if the Center feigned disinterest, maybe other sites would fare better. All search and gather missions still kept an eye out for more of the strange piles, but none had been found over the last year. Duc had flipped through aerial photos of the find from Google-earth and the other hopeful sites.

He double-clicked and one of the golf-sized rocks that had been sawn in two popped up on the screen. He went to a small wall safe, opened it, and removed clear plastic container half-filled with stones. Duc put it on a small cart along with a jeweler's loupe, a small jeweler's hammer, a big, flat knife and some other items. He wheeled them over to Stephan and gave a quick demonstration of their magnetic peculiarities. "They have opposite poles, but not north and south. And the poles drift pretty much all the time." Duc said, "They carbon-date to about four million years old. They're evidently not meteorites, more like granite. They could have been pushed up by continental drift, or possibly from the edge of a volcano, not lava but maybe some crust brought up next to an eruption. To put it simply, we hypothesize they're young earth rocks made by earth-like processes, only with some very un-earthlike qualities."

Then Duc went on to explain that after Robin had started the "Penguin Project", he'd decided to incorporate them in real field conditions and of the tremendous improvement in performance due to a pure magnetic field.

"And that's all we know and the pure magnetic field is really just an educated guess, not a scientific fact," Robin said, "We've been keeping a tight lid on this. The Center is very much committed to preservation. We're not buying into the current scientific world's love affair with publicity. Or as I prefer to call it, funding by public exploitation."

"So-you-haven't-released-any-findings?" Dr. Hollings asked.

"Don't take this too personally, Steve," Robin continued, fully aware of Dr. Steck's obsession with both big government and big money, "but I've no problem letting anyone know where I stand on the subject of big government's record on protecting our environment. The Center here is invading pristine habitats for a profit, sure, but not like the rest of the scientific world, which at times seems to be hell-bent on the destruction of habitat and the extinction of thousands and thousands of species. The only planet we've got is at stake, and I don't see anyone else doing anything more than pass resolutions that are in turn violated by the same nations that voted for them. Save the whale, my ass." He stopped himself from saying more than he already had–it really wasn't his business what Dr. Steck and Steve were involved in. Dr. Hollings was tapping out a response.

"Robin-could-you-take-me-to-my-room-now?" he asked, "And-thank-you-Duc." Robin gave a funny look to Duc, who looked crest-fallen, as if it was he who had offended the physicist, not Robin. Robin pushed Stephan to the door as the geologist silently let them out. No night at an observatory with the world's greatest living expert on the universe, Duc told himself, not now. Sighing, he went back to tell Inga he was done with his monologue, and had decided to take off early. He didn't feel so good.

Robin was guiding the chair down the corridor and kicking himself in the ass at the same time. Never discuss politics with business, how many times had he heard that? He let Stephan in and there was Dr. Steck catching up on his e-mails, probably turning down more degrees and fifty-thousand dollar honorifics while Robin was showing off his rock collection and spouting off in self-righteous indignation on the scientific community being of lesser virtue.

"Well, I better go check on Ian and Zenoida," he said hoarsely, "See you later, guys." Robin heard Stephan typing, but figuring it was for Dr. Steck, turned to go.

"Dr.-Steck-could-you-excuse-us-for-a-moment," Dr. Hollings said.

Robin stopped dead in his tracks- then realized, of course, he wasn't getting out of here scot-free, not without a little lecture on professionalism and respect.

"Why, uh, sure," Dr. Steck replied, who had been most subdued as of late, "As a matter of fact, I really should beat the crowd at the cafeteria. I think I'll just take this with me." He shut his laptop and was out the door a minute later. All the while Dr. Hollings was tapping and tapping away. Robin sat down on the sofa, resting his hands on his knees, facing Stephan.

"Robin-I-think-I-know-what-those-rocks-are" he said, "they-are-probably-from-another-universe. Goget-them-immediately," Dr. Hollings tapped some more, "Those-few-stones-are-from-another-dimension. Say-nothing-to-no-one. Go-now."

Stunned, Robin did as Dr. Hollings commanded. He didn't see Duc, only Inga, who let him in.

"Duc went home early," she said, "I could finish sawing those samples myself." "No!" Robin exclaimed, "I mean, why don't we all take a short day, Inga? I'm going to take the Robin's eggs over to–uh, well, uh, I just need to look at them again," Robin ended dismally–and sounding a little nutty too, he thought, like Gollum. Almost pleadingly, Robin implored, "Come on, Inga, I'll make sure everything's put away and locked up, whaddya say?"

"Oh, you don't have to ask me twice, my little boss-man," Inga replied gaily, "I'm so out of here." She was out the door in a flash before Robin could change his mind.

Mechanically, still in a daze, Robin gathered up the ten rocks left there and put them in the clear container. Inga had taken them all out and had been five minutes away from cutting two into wafer-thin slices to be used as part of Dr. Hollings prototype sensors. Robin had no doubt that the Dr. would have considered that a very bad thing. While the volume hadn't risen as he had spoke, it was more the look in Stephan's eyes that left Robin imparted with a Def-Con One, nuclear holocaust type of urgency. His hands trembled as he went to the small safe, and it took three tries to get it open. Inside were the remaining twenty-two, with two more that had been cut with a diamond-bladed wet-saw. The four resulting wafers from the two cut up stones had been used as implants, with the remnants were stored for future experiments. Well, it didn't sound like that would be happening anytime soon. Robin shut down the lab and went to Dr. Hollings quarters with the twenty-two still intact stones.

Dr. Hollings had been busy while Robin was gone. He had no more gotten back to his room than Stephan wanted to go to Robin's apartment, "away from Dr. Steck." Only after they were there, with Stephan on one side of a coffee table and Robin on the other, the Robin's eggs between them, did Stephen begin. He instructed Robin to go to the Hollings Foundation web site. He had him download a video of a short classroom lecture followed by a question-and-answer period, where in the interests of airtime the questions had been pre-submitted.

The subject was about Einstein's General Theory of Relativity and about the point where the equations stopped working. Stephan was going over material that most of the students in the audience knew–he just gave a review and added a few updates that had been proposed more recently. Even though Robin had studied some advanced physics and had a working knowledge of the subject, he was glad to revisit the basics. Not many people truly understood relativity and he wasn't one of the fortunate few, not yet anyway. He noticed Stephan had a knack for communicating, the lecture was gripping. Then the Q and A began. Could Dr. Hollings give a brief example where Einstein's relativity stopped working? He started on how Einstein knew that there were four forces in nature- nuclear fission, nuclear fusion, electro-magnetism, and gravity. According to Einstein's equations, all these forces should be of equivalent power. Fusion, fission, and electromagnetism are–but for some reason gravity was much weaker. It shouldn't be, but it was. Therefore, it was argued, Einstein's equations must be wrong- after a certain point of explaining perfectly of how everything in the universe works, it just fell apart. Eventually, after no one could come up with a better description or theory, even after eighty years of effort world-wide, one scientist suggested that the reason we saw gravity as weaker than the other forces was because we could only see into part of the dimensions that gravity existed. It could be that there were alternate universes that contained some of gravity's power.

"So like wormholes that might lead to somewhere else in a completely different part of the universe, a similar construct could bleed gravity into a whole other dimension, or even another universe?" was the next question.

"Yes-and-here-I-thought-no-one-was-paying-attention," Stephan said, breaking the audience into laughter.

"Any other follow up thoughts to the alternate universe theory?" asked another. Stephan started by saying that most scientists now accept the existence of dark matter–matter is right here in our universe. It can't be seen, but its there, and is constantly moving around us, even right through us, as small subatomic particles moving at close to the speed of light.

"Some-passed-through-you–as–I-was-saying-this-sentence-and-went-straight-through-the–earth-and-never-slowed-down-never-touched-an-atom-Perhaps-gravity's-force-has-been-distributed-among-the-dark-matter-and-that-would-help-bring-Einstein's–theories-back-to-being-acceptable–In-any-case-conquer-gravity-and-you-own-the-world," he'd said. Then as an afterthought, "And-be-guaranteed-at-least-a-"B"-in-this class," and the audience howled with hilarity. They then all spontaneously rose to their feet, giving him a standing ovation as the video rolled the credits.

Robin listened as Stephan talked of light waves sometimes taking on the characteristics of particles and sometimes particles acting like waves. Some experiments seemingly demonstrated that a particle could and did exist in two different places at the same time. Dr. Hollings told him that his latest research paper was trying to establish a relationship between the very small and the very large that would allow Einstein's equations to co-exist with new findings in Quantum Physics, the science of the very small. His last two papers had been highly controversial, he said, and caused quite a stir upon publication. He went on to say that he had purposely submitted an article over the past year to Nature and followed it up with an interview in Science, subtly and sometimes not so subtly alluding to the upcoming release of his next paper. This major new theory of his, Stephan continued, was scheduled to be read at the Oxford Consortium in June, and was almost certain to be one of the most polarizing publications to hit theoretical physics since Einstein's release in 1905 of The Special Theory of Relativity.

The battle lines already being drawn, he told Robin, and from the tone of his fellow colleague's recent interviews and press releases, most of which had ridiculed his speculations, it looked like things were about to get ugly. His smattering of supporters were all relative unknowns, coming out of almost virtual obscurity. Even then, only with the utmost temerity had they voiced their opinions, fearing the repercussions from the established scientific world. Reputations were sure to be won or lost, with a lucky one or two having the incredible luck to have the right math at the right time, thus becoming the newest authorities on particle theory. Fame, fortune, and prestige awaited the few winners while others would be humiliated and denounced, never to be taken seriously again.

"My-academic-life-is-also-hanging-in-the-balance," he told Robin, "Even-though-I'm-convinced-I'm-right,being-right-means-nothing-if-someone-can-find-flaws-in-your-math. Even-a-small-typographical-error-in-your-supporting-data-could-be-used-to-discredit-an-otherwise-incredible-scientific-revelation. I-find-it-ironic-that-physics-can-be-a-crapshoot-sometimes-thus-serving-as-an-excellent-metaphor-for-the-indeterminancy-of-atomic-behavior.I've-often-wondered-what-if-instead-of-a-god–there's-just-a-mischievous-elf-out-there-with-a-highly-developed-sense-of-humor."

"Someone would try to discredit someone else's work, even if they believe it to be factually correct and a major scientific find, just to protect their own position in the scientific world?" Robin exclaimed.

"Without-a-moment's-hesitation," said Hollings, "It's-an-easy-rationalization. They-can-say-Hold-on-shouldn't-we-wait-a-few-years-for-more-evidence? What's-the-rush? What's wrong-with-being-absolutely-certain?" Meanwhile-they-do-all-they-can-to-keep-their-face-and-name-in-the-spotlight-maybe-get-a-book-deal-or-a-find-a-way-to-put-a-spin-on-it-without-looking-like-a-hypocrite. It's-been-done-before-and-on-something-of-this-magnitude-there's-no-telling-how-far-someone-would-go-to-protect-their-interests. There-are-people-who-would-kill-to-have-those-stones-if-they-knew-they existed."

"Okay," Robin said, "Let's just re-group here and let me see if I've got this right." He took a breath, and said, "You've been working on a major breakthrough in particle physics that is the so-called Theory of Everything. You are planning to release your findings in June at the Physicist's Consortium in a paper that will cause a major upheaval in the scientific world–to the extent certain parties of the opposing field of thought would do just about anything–lie, cheat, steal–to prove you wrong, even if they suspect you're right."

"Yes," said Dr. Hollings.

"These rocks," Robin continued, "you believe are physical proof that validates your research."

"Convinced," Stephan replied.

"And you want to keep this a secret until absolutely necessary. For the safety of protecting these rocks, and if and when you get ambushed you can pull them out and say 'Okay, then explain this."

"That-is-also-correct", said Hollings. Robin stood up and paced the room.

"And you could also protect the location of these rocks and the surrounding habitat by doing it that way, right?"

"Yes," said Dr. Hollings.

Robin continued pacing, thinking he'd missed something important. Then it dawned on him, what Edie said the first day they arrived at the compound and how she came to meet Dr. Hollings. She told him how Dr. Hollings longtime and devoted nurse Sarah had come up with the idea of hiring an English nurse to help Dr. Hollings on his trip to Oxford in the hope of helping him getting settled and familiar with the nuances of an English university.

"She's hoping that I could help level the playing field," Edie said, "against all of his other "esteemed colleagues," who don't seem to think twice about taking advantage of Stephan's impairments."

"Hey, Steve-O," Robin nonchalantly said, "What if you go to Oxford and present your paper and that first "esteemed colleague" attacks your research, what if he also gets to be the first recipient of the debut of Dr. Stephan B. Hollings new voice? You think that might give the rest of those jerks something to think about before the next one decides to take a swing?" Robin grinned wickedly. "Whaddya say, Batman?"

It took a few seconds, but it was a good one.

"News-Flash!-Joker-ambushes-Caped-Crusader-Batman-gets-last-laugh!"

The next day Robin held a 9:00 am strategy meeting, attended by the entire team, which had now grown to thirty-two members. Robin had purposely asked Stephan to stay at his quarters until Edie came for him and Steck.

"I have just been given a new dead-line for Project Batman," he began, and had Edie stand up and tell how Dr. Stephan Hollings had came into her life, "and now yours." Her short but poignant story touched them all, and when she sat down they broke into applause. Robin stood and raised his hands for silence, and while Edie went for Dr. Hollings he told them of the consortium's June 10th date and how Dr. Hollings was expecting to have his authority as the current top expert on particle physics challenged with sleazy underhanded attacks.

"But if everyone here does their absolute best and we can give Dr. Hollings a voice, then what we really will have given him is a weapon to defend himself…" he paused dramatically, as he saw the Dr. being wheeled in, "against those Judas's that are of the same ilk, and lie in the same bed with, the scientists paid by big government and big-money to attack us!"

Then with the booming voice of an announcer at ringside, Robin cried, "Ladies and gentlemen, I give you St-e-e-e-phan Hol-l-l-l-ings!" The conference room erupted in applause and whoops and hollers. Somewhere music started playing. Edie knew Robin was notorious for using music as a motivational tool, proclaiming it "both soothed the soul and awoke the primal." This one she remembered- it was the old 80's band Twisted Sister, playing the classic anti-establishment anthem "We're Not Gonna Take It…" Robin had jumped up on the big table and started singing into an imaginary microphone, and that was all it took as everyone joined in, dancing and singing.

"We're not gonna take it, no, we're not gonna take it, any more…" Edie started singing along with the rest of the eclectic group, bouncing on the balls of her feet. Impulsively she picked up Stephan's hand in hers and started dancing, using her other hand on the handle bar to rock his chair side-to-side in time with the music. When it was over everyone was fist pumping and high-fiving each other, cheering and laughing. They gathered up their notes and marched off to the labs with renewed conviction, hi-tech holy crusaders on a mission from God.

Robin jumped off the table and ran over to Edie and Stephan, chest-bumping Ian on the way. "OK, Doc," he grinned, still catching his breath, "I think I got'em pumped up enough for the kickoff. Whaddya say, let's go kick a little theoretical ass!"

The week and a half went by like a mad dash to the finish, and spirits stayed high. If someone hit a snag, he or she would have more help than they needed at a moment's notice. Ian's crew in fab and prototyping had taken on an uncanny resemblance to a pit crew for a NASCAR race; Ian would have a prototype of a component built and then it flew, literally at times, to testing next door. Ian had, early in the game, put in a half-wall of glass to replace the two previously sealed off rooms. Parts and tools flew through the air, back and forth. Zenoida had two desks and offices, one in testing and the other in the computer lab. Ian would hook up a component to test, Zenoida would shoot some boot instructions into it and then it was off to the races, with Ian probing the logic and using all sorts of gadgets to trigger sensors. Edie never saw anyone that could type as fast as Zenoida- and usually she was talking to a tech at the same time. Most of the time Robin was in the audio-lab with Dr. Hollings and other sound engineers. Randy was in the booth usually, and Robin and Stephan in the main area with all the prototypes and specialized testing apparatus. There was a calm intensity everywhere-

"Man, this is where it's at, it's poetry in motion, baby" Robin had said, commenting on the synchronized teamwork, "We eat this stuff like candy."

Then one day late in May Robin held a short staff meeting. Tomorrow, he said, he and a small medical team would be installing Dr. Hollings bionic trial package. He cautioned, "What's been accomplished so far is nothing short of a miracle, and now we're going for another." Ian stood up and said that they didn't want any of the new members to the team to get their hopes up too high; the "Project Penguin" had taught them that. He didn't elaborate further, and sat down. Zenoida then said the one thing they had learned was how important it was for everyone to relax, and channel their creativity.

Once again we find ourselves in uncharted territory. Any suggestion or plan of attack will be listened to unconditionally, there were some crazy ideas on how to get Fred's brain and equipment to jumpstart into life," she said, "and even some of the zaniest occasionally moved the ball forward enough for a first down." She then had to explain the metaphor to the many non-football savvy members.

Robin explained to Edie how they were going to implant magnetic sensors about the size of a nickel on each side of Dr. Hollings neck. The nerve bundle that connected the voice box to the brain would have two of the discs, creating a small magnetic field that passed through the bundle. As Dr. Hollings tried to say a word, the brain would send electro-chemical impulses down the nerve, disrupting the magnetic field. "Different words create different pulses. Eventually we get recognizable patterns and when Steve thinks 'apple', the sensors send the digitized info from the disrupted field to the wireless computer and if matches up to a previous sampling to get 'apple' from our database. Theoretically," he observed.

Edie noticed that all the team leaders were careful to pre-or-post qualify predictions now, almost somberly. She wasn't sure it pleased her, but went along, speaking in low tones when conversing about the operation tomorrow. Robin explained there was another set of sensors for implanting behind Dr. Hollings ears. This was the feedback loop. She had never totally understood it and said so.

"OK," Robin said, "Say a sentence to just anything, quickly, now!" Edie tried to think for a second. "OK, I'm going to the fitness center later you want to come?"

Robin pointed a finger to her lips. "Now, say it in your mind, don't say it, but in exactly the same way." Edie did and as she was doing so Robin took his finger off her lips and put it on her left ear. She realized she had heard the words without speaking. "When you speak, your brain is sending signals to your auditory system as well as your voice box. It's checking to make sure things are matching up. So we'll use this for a loop, which really is what the brain is doing, to triangulate as it were, to achieve greater speed and accuracy. There's one more component that's used for testing and then wiring, and a transceiver that goes to a small computer that will also be implanted later. Then there's the midi-interface with a hi-fidelity speaker system." Edie's eyes started to cross. Robin laughed, "Don't worry, Aunt Edie, I'll be sure to save the owner's manual!"

Robin didn't tell Edie about all the little electronic wizardry, just to spare her the 'geek-glaze'. He hadn't told anyone else, either, but for a different reason. "Like it or not," Robin thought, "And it's a perfect place to hide them anyway." He reached in his pocket where the Robin's eggs wafers were tucked, reassuring himself that what he was about to do was for the best.

The surgery went off without a hitch. Dr. Steck had been more than a little impressed with the staff. Robin's dexterity and skill with scalpel and suture belied his age, and the use of the tiny robotic arm with the cameras to insert the implants ensured an accuracy of "plus or minus one-tenth of a millimeter," Robin had said, then cracked, "I'm only getting paid to do this once, I sure ain't goin back twice!"

Dr. Steck wasn't totally comfortable with being escorted out near the end, Robin apologetically saying he couldn't divulge all the technology and procedures due to corporate equity agreements with investors, but Robin stood firm, and Dr. Steck finally acquiesced. The entire procedure was over in a little over an hour, from first cut to final stitch and Stephan woke up with no complaints of pain or discomfort. Robin stopped by Dr. Hollings hospital bed later, looking slightly drawn, with dark circles under his eyes. Dr. Steck caught him yawning, as he looked at Dr. Hollings notes.

"Didn't get much sleep last night," he offered, "Guess I was a little nervous about a couple of the components." He saw Stephan was awake.

"Damn," he exclaimed, looking at all the sutures on Stephan's head and neck, "I should have brought Fred, he'd probably think you were the victim of a tiger attack! Hey, Steve, I went ahead and threw in a free vasectomy, professional courtesy and all," He grinned, "We'll move you up to your quarters here in a couple of hours. I'll see you back at the ranch, cowboy."

The next afternoon Robin had Stephan in the audio-lab with Randy, the self-described "Awesome Australian Audio Engineer", in the glassed-in booth. Ian and Zenoida were at two different computer stations, each engrossed in streams of data and jumping bar graphs of light and the occasional "beep" from an error code. Robin was back in his blue-tooth headset and Dr. Hollings was being fed a series of words, one at a time, and asked to try and say them out loud. "We're not expecting any major leaps for a couple of days, so we don't even have his speakers hooked up yet." Robin explained, "I did that just to emphasize the patience we're all going to need to have." Two days later, Robin turned on the interface to Dr. Hollings voice simulator, still preaching patience. Ian and Zenoida had left the lab but were being fed test results at their office desktops.

"Good" Edie thought, "I'd be going crazy if I were Robin or Stephan; I'm going nuts just watching, much less with a ton of people hovering over me." Edie told Robin and Stephan she'd be back, she thought she'd hit the gym for a swim.

"Sure," Robin said, "You're starting to get buff, Aunt Edie, who's the lucky guy?" He grinned, giving Dr. Hollings chair a shake, "Maybe we can up the ante, eh, Stevie-boy?" And of course, Edie had to exit before her complexion gave away her embarrassment.

Jesus, it wasn't like she'd been obese! But Edie knew Robin, like most men, meant no harm. She shouldn't take everything so literally every time Robin said something in front of Stephan, she knew a little brevity went a long way with all the recent stress and tension. And the first of June a week away, Edie mused, as she entered the door to the fitness center.

10

Edie's Idea

At the end of the week Robin held an informal meeting with Ian, Zenoida, Randy and others who had been involved in "Project Penguin." "OK, folks," Robin started, "Oxford's ten days away. That leaves us eight. We've hit a roadblock and I need help. My crystal ball's broke and my magic wand is in the pawn shop."

Zenoida spoke first. "We may have over-designed this one for the time frame allowed. If you look at the level of sophistication between Fred and Stephan's setups, from a purely engineering point of view, you'll see what I mean–Fred's built like an old work truck, and Stephan's put together like a Formula One race car. Now I know the motor's gonna start eventually, but it's not going to be as easy as just pouring gas down his throat and hooking up a pair of jumper cables to his testicles," she said.

"Thank you, T.E., for that excellent use of a mixed metaphor," Robin grinned, "And also for that little mental picture you drew for the guys, I know it's sure to become my newest nightmare. But it's true that we went bigger, better, faster," Robin admitted,

"You know the meds he takes for his Lou Gehrigs, some are for nerve function, right?" asked Inga, "What if we zapped him with a controlled overdose, or his anti-seizure meds, maybe reducing them back?"

"Aunt Edie, remind me to talk to Dr. Steck about that," Robin said, "He's been Steve's physician for twenty years, he'll have the scoop on contraindications and such." Another suggested hypnosis. Ian thought tinkering with voltages in the magnetic fields might help. It went round and round until Robin called it a day, with promises to "try anything that doesn't involve jumper cables."

They tried all the ideas, except altering the medication–Steck had pointed out that the chances of making Stephan too ill to travel would negate any gain. Robin gently broached Stephan with the concept of taking a break from the non-stop testing until after Oxford.

"We'll-try-up-to-the-last-minute," Stephan said, "I'm-fine."

Robin said, "OK, look, I'm going to dig up some old files on 'Project Penguin' and see if I can get any new ideas kicking, do you want Randy to stop feeding you cues?"

"Tell-him-don't-stop," Dr. Hollings replied.

Robin walked to the booth where Randy and Edie were, thinking, "Man, this is one tough hombre."

Robin told them the plan and Randy said, "Not to worry. If he's tough enough to hang in there, then so am I."

"So I heard it was about the same for Fred?" Edie asked, "Was it this strenuous?"

"Oh, yeah, some ways worse," Randy said, "And I was there the whole time. I was the one that heard the first words out of his mouth, I was. See, Fred being a healthy young male and all was always antsy, always looking out the windows, like for a Sheila, or taking off his headset, all the bloody time. I finally tied him down for an hour once, but he just sulked up on me," Randy laughed, "He was mad at me for a week!"

"What's a Sheila?" asked Edie.

"Oh, y'know," Randy shifted a little uncomfortably in his chair, "Like a young looker, a lass." Edie gave him a bemused look. "A girl! A pretty young female!" he finally blurted out.

"Oh" Edie said, "Fred had a girlfriend?"

"No, missy," Randy said, "We weren't sure of what we was doing back then, and someone had suggested that we keep'em separated, as it were. Fred was born and raised in captivity, and hadn't ever seen a female, just his mum's all, and she died when he was six months old."

"But you couldn't get him to sit still because he was looking for females?" Edie asked, "Yet he'd never seen one?"

"Uh, yeah, Miss Edie," Randy replied, taking sudden interest in his switches, "The females were being moved to the cages in the commons here," Randy said, pointing outside to the inner open-air atrium, "And it kept distracting us that day he first talked."

"I'm sorry, Randy," Edie said, "I don't mean to be dense. How did Fred know there were female chimps out there, if he couldn't see them?"

"Well, well, he just smelled them, that's all!" Randy blurted out, ears red, "Two of them were in heat!"

Edie walked out of the booth, trying not to laugh. Poor Randy, didn't he realize she was a nurse? She had caught him looking at her earlier today when his eyes lingered a little too long on her cleavage, as she leaned across to set down his coffee she had brought him. She was taken aback a bit, and then was a little pleased that her hard work of late at the gym was paying off. She had on a V-necked sleeveless tee that she normally wouldn't wear out, but she noticed that when you had an exercise regimen you start to like wearing tee's and jeans. It just felt good to keep that physical state of mind on throughout the day. She started to go sit down, musing on what she and Randy had talked about. The day Fred first talked there had been numerous distractions, a fight between him and Randy, what else?

"Hey, Miss Edie?" Randy asked, seemingly recovered, "Could you turn up Dr. Hollings left ear one or two decibels, and his right just one?"

"Sure, Randy," Edie replied, knowing this part of the cueing process, where a sequence of words that were usually spoken louder would be fed, like "Hey!" or "Duck!" She smiled at Stephan, and he made eye contact and the lips twitched a little into his half-grin. Edie leaned over the wheelchair to get the left ear first, turned it up three notches, and brushed back across Stephan's chest to adjust the right. Oh, wait a second; it was two for the left, not three. Edie leaned back across and felt Stephan's warmth. It made her feel a little tingle, like you get when you brush up against someone whose scent is like an old and remembered fragrance. "OK, two," Edie said, and then looked down to give him reassurance and encouragement- and was shocked to see the smartest man on the planet eyes frozen, staring down her blouse.

"Well, uh, let me go check uh, with Randy, about, er, those settings," Edie stammered, and remembered a little late Stephan couldn't hear her. She did a quick about-face and walked self-consciously back to the booth. The door sprang open.

"Hey!" Randy cried, "I think I just got something!" then slammed the door in Edie's face. Edie barely noticed.

"I should never have left the apartment in this tee-shirt, and now Stephan was"–Wait!! Edie grabbed the knob and marched in the booth.

Randy was on his cell, "Yeah, Robin, definite hit! It's here on the log; it's a sustained exchange between all components, and feedback loop!! You gotta see this!" Randy clicked off, his eyes shining. "Whooo- hooo!"

"Hey, Randy," Edie said, "Is that how it happened with Fred?"

"Yeah, sort of," Randy answered, still caught up in the log.

"What were Fred's exact first words?" Edie casually asked. Randy went from exuberant young scientist to stumbling, bumbling high school nerd.

"Uh, y'know, it'd be better to get that from Fred," Randy uneasily replied, "I mean, seeing how's he's the one who said it and all. I-uh, need to get this data for uh, Robin, uh ready and all, y'know?" So Edie decided to do just that.

She found Fred watching TV in 3-C's day room, munching on a bunch of bananas, peels and all.

"Hey, Fred," she said, nonchalantly, flopping down and throwing her feet up on the old crate, "whatcha watching?"

"Some old Family Guy," Fred muttered, barely paying her any attention. "The one where Peter and the guys try to get Quagmire's job back as a pilot."

"Oh, yeah, seen that a hundred times." Edie said, then, "Say Fred, you remember the first time you talked?"

"Oh, yeah," Fred said, never taking his eyes off the tube, "took forever."

"Yeah, we're getting some of that with Stephan, too," said Edie, "We're trying to get those first words out and it's been awful."

"Hey, Fred," Edie tried to act as if the thought had just sprang up from out of nowhere, "What was it you first said?" Fred looked up at the ceiling, a smile slowly creeping across his face.

"Oh, mama," he said, "Oh, baby," with a faraway look in his eyes, and softly laughed. Edie thought whatever it was it certainly brought back a fond memory. Fred broke out of his trance, looked down at his hands for a second, sighed, and then went back to watching TV.

"Uh, Fred," Edie said, gently, "You were saying, y'know, what your first words were? It could be important- it might help Steve."

"I just told you," Fred replied, "Oooooh, mama. Oh, baby." He turned to her, and Edie was surprised to see Fred a little misty-eyed. "Nothing like your first love."

Edie and Fred talked for a half-hour, about the first time he'd ever seen a girl chimp. "Her name was Angie," Fred said dreamily, "I never knew anything could be so pretty." He went on to describe how Angie had slipped out of her cage in the compound and had been exploring the inner walls, trying to find a way out when she looked in the windows right where Fred was sitting in the audio-lab. Fred was dumbstruck, he said, Angie just three feet away, looking at him with those big beautiful eyes.

"I could smell her, it was like nothing I'd ever felt," he continued, "I thought I was floating in thin air. Then she tried to climb this pipe, a gutter that went up to the roof and I got a good look at the whole package. She was so hot!" Fred exclaimed, "And all I could think of was, 'Oh, mama, oh, baby!', and damned if I didn't hear those same words said out loud."

"Next thing I know, Randy's whooping and hollering, jumping up and down like a fool," Fred grinned, "Hell, I thought he was all fired up about Angie, too! Soon, they had me talking a kind of baby talk, and it was easy after that." He shrugged. "Robin was the one that made it go so fast. If me and him hadn't wired up, I'd still be stuttering and talking like an idiot."

"Wired up?" Edie asked. "What was that?"

"Oh, that's when me and him switch our simulators over to what he calls 'silent running', to where only we can hear each other," Fred said. "That's when it all really clicked."

"You mean," Edie said, "Robin has had the same surgery as you and Stephan had?"

Fred winced. "Uh-oh, I think I just screwed up." He grabbed her arm. "Edie, Robin said to keep it down about him having'em, too, I just forgot! I don't think it's a big deal, but let's keep it to ourselves, OK?" Fred brightened. "Hey, I told you what got me started talking, huh? That give you any good ideas on helping out the doc?"

Edie stood up, and smiled enigmatically. "Fred, you have no idea."

11

Doctor Hollings Is Motivated

Robin was uncharacteristically quiet, but his mind was racing. Trying not to give anyone a reason to slack up while yet still maintaining an aura of an impending breakthrough was a slippery slope indeed, he pondered, as he went once more over the data with Randy. He had been over everything twice, and had gone through the same audio sets again and again, to no avail. He glanced over at Randy and got back a stubborn look that stopped him if he was sure that he'd seen something.

"No, it was there, Robin, I saw it happen. He did everything but speak!" Randy insisted, now starting to show the pressure.

"All right, but what are we missing, then?" Robin asked, his brow furrowed in concentration. "Hey, maybe we ran through the cues too fast. Might be something as simple as that, y'know." He shoved back out of the chair, heading out of the booth to rejoin Dr. Hollings in the lab.

"Put on a little music, something slow and bluesy," Robin said, "I think it could be that we're all just pressing too hard." He looked at Stephan, knowing what hell this must be for him.

"Hey, Stevie-boy," Robin said suddenly, "You ever watch basketball, like the NBA?" Not waiting for an answer, he continued, "Me, I think Michael Jordan was the best, at least under pressure. I've only seen the high-lights of back when he played, but that guy was so smooth and relaxed, even at the end of a close game." He leaned back in the office chair, and rolled himself across the room, wadding up a printout from earlier in his hands. He took aim at the wastebasket in the corner, acting like he was getting ready to shoot a free throw, imitating the practice dribbles, then placing the improvised 'ball' over his head to take a shot.

"I remember seeing him win this one in overtime on ESPN Classic against Detroit," he said, taking a few more fake dribbles, "and later in the post-game interview, someone asked him about the shot, where he faked Byron Russell right out of his jock, hitting the jumper as time expired. The reporter asked Jordan, "What was the hardest part of making a shot like that?", and Jordan just smiled and said, "Making it look so easy." Robin launched the chair and the wad of paper in the air as he slid across the room. The printout plopped into the wastebasket with a satisfying ker-plunk.

"Man, did he know what he was talking about, or what?" He winked mischievously. "So how about us so-called geniuses stop making this so hard, huh? I mean, it's so easy an ape can do it, for crying out loud!"

Edie walked up the corridor to the audio-lab, more than a little subconsciously. She got a couple of approving looks from the maintenance men as she passed, and could feel their eyes following her backside as she passed. Edie was silently thanking her stars that she had had the presence of mind to throw on a lab coat. She had on more make-up than she could ever remember, and the rest of her ensemble was a first as well. Opening the door to the lab, Edie was surprised to hear music playing.

"Don't stop, don't think, just go." She took a deep breath and stepped on in.

There was Robin shooting a wad of paper at the trash can, rolling in a chair across the linoleum. He said something to Dr. Hollings and slapped him on the back. He swiveled around to say something to Randy, but caught sight of Edie first.

"Hey, Aunt Edie, what's up?" he cried, and then, "Gosh, you look hot tonight, got a big date?" But thankfully he changed the subject in the same breath.

"We think we're getting closer, Randy got a bite earlier. A big bite."

"I know, I was here," she said.

"You were?" he exclaimed, "Great, because we're trying to replicate what happened. Maybe you'll see something Randy missed or see what we're doing wrong."

"You never know," Edie said, "and I like that music. You know, I need to check Stephan's vitals."

"Hey," Edie lied a little, "that's what I was getting ready to do earlier when Randy got his, what did you say, bite. If you want an exact reproduction I probably should pick it up where I was before, and maybe two sets of eyes on the board wouldn't hurt, either, huh?" God, she tried to make it sound natural, but it came out flat and artificial.

"Hey, right now I'd try anything," Robin said, evidently buying into the act. "I'll set everything back to exactly how it was." He was halfway across the room, heading towards the booth.

"Oh, and Robin," Edie said, and Robin looked back over his shoulder.

"Yes, Aunt Edie?"

"Leave the music on, OK?"

Robin sat down next to Randy. "Aunt Edie said she was with Stephan when you got the hit."

"Yeah," Randy replied, "I'd totally forgot. She went to go find Fred or something." He stretched his arms above his head. "I'm a little poop-goofy right now, boss, but I'll hang in there as long as you do."

"OK, Randy, let's roll the first set." Robin said, putting on his blue-tooth, "Les bon temps roulle!" Edie slowly walked over to Stephan, dragging the office chair behind her, her extended fingers resting lightly on the back.

"Hello, Stephan," she breathed, "Did you miss me?" Edie sat down in the chair, strategically crossing her mini-skirted legs in front of the physicist.

"Hey, Aunt Edie, we're getting a reading! cried Robin from the booth. "Whatever it is you're doing, keep it up!"

"I know you men are busy," purred Edie, "Let me just check your heart rate real quick. My, it's so warm in here, I'll just take off this bulky thing," she said, getting up and slipping out of the lab coat.

"Oops, I dropped it," Edie said, letting it fall, "Now where is that stethoscope?" Straight-legged, Edie bent over and picked up her lab coat, her mini-skirted derriere not more than a foot away from Dr. Hollings wheelchair.

"Randy, I'm getting audio!" yelled Robin, his hands flying over the dials, craning his ears, "It sounds like, Oh mi–Oh mi–, something else, but I can't make it out, can you?!"

But Randy wasn't answering, not believing his eyes, because what in the hell was Robin's aunt doing out there?

"Now, Stephan, today I want to get a very accurate reading, so I'm going to slide open your shirt for my stethoscope to get as close to your heart as I can," Edie murmured, unbuttoning his shirt, her glossed lips mere inches away from his.

"Listen, Randy, he's saying 'don't stop, please don't stop!" Robin hollered, then, "Wait–was that on the cues?"

Randy answered with a jab to his ribs. Robin looked up from the sound board, surprised. Randy's mouth was agape and he pointed wordlessly to the lab. Edie was gyrating slightly with her hips, and her upper torso was brushing against Stephan, while her hand, inside his undone shirt, was gently caressing his chest.

"Oh, my, Stephan," she tongued the words into his ear, "What a strong heart-beat you have!"

"Can you tell me why it is so warm in here?" she continued, her free hand grabbing the large, decorative ring that hung on the short chain that connected it to the zipper running down the front of her purple mini-dress. Edie tugged it down an inch, exposing more cleavage, noticing that the red power light had come on for his speaker system.

"Robin must have turned it on from the booth–that means he must be starting to get through!" she thought excitedly.

What she didn't notice was that the brass ring she'd just let go of had caught itself on the protruding rod used for Stephan's temporarily removed video screen.

"Wh- Wha- What..." Edie heard emanate from the speakers. "He's got it, it's working!" she thought, and stood up abruptly–but the miniskirt's ring stayed, hooked on the brace.

"What's the matter, Cat woman got your tongue, Batman?" Edie seductively teased, not realizing her ultra-modern purple mini-skirt with the large, full-length zipper was now undone to her belly, her breasts cheerfully bobbing out, almost fully exposed from her sudden upright movement. Robin and Randy caught the next words in the booth as clearly as Edie heard them through the speaker system.

"Oh, my God, what a rack!" came out, perfectly, crystally-clear, "What a set of jugs!"

"Well, Randy," Robin jubilantly exclaimed, "This is a truly momentous occasion!" He flipped a switch to broadcast his voice into the audio-lab for Dr. Hollings and his beet-faced aunt, who was now struggling to zip back up without snagging anything else and risking bodily injury in the process.

"For on this day, not only have we established that Dr. Stephan B. Hollings has achieved the ability to speak, thanks to the assistance of modern technology," Robin's voice boomed in a fake tenor that would make a Senator proud, "But more importantly, that he is most definitely a boob man!"

12

Doctor Hollings Credibility In Question

The next week was a blur, filled with non-stop activity. The most disturbing news came on Monday, the first of June, seven days from the symposium at Oxford. Dr. Steck had walked in the guest quarters living room where Stephan, Robin, Edie, and Inga were sitting, taking a short break from the speech therapy that Inga, a speech therapist, had designed. He threw down printed out articles, one from Nature and another from Science.

"These just came out, Stephan," Steck said soberly, "We've got ourselves a fight. Beardsley is calling you a 'hack' in an interview, and that jerk Stoops has an article in Science stating "Dr. Hollings has obviously debilitated to the extent his upcoming "major paper" shouldn't be allowed to be formally presented to the Consortium, but perhaps be more suited to a reading at Piccadilly Square."

Dejectedly, he sat down and stared at the group. "We may want to reconsider our position. We might not want to attend at all," he ended.

Dr. Hollings told Inga to go ahead, she and Edie should take lunch, he wanted Robin to read him the articles.

"Alone," he said, and Dr. Steck took the hint, exiting as well.

Stephan had taken Inga's instructions to "talk as much as you can" very literally, using most of the time teaching Robin the more esoteric tenets of modern physics in general and his controversial new findings specifically. Stephan had been amazed at Robin's quick grasp of the subject, and grateful to have such an educated and gifted mind to bounce his thoughts and theories off of. Robin read the articles back to back and the two amounted to a united attack on Stephan's unofficial title as the leading authority on Quantum theory. He understood most of their basic equations and followed the rest as best he could.

"One thing's for sure," Robin said, "It's a real setup for a showdown at 'Ye Olde Oxford Corral. And its two dozen against one," he noted sourly, "Talk about swimming with sharks."

"Could be, but then again, maybe not," Dr. Hollings replied, "They think so, yeah, but they could be wrong. And that, my friend could prove fatal."

"I don't get it," Robin said, "these two guys, from what you've said, have managed to garner support from all the leading theoreticians, at least the ones that matter, either by political strong-arming or cajoling. What did I miss, Steve, where's your secret weapon?"

"Why, Robin," Stephan answered, "I'm a little surprised to hear that, especially from you. It's right here in front of me."

Stephan had expected a power struggle at some point, ever since he had dropped the first hint of his radical new theory–he just hadn't passed this onto Dr. Steck. Stephan knew that Steck wouldn't agree that drawing his enemies into what hopefully would be an ambush, to expose and dispose of them all, would be worth the risk.

The Consortium at Oxford was a formal and official attempt to organize the world of Quantum Mechanics into a voting body with elected leaders. That he could just waltz in there and assume presidency would have been presumptuous–if there was ever a perfect time for a challenge this would be it. He told Robin this as calmly as discussing whether it might rain tomorrow.

"So you've been planning this all along," Robin said.

"With or without the symposium, my paper was going to set off a war," Stephan said, "the stakes are just higher now."

"So what's the plan of attack?" Robin asked, "I'm new to guerilla physics."

Stephan had thought this through to the last detail, and for the next hour his strategy unfolded- by the end even Robin was dumbfounded.

"You want me to go to the symposium, too?"

"I'm going to need a linguist, you fit the bill. You, me, and Edie, we take in the sights, maybe kick some mad scientist ass, what's not to like?" Stephan said, "Plus there's that other little detail."

"Oh, what's that?" Robin exclaimed, not believing his ears–helping Dr. Stephan Hollings, the world's eminent leader in physics, in a caper worthy of a spy novel!

"That little detail of how you've got a voice simulator implanted in you as well," Stephan said, "and how you can read my mind."

"How did you know?" Robin asked, astonished.

"It all added up," Dr. Hollings said, "You probably would have succeeded with Fred without it, so something else made you do it, right?"

Robin explained how he was able to coach Fred through the hardest parts by 'connecting', wirelessly feeling in his ears and vocal chords what Fred was experiencing and vice-versa, Fred his.

"By extension, we developed an innate form of communication," Robin said, "But how did you know for sure?"

"It was simple." Dr. Hollings said, "Fred's intelligence is vastly superior to an average chimp, your mentoring on such an intense level led to an optimized level of brain activity. That thing about how a human utilizes only ten percent of their brain at any given moment, right? So what's Fred up to, maybe forty percent?"

"Uh, he actually hit fifty-two once," Robin admitted, still stunned, "But my initial decision to have myself implanted had nothing to do with that," he admitted, "It was because I wanted to be able to say, if I ever was accused of unethical experimentation, that I was first and had verified the relative safety of the procedure."

"I see," Dr. Hollings continued, "have you been eavesdropping on me, Robin?"

"Just a little," Robin said apologetically, "But only when I thought you were close to getting hung up–I'd check to see if I could figure out if I should change the cues we were feeding you."

"Of course, the temptation was always there," Robin said, "And I rationalized with "it's in the best interests of the patient."

"No blood, no foul," Dr. Hollings said, and went on with his plan.

"I'm always been a target in the public arena," he said, "For the most part I've been able to pick my battles and have held my own, thanks to spotting some flaws in theories from second-rate scientists."

He smiled that funny half-grin. "But now that I have the same verbal ability, and perhaps more importantly the element of surprise, maybe now I won't have to listen to the lies that would have never been thrown in my face if I had been able to defend myself more adequately. If you could be my invisible little research assistant, I could draw them out, perhaps even uncover some falsified results, which I'm convinced is going to be buried in their supporting data somewhere." He paused, letting it all sink in, then continued on. "There might even be opportunities to eavesdrop on my 'esteemed colleagues' conversations, however, this would be in their respective tongues. That's where you, with your language skills, come in–my nurse's young nephew on holiday, spending a few days taking in the world of big-time scientists. They'd take little notice if you play it right. Maybe a directional mike, a little recording equipment, things like that, you know."

"Holy cow, real cloak and dagger stuff" Robin laughed, "Where do we start, Batman?"

"Quick, Robin, to the Batcave," Stephan cried, "Where else?"

"Well," Ian said, "Hi-tech espionage just happens to be a hobby of mine." He picked up a mechanical pencil and started a list. "Small pinhead microphone, with variable gain, wireless, of course. Digital recorder and transceiver, with multiple feeds for additional planted bugs. Video-capable as well, monsieur?" Ian had affected the tone of a snooty French waiter. "And perhaps I might suggest a dozen tranquilizer darts, followed by a round of truth serum to cleanse the palate?"

"Well, at least we're in the right place," Robin said, "Whaddya think, Steve?"

"Sign me up," Dr. Hollings said, "With every upgrade you can imagine." He added on a somber note, "We're only going to get one shot at this, we better make it count."

13

Learning From Fred

One day before they were to fly to England, Robin and Fred dropped by Dr. Hollings apartment.

"Hey, doc, got a minute?" Robin asked.

"Sure, what's up, guys?" Dr. Hollings replied.

"We're here for your final lesson," Fred said, "Then you get to join the club."

"Oh, really," Stephan came back, "And exactly what club is that, assuming I pass the test, right?"

"You'd be a full-blown Jedi," Robin said lightly, "But only if you pass the test." He turned to Fred and nodded.

"Robin told me you guessed that he had the same equipment as me," Fred said, "and how it improved my brain function by being exposed to the human mind. Pretty impressive, but no one ever stopped to think that maybe that would be a two-way street, did they?"

Fred took on a superior tone, "Nothing for you humans to learn from a lowly ape, right?" He slammed his fist down on the coffee table. "Well, you'd be wrong, buffalo breath!" He broke into a grin. "Man, it feels better every time I say it! Wrong, wrong, wrong! There's plenty you could learn, you bet'cha. Tell him, Robin!"

"I will, Fred, but not before I commend you on your touching display of humility, and for not stooping to flinging feces at us lowly humans for sullying the sacred air of your presence."

"Hey, that only happened once!" Fred said, "I thought we agreed to forget about that."

"OK, Steve," Robin continued, "Turns out that Fred opened up a whole new paradigm of looking at things from an animal perspective. Did you ever hear of those tests where a chimpanzee will outscore a human every time?"

"No, but I'd love to hear more," Dr. Hollings diplomatically said, "What kind of test were those?"

"The most dramatic example is where researchers took a chimp and placed him in front of a computer display," Robin said, "And these numbers pop up on the screen and off again before you can get a good look at them, seven or eight numbers in a row." He looked at Fred. "Would you like to describe the results of those tests, Mr. Smarty pants?"

"It turns out that when all the numbers were redisplayed, all together on the monitor, the chimps could point out the sequence that the numbers had been flashed across the screen, every time almost. But perform the same test on humans, and their recall was less than fifty percent," Fred said, "You humans can't remember shit, man, not visually. You're optically retarded idiots that wouldn't last a day in the wild on your own."

"That's not all I learned," Robin said, "You know how some animals possess incredible homing abilities, like Ridley sea turtles? Chimps have some of that, too, but with the implants it seems to have had a multiplier effect." Robin got up and walked out the room. "Take it from here, Fred."

Fred got up and turned the TV on, walked to the fridge and grabbed a pear. He loped back to the couch, and plopped down, never saying a word. He munched his pear, pointedly ignoring Dr. Hollings.

"What's this all about?" Stephan started to say, but Fred's hand shot up, as if to say stop, and then put his finger to his ear.

"If you listen, you can see him," the primate admonished, "Just listen with your mind, try to feel him with your nose, it'll work."

Steve was left speechless. Fred suddenly took the same finger and pointed to the phone on the coffee table that Dr. Hollings had, a little something that Ian had rigged up to activate by Stephan's voice.

"It's for you," Fred said, and it started ringing, "its Robin, calling from..." Fred closed his eyes for a moment, "the cafeteria, I think by the bakery."

Dr. Hollings said, "Answer, phone," and the ringing stopped. Robin's voice came on.

"Hey, anybody want anything while I'm at the deli?" he asked.

"Fred thought you were at the bakery." Dr. Hollings said, still mightily impressed.

"I was when I was dialing; I just now walked over here this second. What's that Fred's eating? I felt him go in the kitchen."

"A pear," Fred said, then looked dismissively at Steve, "got any questions, Doc?"

"Yeah," Stephan said, "How soon do I get to be a Jedi, too?"

Robin came back and went into deeper explanations of how Fred would know where he went all the time and was surprised that Robin didn't know the same. They worked together and Robin started to pick up the subtle vibes almost immediately, an inner compass rediscovered that had been lost somewhere back down the evolutionary trail. Then he and Fred practiced optical recognition until Robin was reasonably proficient.

"You ever wonder how a wild animal's reactions are so quick, so unerring, whether it's a monkey leaping from branch to branch, or a cheetah running down a gazelle?" Robin said, "They've all got this incredible field of vision, and man, they see it all, every blade of grass, it's like..." Robin grasped for words, "this perfectly absorbed preoccupation with their surroundings."

"We humans filter out the background in order to better analyze whatever we're focused on," he continued, "but a chimp, they see every leaf and branch of that tree they're jumping into, equally." He breathed deeply, "Man, it's a rush! You feel, you become part of it all, one with the natural world. You don't think as much as react."

For the rest of the day Fred and Robin had Stephan practice by "feeling" how Fred looked, smelled, thought, or even more difficult, didn't think. It was slow going, and finally Robin suggested to Steve "to try not to try so hard, dude, I think you're over-focusing. Try to clear your mind; you're falling into a mental block. Here, let me give you an example." He stood and bowed to Fred, like a martial arts student to his master.

"There's this article I read once about how Bruce Lee gave this interview to some journalist who didn't know the first thing about karate, back in the day when martial arts was just beginning to become popular in America," Robin said, going through a series of karate moves, "This guy asked him for a demonstration. Bruce Lee had him take a boxing stance, and even though the writer was way bigger and had braced himself, Bruce knocked him on his butt by punching him in the chest with just one finger. The man was astonished and asked if he could teach him how to do that, that was the coolest thing he'd ever seen.

'Sure,' Bruce Lee said, 'but first you will have to empty your cup.' 'Empty my cup?' the writer said, 'I'm not following you.'"

Robin struck a kung-fu stance and Fred leapt to his feet, circling his opponent and slashing the air with the edges of his hands, snarling menacingly.

"Lee said, 'I can show you how to strike a man's chest with your finger, but it won't work until you empty your mind of all its preconceptions." Robin continued, snap-kicking at Fred's front knee, "He told him, 'Your mind is too full, there's no room for anything else! Empty your cup, come back, and then I fill it back up with the knowledge you seek."

Robin charged Fred and leaped sideways in the air, executing a flying kick at the chimp's head. Fred ducked under the kick and with lightning quickness blocked Robin in the chest, his hairy arm a blur. Robin fell to the carpet and landed on his side. He rolled over into a sitting position..

"Man, I thought I had you that time, monkey-San!" he cried, slamming the floor with his fist in disappointment. "I swear I saw your eyes looking the other way!"

"That's the problem with all you humans," Fred said, "Always thinking. And expecting a chimp to only use his eyeballs to see."

At long last, late in the evening, Fred left for a minute, saying he wanted some grapes he had in the dayroom. After a few minutes of talking about their flight the next day, Robin abruptly stopped talking.

"OK, Steve, its test time!" he exclaimed, "Do you know where Fred is, and better yet, can you tell me what he's doing?"

Stephan was taken by surprise. Then closing his eyes, he tried the relaxation techniques they had worked on. He began to ebb in and out, searching for that state of sub-consciousness where everything and one thing were of the same value, a flat screen where there were no corners, no center, because all things were a center. He started feeling a presence, a point right in front of his left temple. Without opening his eyes he swiveled his chair towards the now faint buzzing pressure until it was between his eyes, deep in his sinus cavity. He suddenly connected–his hands were moving to grab a small box, saying something, and he could feel a slight twitching in his throat. He could both taste and smell something in his nostrils, another presence, close and sweet. Stephan's eyes fluttered open.

"Fred's in the dayroom of 3-C," Stephan said, slowly, as in a dream. "He's changing the channel on the TV. And I think he's talking to Edie?" he asked, more than said, to Robin.

"Ah and well learned have you, young Solo," Robin said, bowing with his clasped hands to his student, "To the club, welcome."

14

Arriving In Oxford

The chartered jet landed at Heathrow late the next morning, and they were escorted through customs with typical British efficiency. Robin was like a kid at Christmas, twisting his head this way and that as they went through the city. The limo arrived at the Wilshire, where the symposium was to be held, and as they approached the front door photographers and news reporters swarmed the car. Dr. Steck immediately took charge.

"Every stay in their assigned places," he barked, "Let's give them their dog and pony show, and not a thing more, now's not the time."

As soon as the limo stopped, the driver and his aide jumped out, looking as much like well-dressed bouncers as drivers. Dr. Steck exited one side followed by Edie and Robin. The two drivers went to the door closest to the hotel's front doors, and unloaded Dr. Hollings. The TV news cameras and reporters were surrounding them, and Dr. Steck pushed his way to Stephan's handlebars, a bouncer protecting each side. He smiled at the various newsmen as he pushed Dr. Hollings through the horde.

"Dr. Hollings, do you want to comment on the remarks by Dr. Beardsley?"

"Are you angry with Stoops for his Science interview about your paper?"

"Are you afraid your paper might not be allowed at the conference?"

All the while Dr. Hollings was typing and saying with his mechanical voice, "No-comment–thank-you…" as Dr. Steck kept saying "Ladies and gentlemen, please, Dr. Hollings will make an official statement at a later time." Edie and Robin were ignored for the most part, and that was fine by them. Their luggage would be brought up later, Steck had said, but Robin insisted on keeping the one large backpack by his side.

Eventually, they all made it to their rooms on the eleventh floor, Robin next to Edie's room, with Steck and Stephan in a suite at the end. The rest of the floor was filled with assistants to several other scientists, Robin learned, three from Spain, two from Italy, and two from China. He made several trips up and down the elevator, just to familiarize himself with the different dialects. From what little he heard about the symposium, it was certain a battle was imminent. Some expressed surprise that Hollings was even here–others were excited, stating that they felt fortunate to be here to witness such a historic watershed.

"Remember how it was with Einstein and the eclipse?" said one Russian to another. "This will be no different. Peoples reputations ruined, careers shattered in the space of a weekend!"

Robin planted a bug in a corner of the elevator to practice and spent the afternoon with the I-pod looking tracking device Ian had given him, getting a good feel for the equipment. He felt a little guilty at first but all he had to do was remind himself that his was a just cause, for a scientist he had come to know and respect was under attack. He was there to protect Dr. Hollings standing and the presentation of his latest major paper against those who condemned him and his theory without even having heard it yet. And while Robin had made up his mind on the matter, it did occur to him that it was just a theory, and there was always the possibility of it being wrong or perhaps possessing a flaw.

He still had trouble grasping entirely what Dr. Hollings "General Underlying Principal for a Unified Theory" exactly meant or why it was going to be such a polarizing publication, but Stephan had said even he himself didn't comprehend all the ramifications, he just did the math. Robin knew that was self-effacing, but now he tried to remember the basic overview Stephan had given him, that one night he'd had showed the doctor the Robin's eggs.

"Most physicists today are in agreement on the existence of black holes, big bang theory of the creation of the universe, things that hadn't been fully explained, but are less controversial that they were when first proposed," Dr. Hollings said, "But after that numerous schools of thought have diverged with wildly divergent theories on the one theory to link all four fundamental forces in nature. These are one, the strong nuclear force that hold the nucleus of atoms together, two, weak interaction (which holds protons and electrons to the nucleus), three, electromagnetism, and four, but most perplexing, gravity. Now quantum mechanics is the study of the subatomic world, whereas Einstein's Theory of Relativity dealt with the very large phenomena of the physical world. For the most part, his theory of General Relativity does an excellent job of describing the universe, except for the very large and the very, very small. Then it all falls apart. There's missing mass, there's a problem with gravity being so weak compared to the other forces–gravity should be much, much, stronger.

Then someone said, maybe there's other dimensions that contain this missing gravity, and all of a sudden someone else came up with string theory, where particles of subatomic matter could vibrate like a violin string, in an out of different dimensions."

"There's a lot of mathematics I'm skipping over," Dr. Hollings said, "But just remember the descriptions are an attempt to unify the equations into a Theory of Everything that covers everything from subatomic foam where time starts to bubble, to black holes where the mass is so dense that even light cannot escape and for all we know opens up into another part of the universe." He paused. "I have developed some new equations that point strongly to the existence of an alternate universe–that particles resonate in and out of. This isn't maybe, sort of, coulda, woulda, shoulda," Dr. Hollings said, "I'm putting my entire life's work on the line."

He went on to describe to Robin of how as they spoke the matter that they were made up of was only here in the present four-dimensional reality only part of the time. "As we speak, the atoms we are made up of are bouncing, literally, from here into another universe and back."

He gave some other examples. "You know how film works–you see a continuous stream of action from thirty-two frames a second of photos. Imagine you're living in sixty-four frames a second and depending where you are standing determines which of two movies you're watching." He talked of gravitons, anti-matter, quarks, anti-particles, and such at great length. At one point Stephan saw Robin's eyes glazing over and stopped. "Any questions?" he asked, in jest.

"Yeah, how do the Robin's eggs help you prove this existence of other dimensions?" Robin replied, trying his best to keep up.

"Well, because they're magnets," Dr. Hollings said, "but of a different type of matter."

"A different type?" Robin said.

"Yes, the kind that my equations predict would exist–in another universe."

Robin hadn't told the doctor he had them in his implants-Robin justified it as a means to an end. Plus it wasn't like they were going to get lost or stolen. And the stones had already been cut up so he'd gone on ahead.

"I'll tell him after the conference," he'd reasoned. These were his thoughts this morning as he dressed the small microphone into place and ran a sound check. Satisfied, he went to check on Aunt Edie.

"Oh, good, you're ready," he heard as Edie came down the hall. She seemed a little nervous. "I know it's a little early, but first day and all, I thought we might play it safe and go over Stephan's agenda one more time." Edie said, "I hope he's doing better than I am!"

They walked towards the other end of the hall to the corner suite–just then the elevator opened and out stepped a large well-built man in an expensive suit. He had a badge on that said security. He eyed Edie and Robin warily, almost with hostility, then broke into a smile, like one would expect from a concierge.

"Oh, Dr. Hollings nurse, its Edie, correct?" he asked with a slight accent, "I was just coming to escort your party down." Robin saw another big, foreign-looking man holding the elevator door.

"I thought the conference was at 9:30, it's just now 8:20," Edie said, a little surprised, "Aren't you a little early?"

"There's been a small change in plans," the swarthy man said, smiling superciliously, "But just for today, I assure you." Robin noticed the man in the elevator come out at Edie's remark and he now saw another security guard behind him step out and put his finger on the 'door open' button. What kind of security is this, he thought, a little over the top for a trip down to the mezzanine. The one who had exited had said something in a foreign language he didn't place right away, but then he'd heard only the last of a short phrase. What was that, some dialect he hadn't heard in a long time, sounding ancient and coarse? But he now saw the first guard at the door to the doctor's suite, knocking rather loudly, and forgot all about it as Dr. Steck came to the door.

"What in the blazes, do you have to beat down the door?" Steck said, knitting his silk tie.

"I'm, sorry, there's been a slight change of schedule, we need to go down a little early," the lead security said, "Just for this morning, we had a small miscommunication with the press on what time the networks would have for opening remarks." That was all Dr. Steck, media-hound that he was, needed to hear.

"We'll be right out," he said and one minute later whisked Dr. Hollings out the door. They all proceeded to the elevator and got on.

As the door started to close, Robin darted out.

"I forgot my laptop," he said, "I'll meet you down there at the conference room." The doors slid shut and he ran to his room and grabbed his computer, tearing back out to the elevators. He pushed the down button and watched the one that had just left go past the mezzanine, down to the basement- what? Why would they do that? Did someone push the wrong button?

The other elevator dinged and Robin got on and pushed basement, a funny feeling starting to gnaw at him. Foreign security guards, strange explanations, wrong floor?

"Oh, stop it!" he said to himself, all that spy versus spy gadgetry he had been playing with had him imagining things.

Still, what was that dialect–it sounded so unfamiliar and old, like a dead language.

Ruminating on this, Robin forgot to push M for mezzanine and when the elevator doors opened he looked up at the indicator and saw he'd pushed B for basement. The doors opened as he went to push the button for the mezzanine–wait! Was that Dr. Steck's voice? He sounded angry and loud. Robin stuck his hand out and stopped the doors.

"What's going on? Where is everyone?" Robin crept around the corner and looked down a long hallway. He saw a fire door closing shut, and caught a quick glimpse of chrome, and there was Dr. Steck, slumping against the wall. Where was Edie and Dr. Hollings, what were those guys doing, kidnapping them?

Robin ran down the hall, and then drew up short. He should go get help, did 911 work here? He remembered he didn't have a phone; his didn't work here so Robin had left his in the room. He sneaked up to the fire door, and looked through the small glass pane above the door bar out onto a small loading dock that connected to the underground parking area. A white cargo van was backed up to the dock and Robin saw Edie, blindfolded and hand-cuffed, sitting on a bench in the back, next to one of the security guards. The other two guards were dragging Dr. Hollings chair into the van. As soon as they got him loaded in the back, one of the guards jumped out, slammed the two doors, and ran around to the front, throwing himself into the passenger side of the vehicle. The second he had his door closed shut the large van lurched away from the dock and with tires squealing, shot up the ramp towards the light of day.

Robin pushed through the door, not believing what he had just seen. He turned to run for help and saw a fire alarm on the wall. He yanked it down and tore up the ramp. He made it just in time to see the van swerve around a corner to his right. He turned, looking the other way and saw a motorcycle, with some sort of logo on the rider's jacket pull up to a door of a real estate office. The rider stopped, hopped off the bike, and strode into the office, his helmet still on, a parcel under his arm. Robin sprinted up to the bike and was relieved to see a key in the ignition, motor still running. He leaped on the mid-sized motorbike and sped away, hearing exclamations of surprise turn to shouts of curses as he made the turn where he last saw the van.

His mind racing, Robin fought to remain calm. He knew something was wrong the second he saw the third goon, he felt it, a definite tingling running up his spine, it was true, damn it, he could still feel it right now, tingling in his brain. Robin suddenly realized he knew where, or rather which direction, Dr. Hollings was! He veered left at the next intersection, and now the sensation moved from behind his ear to his forehead, not exactly dead center but close. Another revelation occurred to him and in a quick movement Robin reached inside his suit coat and flicked the audio recorder on that was wirelessly connected to Dr. Hollings implants, and also to Stephan's wireless mike that was in his lapel. Ian had outdone himself, and now it might payoff, Robin thought grimly. He gunned the bike down the street, intent on staying in range.

The van was now driving east toward the harbor, at normal speed, in an attempt to remain inconspicuous. He heard through his implants the two guards in back jabbering away in a foreign tongue, their sentences punctuated with obvious relief. A two way radio cackled up in front of them, he recognized the lead guard's voice responding to his front left.

"We have the doctor and his nurse, the woman," he said, "Birki had problems with the Dr. Steck, and had to disable him."

"That fool!" an angry voice reprimanded the guard, "He could have still brought him. What's your precise location?"

"We're on St. John's, coming up on Wharfside," replied the captor, "We'll be there in five minutes." He clicked off the radio and said something in that other language Robin didn't recognize, but that sounded different that the other two in the back to the driver, who laughed and said, "Exactly fifty hours from now we'll be back home. I can wait till then–those native women suit me–that is, as long as you like big ears!"

Robin hurtled down the busy street, passing cars in zigzag fashion. He was gaining ground; he could feel the pressure building in his sinus cavities. He could almost sense each turn the van was making now. "There!" It had just turned left! Robin down-shifted and cut to his left, right across the front of a checkered cab. The driver's horn blared and Robin instinctively swerved away from the deafening sound, almost losing control. He barely missed striking a police bobby, directing traffic. The honking of the horn was now joined by the policeman's whistle, just as Robin spotted the cargo van turning right on the next street up. Up shifting, the bike shot like it was out of cannon–so intent was he on his prey he didn't see the little Fiat that abruptly changed lanes, cutting him off.

Robin tried to whip around, but the motorcycle's tires slipped on the cobblestone pavers, jackknifing the bike back into the path of an approaching Mercedes. Robin clipped the front bumper, and flew up in the air. In what seemed to be slow motion, he saw the windshield of the sedan come rushing up to meet him. Then all turned to black.

"Aye, the little bugger's coming around. I'll ring you back later, got to hear this one's heart-rending version of how he's a victim of society, and at such a wee age, the poor lass."

Robin heard the voice from a distance, sounding tinny and distorted. Groggily, he opened his eyes, and winced at the brightness of the room. He went to sit up and didn't get far before his head started spinning, and he lay back down. God, his head hurt! He went to touch his throbbing temples, but his hand stopped almost as soon as he raised it–what the devil?

He was handcuffed to a rail that ran down the side of the bed he was lying in. Robin took all this in, but everything wasn't fitting together, like a jigsaw puzzle with pieces missing, until he looked up and saw the bobby from the intersection. The cop was looking at him sternly. The sight of his uniform and badge brought Robin back to reality and out of his foggy state.

"Where am I?" he asked, his voice cracking.

"Aye, well, you're in St. John's Hospital, young man," the policeman replied, "But your more permanent quarters will be the eleventh precinct's jail, if you'll be expecting postal delivery's."

"I'm Robin Langston, Dr. Robin Langston," Robin said, "I was witness to a kidnapping." The bobby had a small notebook flipped open and a pencil in his hand. "Ah yes, doctor," he said, exaggerating the honorific, "I must complement you on that excellent choice of a profession, and I must also say that your fake ID's are of the highest quality. I was just wondering, did the ladies at the bars buy into such a novelty as yourself, Dr. Langston?"

Robin caught the sarcasm and realized he needed someone from the hotel to verify his papers–surely the police must have been alerted by now of a kidnapping. He started to speak, but a loud voice out in the hallway cut him short.

"You most certainly will allow me in there, you idiot!" Dr. Steck was shouting, "There's been a crime committed, all right, and if you don't get out of my way this instant you'll be arrested for–for unlawful arrest, and under investigation for incompetence, you arrogant bastard!"

Robin saw the door burst open, and for once he was glad to see Dr. Steck's pompous ass. Dr. Steck had a large bandage on his head, but otherwise seemed ok. "You there, un-cuff this young man at once!"

"And who might you be?" the bobby demanded, putting his hands on his hips.

"I'm Dr. Richard Steck, from the United States of America," Steck retorted, "Dr Langston is a witness to a kidnapping, as was I. I want him released from those manacles and Scotland Yard notified immediately!"

Looking at the disheveled, raving Yank the bobby said calmly, "Well, you and… Dougie Houser here are going to have to do better than that."

Steck glared at the cop. He was even more incompetent than the security at the hotel who, upon seeing him unconscious, had gotten the idea that he had been mugged, and called for an ambulance, not the police, wanting to not upset the other guests. He had come to in the emergency room, and an intern had commented on the other "foreigner" who had just been brought in, a young kid with fake ID's stating he was a doctor of all things! Steck had jumped off the gurney and proceeded threatening everyone within shouting distance with lawsuits of unimaginable magnitude if he wasn't taken to Robin's room immediately. Now this imbecile!

He started to inform the bobby of just who had been abducted, and then quickly regained his senses. Dr Steck smiled and pulled out his Blackberry, picking up the bedside phone.

"Hello, Nigel?" Steck said, turning his back on the cop, "We may have an incident here of international proportions. Do you have a minute?"

Steck ran down what he knew, and from Nigel's reactions he knew he had made the right decision. He hung up and waited patiently by the window, humming a little tune, ignoring Robin and the suddenly nervous policeman.

Robin started to say something, but couldn't piece anything together in his brain that would come out lucid enough to help the situation. Just then another officer came in the room; obviously the bobby's superior, as the bobbie quickly snapped to attention. "What are you doing interrupting an official police investigation?" the officer raged at Steck, "This person has committed theft, evading and eluding, and recklessly caused a serious accident! Who do you think you are, mister?"

The bedside phone began ringing, and Dr. Steck calmly answered.

"Yes, that is correct, he has been kidnapped. Perhaps we should continue this conversation at your office. However, we seem to have been detained by the local constabulary. Perhaps you could have a word with them?"

He handed the phone out to the senior officer. "My name is Dr. Richard Steck, and this is Dr. Robin Langston," he said, "and this is for you, Sergeant." Steck smiled icily. "It's the prime minister's office."

Later that day, Robin and Steck met with Scotland Yard back at the Wilshire, where they had been whisked up to the doctor's suite. Neville McDougal, from the prime minister's office, was there as well. The floor had been cleared of all the other guests, and the elevators locked out. The crime scene unit had come and gone.

"Not much to find up here–a hundred people have come and gone. We dusted for prints, we might get something there," the unit's leader had said. They sat in the suite, waiting for contact by phone or otherwise; the experts pondering the next move.

"We debated even attending," Dr. Steck ruefully noted, "The symposium had all the earmarks of a witch hunt, anyway."

This evoked great interest among the detectives, who after much deliberation, proposed to use the controversy to their advantage.

"The less publicity the better," said head detective Elton Wilkes of Scotland Yard. "If they get spooked, that's usually when bad things happen." He didn't elaborate on what bad things could be.

Therefore a leak to the press was engineered, to the effect that Dr. Hollings had chosen discretion over valor–"his paper wasn't ready to withstand the rigors of scrutiny it was sure to receive," was the official statement on his sudden absence. Dr. Steck became the obvious choice to be the contact person, now it was just sit and wait. Robin spent some time with a sketch artist while he recuperated, luckily not having sustained any broken bones, and gave a description as best he could of the guards. The license number of the van he'd remembered, and as expected was reported as stolen the same morning.

Robin spent the majority of his time trying to retrieve data from the miniature hard drive of the audio recorder, which had been smashed in his collision with the Mercedes. He finally got one working, the one that recorded Dr. Hollings 'spoken thoughts', and downloaded it immediately for fear the drive would crash. He toyed with the other drive late into the night, and at last it started spinning, hesitantly at first, and then finally rose to full speed. Robin held his breath while the drive limped along–and at last, "download complete–100%" came up on his laptop.

He exhaled thankfully and wiped his brow. Robin's body ached and every time he shifted positions he discovered another bump or bruise. He emailed Ian and had another unit Fed Exed to the hotel, just in case he ended up involved in negotiations with Edie and Stephan's captors–not to mention he liked toying with the electronics, at least it was something to take his mind off the present.

It arrived next morning as he was finishing up with another briefing from the detectives. No demands as yet, but they hadn't been surprised.

"If they're pros, they'll lay low for at least three or four days, then make contact." Detective Wilkes informed Robin and Steck, "Time is on their side."

Robin downloaded the two files from his laptop onto the new I-pod looking replacement, plugged in the headphones and lay back on his bed to see what if anything he had picked up.

"Robin, this is Stephan," Dr. Hollings 'voice' was calm, "If you can hear this, Edie and I have been kidnapped. We are in a white cargo van and Dr. Steck is in the hallway down in the basement, hurt. We've been kidnapped and are heading east by the way the shadows are falling off the buildings. Robin, turn on the other channel to the mike in my lapel, the guards are talking in some strange language, maybe they'll say something to help the police. I'll relay any information I see or hear, but right now it's hard to see out, and I don't know the range of my implants transceiver, but I'll keep trying." There were periodic updates on what direction Dr. Hollings thought they were headed, and then finally nothing, most likely when Robin hit the windshield of the Mercedes.

Robin switched over to the other file from the lapel microphone. He heard the two guards talking and began to make out snippets of the strange dialect. What was that, he couldn't believe his ears–it was a language he had only heard once or twice in his life. What was it called? Balaluka or something like that, and ancient Polynesian-Samoan derivative spoken only in a few isolated island chains, interspersed among the thousands of islands of the South Pacific. What in the world would such a rare culture, almost extinct, be involved in a kidnapping of a world-famous scientist?

He had only stumbled upon the language recently researching old tales of piles of rocks used in religious ceremonies in ancient cultures, back when he first was trying to ascertain if the

Robin's eggs had significance in archaic religious practices. He had been intrigued by the exotic sing-song dialect that less than ten thousand spoke as a primary language. His natural gift for linguistics took over and Robin started picking out bits and pieces. He started to call the detectives and stopped–he had already been ignored and shoved to the side more than once with that "let the police handle things" condescending attitude, that was made even worse by his age. Besides, Wilkes and his team hadn't made much of an impression on him anyway. Robin decided then and there that he had enough resources and intelligence to proceed with his own investigation. He went back to the conversations recorded in the van, with strengthened resolve and the beginnings of a plan already starting to gel in the back of his mind.

15

Searching For Doctor Hollings

It took three days, but Robin had translated the entire ten-minute recording. There had been no word from the kidnappers, and Scotland Yard was running out of ideas. They had found the van, down by the docks, abandoned in a side alley, but it provided nothing solid to work with. The more Robin saw the more he was convinced the momentum of the investigation was waning.

He called Bob, his godfather and director at the Center.

"Bob, I need your help," Robin said. He outlined his plan, and Bob promised to get everything moving right away.

Robin went down to London International Bank and opened up a bank account. He had a short meeting with one of the vice-presidents, who almost fell out of his chair when Robin told him to expect a million Euros to be wired from his Swiss account the next day. He went back to the hotel, and up to Steck's room.

"Doc, we gotta talk," he said, "I've gotta do something, and I'm gonna do it with or without you. But since you got a dog in this hunt, I think you'll like what I'm about to say."

Robin explained how he thought that it was certain that Dr. Hollings and Edie were out of the country.

"Have you told Scotland Yard?" asked Steck.

"No, and here's why," Robin replied, "First of all, if what I said isn't true, the local investigation into the matter would suffer, because it would take the heat off of them. They could slack off by saying now it's an international matter when there's still a chance they might yet uncover some clues. On the other hand, if I'm right, it would be huge news, and the last thing we would want is to take a chance on it leaking out. That would be bad because the abductors would then know there's an international effort and then they might resort to drastic measures."

"What is it you want me to do, Robin?"

"You've got all those connections with the federal government back in the U.S., right? I want a name and a number from the State Department of someone with covert operations clearance in the Pacific basin." Robin gave Steck a fierce glare. "Because when I find Aunt Edie and Stephan, I want the CIA to be the first to know."

The next day Robin checked with Scotland Yard. He got a weary sounding detective Wilkes on the line.

"Hey, Detective, I thought I'd go down and look at where the van was abandoned. Could you give me directions to where it was discovered?"

"Good," thought Wilkes, "give him something harmless to do, keep him off my back for a while." Besides, his team had already interviewed all the local hoodlums and had swept every square inch for a square mile, anyway. Robin then called the bank and verified the funds were in place. Next he took a cab to the airport to pick up his guest, flying in from the Congo.

He was easy to spot, six feet two, with brown wavy hair, broad-shouldered with an athletic build not totally hidden by the business suit. Robin thought Lt. Colonel John Conrad could pass as Antonio Bandera's big brother. Much bigger brother. Robin strode up and without wasting words said, "I'm Robin Langston, I've got a car waiting."

Conrad said, "Over there, right?" and briskly started for the sedan, Robin striving to keep up without breaking into a run.

They headed to the hotel, Conrad asking to see the file Robin had promised him that contained all the info he could assemble. He flipped through it and said little. When they checked into the hotel, Robin said, "We'll meet later with Dr. Steck and, uh, another party of interest." That Robin offered no further explanation or name seemed to have no effect on him. "Seven o'clock," he simply said, "and went to his room.

At seven sharp, Robin, Col. Conrad, Dr. Steck and another man only introduced as "Dafoe" met in the corner suite. Dr.

Steck began with the kidnapping, Robins pursuit, and accident, the cover-up, and subsequent progress (or lack thereof) by the Yard in the case. Then Robin took the floor.

"Col. Conrad, here comes highly recommended in matters of delicate international relations and enforcement. He is on temporary assignment from the Center's security force. He is the leader of our mercenary team in Africa," Robin stated bluntly, "He is here to assemble a task force. We are going to attempt to find Dr. Hollings captors. If we find Steve and Aunt Edie, his team will rescue them, by whatever force necessary, with lethal and extreme prejudice."

Mr. Dafoe, here," Robin continued, "Well, he was never here and I have never heard of him in my life." Robin smiled. "Now let me tell you what part of the world Dr. Hollings is in and then you all can tell me how we're going to find exactly where they are, and we'll worry about the rescue after that."

Robin played the audio recording, "That's a language called Balaluka, an almost extinct language from the Pacific basin. These men are from some island or island chain and I have interpreted this conversation personally and I'm convinced they are talking of heading home to the islands. We find home, Aunt Edie and Steve are close."

Robin projected a map on the large flat-screen monitor hanging on the wall, depicting the South Pacific basin.

"They said fifty hours from here in London." He clicked a mouse and a circle appeared.

"Fifty knots max times fifty hours gets them anywhere here, but there's more details to go on to help narrow it down. At one point they talk of a main island trading post, and two or three, I can't tell which, islands where they're going that's a half day away by boat. The driver of the van spoke Samoan, a dialect found in this area also. My guess they speak the dialect on the main island with the trading post and Balaluka on the smaller two or three. Those islands could still be in the Bronze Age, many are, and an excellent place to disappear."

He clicked again and Google Earth's site appeared. "I have assembled a team back at the Center that are searching and documenting all sets of islands that fit these criteria. There is a research ship that is heading for the South Pacific as we speak. Col. Conrad, you want to take over?" Robin sat down.

"To maintain the element of stealth we will be using the research ship to pose as a documentary group retracing old trade routes of the Polynesian on the pretext of looking for anthropological and scientific evidence that Native Americans had Polynesian ancestry. That is, that the Polynesians were the original settlers of North America. That's our cover story. I'm assembling a strike force that will be trained to pass as a film crew and support staff. Dr. Steck will be presented as the 'producer' of the series, staying on the main vessel, while our team will be utilizing auxiliary craft to film me, the host of the series, documenting our adventures in the South Pacific. Robin is the producer's nephew who gets everything he wants–as a spoiled adolescent he can be anywhere anytime and the crew tolerates it, giving Robin an excellent chance to spy out our prey with his particular skill with the native languages. The film crew," Conrad emphasized by making little quotation marks in the air, "is being assembled from all points of the world–not only for their military training but for their other, more eclectic traits as well. We don't need a bunch of grunts–this is a very sophisticated group of skilled paramilitary specialists. Okay, who has questions?"

"Well, yeah," Robin jokingly said, "Where do you find a bunch of poised, hip, socially presentable paid assassins these days, Antonio Buttkickus?"

"We always look first for unemployed politicians, but have been known to accept the occasional paroled CIA agent," quipped Conrad, looking at Dafoe, "qualified assholes are so hard to find these days."

The next three days were spent outfitting clothes, accessories, and implementing their exit strategy from Scotland Yard. In the daily briefings Dr. Steck gently began to let Detective Wilkes off the hook, hinting that while not giving up hope, there were pressing affairs that could not be put off any longer. He was a little more resolute every passing day, and Robin complimented him more than once on being a "natural born bullshitter."

Robin and Conrad spent sometime each day on the finer points of surveillance and espionage. On the next to last morning Conrad suggested a quick trip down to the docks for a field exercise in "interviewing locals without letting them know your intentions."

"That's why the Yard got nada," Conrad explained, "because everybody knows they're cops, and snitches wear stitches in that neighborhood. Investigation is an art form, best left to artists, not civil servants."

Robin took a new device Ian had sent, a sort of bug detector that he wanted to practice with. Conrad said, "Maybe Dr. Hollings or Edie dropped one of your little mikes somewhere," and Robin's mouth dropped in amazement.

"I don't know if he could have, but I gave a couple to Edie when I was practicing the night before! She put them in her jacket, I know, and she knew where Steve's were. As a matter of fact he had one on his cuff that he did knock off once, so he might have had the chance!" He suddenly grimaced. "How could I have missed that, and you thought of it just like that?"

Conrad grinned. "That's why they pay me the big bucks."

Conrad rented a beat-up old pickup from a hotel worker he had spotted in the parking garage, thirty Euros for a half day. He had put on dirty old Levis, scuffed boots, and a cardigan sweater with holes and oil stains. He stopped at a thrift shop and had Robin go get a similar outfit, but for a young hoodlum, instead. Robin walked out thinking he had done a decent job from what he had seen on TV, as to what constituted a "gang-sta". Conrad laughed and back in they both went.

This time when they came out Robin felt foolish but he had to admit he looked "Like a freaking punk". Conrad had him tuck a pack of cigarettes in his shirt pocket and a lighter in his pants, and as they drove down to the harbor he made him practice taking out a cigarette and lighting it. "Try to squint and let it hang to one side."

They drove down to where the van had been found. Conrad went into a liquor store and a few minutes later came out with a carton of Newports and a sack full of cheap wine and half-pints of whiskey. He tore open the carton and tossed it on the dash.

Next the mercenary raised the hood of the truck, lit a cigarette, and opened up a beer from the six-pack he pulled out of the bottom of the bag. Conrad tossed a Mountain Dew and a fountain drink cup to Robin.

"Pour the soda in the cup," he said, pouring out some of the wine from one of the fifths on the ground and putting it on the seat by Robin. "But when someone walks up, you tug on the rot-gut, okay, we're hard guys, right?"

They kicked back, boots propped up on the jams of the open doors, and it wasn't long before a rough and tattooed dock-hand came swaggering by.

"Hey, mate, know where I can get a jump," Conrad asked, then offered beer and cigarettes, and before Robin even had a chance to take a swig of his wine they were joined by another. It wasn't another ten minutes before 'tough' came driving by with an old car and the men waved him down. They dug out a pair of cables and jumped the truck, but it still wouldn't start.

"Go call Gabe, T-wreck, see if his sorry ass is home," Conrad said to Robin, who was caught off-guard by his new nickname.

"T-wreck, where did that come from?" Robin wondered, but Conrad was eyeing him like he was screwing up, so he walked across the street to the liquor store. Robin, or T-wreck, went over to the payphone located outside and tried to make it look like he was dialing some numbers. He didn't know how long to take so he stayed and counted to fifty, and then sauntered back over. Conrad was handing over the sack with the alcohol to the tattooed biker looking man in the car. The biker said something to Conrad and he laughed as he reached back into the dash of the truck and tossed a couple of packs of Newports in the car.

"Alright, school," Conrad said, "Keep that on the cool, easy-breezy, feel me?"

"Hey, I gotcha, dog," biker-man said, "Holla." The car eased on down the road.

"Ready, T-wreck?" Conrad grinned, putting the ignition wire he'd pulled off earlier back on the truck.

"Ready for what?" Robin asked, "and why did you send me over there to the phone, and why is my name T-wreck all of a sudden?"

"Are you ready to go see what the Yard missed?" Conrad said, and turned the old truck over, gunning the motor to life, "And I sent you to the store to keep us from getting made, because all of a sudden you lost your Cockney accent. And I called you T-wreck because I was trying to get you to check yourself before you wrecked yourself, okay? What was I supposed to say, hey assholes, meet my friend Robin, the boy blunder?"

Conrad let out the clutch, squalling the tires as they headed out. He laughed and shook his head, "How the hell did you forget you were a punk-ass thug?"

"Someone saw the foreign dudes down by the docks," Conrad said, "They told the bikers buddy, buddy told biker, biker told me."

"You know where they were?" Robin asked.

"I know the exact pier, and I'm dropping you off there to play with your new toy." He looked over at Robin, "While I go make some new friends."

Five minutes later Robin was getting out of the truck, and he couldn't believe that what he saw was a usable dock. They were in a back corner of the harbor, tucked behind some dilapidated and burned out buildings. Weeds grew knee high and the pier was leaning in places and missing planks in others.

"Perfect," Conrad had said, and as Robin looked at him quizzically, "Perfect for someone who doesn't want any unexpected attention."

Conrad told him he'd be back and for Robin to see what his detector might turn up.

"Use your eyes as much as the detector," he said, "Every picture tells a story."

Robin started at one end and worked his way to the other of the over-grown lot that led down to the decrepit seawall, towards the rickety gangplank style ramp that led to the dock. The small wand resembled those of airport checkpoints, but had a few extra features, such as the capability to detect wireless transmissions for bugs. Ian had also come up with an innovative device that could pick up electronics by virtue of its metallurgical contents, depending on the principle that many circuit boards contained small amounts of gold. There were different settings you could use to fine tune for what you were searching for, and Robin first used the general scan setting that would be the equivalent of a standard metal detector.

He found several coins, shillings and pence, some of which appeared to have been in the dirt a long time. He also spotted a few plastic bottle caps that had strange, foreign writing on them-upon further inspection he recognized it as German. Then, on what Robin thought must be a significant discovery, came when he located some brass casings from a handgun, shiny and fresh looking. He duly noted on a notepad the locations of everything he'd found.

On the second sweep Robin hit some serious pay dirt. First he found a small electronic device that looked similar to a garage door opener but had a keypad and display, like a scientific calculator. The unit was new and the lettering was in Spanish, having keys that were lettered for specific functions, like 'enter' or 'exit'. Then on Robin's third and last pass for wireless transceivers he got a solid hit, down by the ramp leading down to the dock.

Robin was down on his knees, probing through the grass, when he heard the sound of cars approaching. He stood and saw the old truck creaking on its springs, bouncing down the neglected road full of potholes. Following Conrad was a newer utility truck, like a phone repairman would use. He spotted a welding generator with coiled up cords and hoses, and ladders mounted in the overhead rack of the truck. There were also tanks for gas or maybe oxygen for scuba diving, he couldn't tell, in special built-in racks.

Conrad parked next to the seawall and the repair truck pulled right up to the ramp, close to Robin. Robin put the wand down by some large rocks that used to be part of the seawall, but were now just another part of the crumbling landscape. He reminded himself that he was a cockney-speaking punk, and lit a cigarette with practiced nonchalance. Squinting at the two men clambering out of the vehicle, Robin tried to convey an air of indifference. It was all for naught as Conrad was now Col. Conrad, all military and businesslike.

"Robin, come on up," he called, and introduced the two men, Jon and Alphie.

"These are dock and harbor repairmen, who wager they can tell if and what kind of maritime activity there's been going on around here, by virtue of their many years of servicing this very harbor. Is that a fair assessment of your skills, gentlemen?"

"Aye, sir," said the leader of the two, "All ships leave marks and scrapes, like for their height. And then there's other signs, such as of their tonnage and hull silhouette, as it were. If it ain't on top, it's down on the pilings, or in the mud. You'll be losing this bet mate, eh, Alphie?" the swarthy dock hand guffawed, looking over at his companion who was carrying swim fins and a wet suit down to the dock.

"Tis a foolish bet indeed, might as well be counting out the quid right now, and save us the time from O'Leary's bar," Alphie replied, then quickly, "No disrespect there now, govnor."

"None taken," Conrad said good-humoredly, "But remember, I want proof, and I want specifics. Two hundred Euros is a goodly amount, even for "the best in all of London"," he added with a touch of severity. The two men looked at each other with a new found apprehension, all beer talk now having been put aside.

"Right, right," Jon said, "Alright, Alphie, let's go see what kind of fish has been lurking about for the gents." And the two went to work.

"Find anything useful?" asked Conrad turning to Robin.

"Oh, wait, where was I?" Robin said, thrown off by the slightly inebriated workers bravado. "Oh, yeah, maybe. Give me a minute to find my spot." Robin poked around and suddenly cried out, "Oh yeah, baby, come to poppa!" He stood triumphantly. "They were here; Conrad, Aunt Edie and Steve were really here!"

Robin held up the small metal disc, its stainless steel housing shining in the sun. "This is off Stephan's cuff; he knocked it off going down the gangplank."

"Great!" Conrad exclaimed, pulling out a cell phone handing it to Robin. "Now call Steck, we're gonna need a couple hundred Euros, quick." He looked at Jon and Alphie, who were having an animated conversation out on the creaky pier, "I think we're getting ready to lose a bet."

Jon was shaking his head, "No way, we can't say that, Alphie, they'll Welch on the bet! We got to come up with something better than that! He'll think we're daft!" Daft I may be," Alphie retorted, stripping off his wetsuit top, "But that's what was here! And another thing," he added angrily, "He's military, some kind of ex-seal or ranger. You weren't in the service, but I was and he's not one to mess with!"

It's two hundred Euros, for Chrissake," Jon pleaded, "We can tell him anything as long as we get our story straight and stick to it! He ain't gonna buy it, I tell you, even if it is the truth."

The truth is what I'm going to be telling him," Alphie countered, "And if he wants proof-positive then he can bring any naval officer out here to verify what I saw." He shook his head as Jon began to beg his case, resolute. "That's my story and I'm sticking to it, no matter how crazy it sounds!"

A submarine?" Conrad exclaimed, "You're telling me a sub was moored here?"

Alphie nodded solemnly. "I spent ten years in Her Majesty's Navy, and I worked as an underwater welder for seven of those ten. I spent plenty of time around subs, as much as ships, and only submarines makes marks like that at mooring." He spat on the ground. "Tell you what mate, double or nothing, you go get another bloke out here that's worked on subs, he's going to say the same thing. It's plain as day, I tell you!"

Alphie was standing firm, of that there was no doubt. Conrad was looking out at the harbor, pensively, hand on his chin.

"N-now, mister, we don't want any trouble here," Jon stammered, "We held up our end of the bargain, see and-"

"What kind of sub?" Conrad cut him off, "Nimitz class? Nuclear?"

"No, smaller, not American or British," Alphie said, sounding encouraged, "About thirty-five meters long, I'm not familiar with anything like that. No new submarines have been commissioned that size, not that I know of. Must be top secret or a prototype or something," he ventured. A cab pulled up to the dock and Dr. Steck got out and headed towards the men.

"Well, boys, there's the money man," Conrad said, "Alright, so they had a damned submarine. Who the hell owns their own submarine?"

Back at the hotel, Robin, Steck, Conrad, and Dafoe looked over Robin's discoveries, one by one.

"Well, the money could have been there forever, no surprises there. The bullet casings are fresh, less than two weeks, I'd say, probably someone taking some target practice before they go into action, see it all the time." He paused, reflecting. "Some guy's always want to touch off a few rounds before they go into action, see it all the time in the military. Just a few, like they have to make sure their gun still works or something." He shrugged. "The bottle caps are German bottled water, not readily available here in England, I'm told, so we've got a German connection possibly. I'll make some calls, I've got some people that can snoop around over there, see if they can dig up any info on any hi-tech military prototype. I'll also have them check to see if the German underground has any heavy hitters working on a major lick."

He noticed the confused looks from Robin and Steck. "If any highly skilled individuals have hired out for a major heist on a contractual basis," he clarified. "Now we come to this." He picked up the electrical device that looked like a calculator.

"This intrigues me," he passed it around.

"I could send a photo of it and some serial numbers to Ian," Robin said, turning it over in his hands, "That is, if I find some."

"You won't find any," Dafoe said, and then he took it from Robin, looking at it with some degree of familiarity, "It's a Spanish language translator and encryption device, very hi-tech communications device. It provides for translation between two languages, but with encryption. Used mainly by hi-level agencies," he smiled a little ironically, "and Columbian drug lords."

16

The Mercenaries

The next morning Robin, Steck, and Conrad split up, with Robin and Conrad taking a commercial flight to Hawaii, then by small plane to American Samoa. There they choppered out to the research vessel 'Real Genus', appropriate enough, Robin thought. He and Conrad were welcomed by the captain, and were taken below decks to their quarters. The 'Genus' was a floating laboratory, one hundred and fifty feet long, with a wide beam. Col. Conrad and Robin each had private rooms, with Conrad's resembling a captain's quarters room and Robin's a large closet. But he had a window, Robin consoled himself, and a small built-in table next to his bunk that his laptop barely fit on. Much better than the crew's quarters, bunks stacked on each side of a hall that had a narrow metal bench, picnic table style. The crew had a day room with a TV and books. It could fit about one-third of the crew at any one time. Conrad assured Robin these accommodations were standard fare and better that most. "Try sleeping in the in the jungle for a couple of weeks," he'd said. "This setup would seem like a room at the Hilton."

That afternoon Steck arrived and over the next thirty-six hours the dozen men Conrad had hand picked began arriving as the 'Genus' continued her southerly voyage at a steady eighteen knots. Conrad saved the formal introductions until the entire force was assembled. The evening after the last of the 'mercs' had arrived; Conrad called them all together in a stateroom topside off the navigation room. He introduced Robin and Dr. Steck and launched into a briefing that described what they knew, what they were hypothesizing, and "some out right guessing." He passed out thick folders with pens and notebooks, then proceeded with the introductions, going clockwise around the large mahogany table. "This is Chance McCoy, ex-seal and linguistics. Next we have Jose Wolfe from Spain, chopper pilot, medic, and sniper. Mark Drake from England, communications, interrogation, mechanics. Red Jones, American, fighter pilot, computers, tactics. Eddie Warlow, but everyone calls him 'Warlock', Texas, driver, explosives, and special weapons. Herman Geissen, Israel, pilot and counter-intelligence. Steven Koenig, South Africa, combat and reconnaissance. And last but not least we have Vlad Romanov from Russia, weapons and demolition man." Conrad paused. "Every man here has extensive combat and special forces experience–I just wanted to emphasize the fact that each of you were retained as much for your individual specialties as for your fighting skills." He looked around. "We are a surveillance team posing as a video crew filming a documentary. We get lucky and locate our objective, we will immediately transform into a paramilitary strike force with the stated goal of rescuing Dr Stephan Hollings and Edie Langston, alive and unharmed. As for their captors," he said, his eyes as black as coal, "Kill'em all, let God sort them out."

The 'Genus' had just completed a similar research and documentation mission, where the travels and discoveries had been filmed, and the captain explained, most of the equipment and some of the crew had remained to train the 'mercs' to reasonably pass as a film crew. The real film crew was an avant-garde collection of 'fruits and nuts', McCoy thought, after their first day of film school. The mercenaries had tripped over each other, cursing and forgetting what to do and when to do it. The director was a stereotypical raving lunatic and the plan was for a mock taping of Conrad taking the 'viewers' on a tour of the 'Genus'. McCoy being a surveillance specialist, was made a video man, with Jose Wolfe, or 'Wolf', on the other camera, primarily for his extraordinary balance and deft movements, being a fifth degree Black belt in Moi Tai. Drake, the Englishman was, at six-three, the tallest and for his height alone the director Klaus selected him for the boom mike. The others were designated as grips, or equipment men, with Warlock elected as Klaus' hovering assistant. But the Biggest laugh was when Klaus turned to him and said, "That leaves you for make-up," and thrust a cosmetic case in his hands. The mercs burst out laughing, for the Texan was known to be a bit of a homophobe.

"Hey sug, how's my lipstick, does it need freshening up?" Red, a fellow Texan, yelled, and Warlock said, "Ya'll keep it up, God's gonna have some sorting out to do." They got dead serious though, after Conrad reminded them that their foe had a 'freaking sub, you know, he's got to have top notch security, and if we're made the last thing you'll film is probably is your own death."

Klaus kept yelling, "No, no, listen, people, vat are you doing, you bunch of dumb jocks?" But they finally managed to film a two minute segment of Conrad (who was actually quite believable as an actor) walking the ship, starting on deck with the Zodiacs, their inflatable, motorized auxiliary craft, and going below decks to the lab, without a hitch. Later, watching the video play on the big screen up in the topside stateroom, the team took greater interest in their roles and vowed to do better the next day, criticizing their mistakes, down to the last detail.

"It's all the same," Robin thought, "These ultra-competitive alpha males don't like losing at anything." He was right, the next day even the hyper-critical Klaus slipped up and complemented the crews progress a couple of times. For four day's they practiced video techniques, but that was only part ot each days activities. Robin and Conrad received a short briefing from Steck every day as he was the de-facto liaison to the outside world. Scotland Yard had received no demands, and had no new leads.

The team in Africa had come up with a primary target island called Kilakou (pronounced 'kill-a-cow'), and the 'Genus' would arrive in the morning , anchoring out in the deep waters off the bay. The 'Genus' sailed into Kilakou the next morning. The tropical sun warmed Robin's face as he sipped coffee at a table mid-ship on the deck. He watched the captain's crew lower the Zodiac into the clear blue waters below, one of two of the 'Genus' auxiliary watercraft. After the rope ladder was thrown down, Conrad, McCoy, and Warlock descended–then it was his turn. His stomach did a little flip-flop as he looked down at the bobbing launch; it took all his nerve to force himself over the railing and down the swaying ladder.

"Come on, girl," Warlock drawled, "We ain't got all day!" Robin finally made it and he hoped the others hadn't noticed his shaking knees. McCoy was at the helm, Conrad was checking the communications to the ship, with only Warlock sitting there, grinning at him with a condescending look on his face. "Well, glad you could make it," he said, "Thought I was gonna have to shake you off that rope like a kitten out of a tree." Robin could tell Warlock had a low opinion of his physical ability and had already made a couple of snide remarks about the wisdom of having a "punk kid on a serious mission," under his breath to no one in particular. Conrad had overheard him once and gave him a sharp look, but, thankfully said nothing. Robin was secretly glad–he didn't want the Colonel sticking up for him and thereby taking a chance of alienating the entire crew. He knew he was going to have to prove himself at some point and he made a promise to not let his attention wander, perhaps his readiness could compensate for his physical shortcomings and lack of experience.

"No worries mate," Robin said, "A bit shaky, but I'm a quick learner." Warlock merely grunted, checking the video equipment in his bag, digging deep. Robin had seen the nine millimeter handgun with the silencer packed first, he remembered the casings sown by the dock and what Conrad had said about some people obsessing on their weapons before battle. He glanced at Warlock's face and thought it seemed unusually set. "He's nervous, too!" he thought, and wondered why. As far as he knew this was a simple reconnaissance to check to see if there were Balaluka speaking tribes in the area. Sure, he was nervous too, but no more than Warlock–it gave him a sense of encouragement. Robin looked over at Warlock and grinned. Warlock stared at him for a moment, and then zippered his bag shut with a vicious yank. They were heading to a small pier that led to a building with a thatch roof. Conrad sat down next to Robin.

"Ok, McCoy's sticking with me," he said, "And while we make small talk with the proprietor, Warlock starts playing with his video-cam up and down the beach or wherever there might be natives. You just do your thing, see what you can overhear-but remember, don't say anything except in English or Spanish. I doubt anyone here speaks those but stick to the plan–don't get us made."

"Yeah," Warlock said, "Don't get us killed, OK?" Conrad gave Warlock an annoyed look, but agreed.

"Don't press, if you get a bite, stop and think, won't that chance still be here tomorrow, and more importantly, do you want to chance not being here tomorrow?" He slapped Robin on the back and went back to the helm with McCoy. As they neared the dock, Robin saw some canoes with outriggers pulled up on the white sand. He saw a couple of small children playing at the water's edge. They stopped and stared as the skiff coasted up to the dock. Warlock jumped nimbly out of the moving boat onto the pier in one fluid, graceful movement. Robin was amazed by the sheer physical prowess, shared by all the mercenaries. They were all big strong men, but quick, sneaky quick, with the practiced ease of gymnasts. Robin saw a large fat man waddling out of the storefront onto the sagging porch. He had a bald head and was mopping it with a dirty handkerchief, his wife-beater t-shirt stained and soaked with sweat. He sat down heavily on the bench next to an old "Drink Coca-Cola" sign that had a thermometer in it. There were old license plates and street signs nailed to the façade; Robin wondered how far they were from a paved street and how they ended up here.

"Okay, McCoy, don't forget you're my translator and I'm London Frye, minor celebrity." Conrad got out of the skiff, waving to the owner and grinning like a fool, "Olla! Hello, I'm London Frye, host of 'Polynesia, the first native Americans?" Conrad said.

"Welcome to Kilakou," said the fat man unenthusiastically. "What do you need?" Conrad realized that his best impression would be with his wallet, not like the civilized world where people were willing to do anything to get on TV. "We'll be sending the cook's list over later," Conrad said, "He was glad we stopped, we're in need of substantial reprovisioning." That got him the reaction he was searching for.

"Well, come on in, Mr. Frye!" the trader said, bolting off the bench, "Let's start with a drink, shall we?" He opened the screen door to the store, and barked an order inside in another language. Conrad looked at McCoy, who shrugged his shoulders. That meant it wasn't Spanish, German, or Russian.

"Get your video-cam going, and make sure the audio's on," he said quietly, and faced the camera, "And this is why we brought 'that punk kid along on a serious mission." Robin and Warlock walked down the beach, towards the small children, who immediately ran away. They had disappeared into the palm trees and lush underground, chattering excitedly to the other, but Robin was considering going up to the small group of huts that he could see, sitting up from the beach on a low hill. He could smell smoke from a campfire and something was cooking. The exotic smell wafting across the light breeze, but when he turned back to Warlock to see what he thought, he wasn't there. Robin walked back out of the jungle, and Warlock was fiddling with his video-cam, down by the shore.

"Is it not working?" he asked, and was pleasantly surprised when Warlock didn't come back with a smart-ass retort.

"Look," he said, pointing out to sea, "I'm trying to remember the zoom function on this one; I only used it once in practice." Robin saw a few gulls circling and diving out almost out to the horizon. Warlock stood up from the one knee he had been using to prop the camera on and hoisted it to his shoulder, peering through the eyepiece. "Come on," he said to Robin, lowering it back down, "We got company." They traipsed back to the general store, staying down by the water, where the wet sand was firm. Warlock strode up to the porch and into the store, leaving Robin the video-cam.

Robin turned it on and found the zoom, leaning against a post that supported the overhang of the small porch. He swept the camera back and forth until he spotted them, four natives in two canoes, without outriggers, that were loaded with baskets in the middle. They weren't paddling, but had paddles in their hands, with the two rear riders trailing theirs in the water as if they might be steering. "Are they in a current or incoming tide?" he wondered, for the canoes were moving closer but the natives were looking east and talking amongst themselves, gesturing. Robin realized that they could see the 'Genus' from out there, and no doubt were awed by its statuesque form, a sleek yet formidable vessel. They drifted onto shore, the canoes cresting the small waves with ease, and the natives were all paddling now, strong sure strokes, putting their backs into it. Timing the landing perfectly, the canoes rode a final wave right up to shore, the two older men in front stepping out onto the dry sand with a certain privileged air, both walking up the beach to where Robin stood without even glancing back at their younger companions, who had jumped out into the surf, now dragging the carved boats out of the water.

Robin had sat down on the bench, acting like he was busy with the camera, but in reality he was turning on the audio function. The chieftains regally dressed with brightly colored tattoos and headdresses wordlessly went into the store. Robin pointed the camera at the two younger men, who were unloading the baskets and now heading towards him, each with a woven basket slung over a shoulder. They stopped at the edge of the raised porch and sat the baskets down onto the warped and rotten planks, and after giving Robin a somewhat disdainful look, went back to the canoes, at one point trying to trip each other, like a couple of jocks on a football field, horsing around.

"Jerks, I bet they're not three years older than me, either one!" His temper flaring at the pronounced insolence they had shown him, just like thugs on a London sidewalk, making you step aside as they pass. He then remembered his acting debut with Conrad, pretty much doing the same thing and he couldn't help but smile as it occurred to him no matter how far you went some things never changed. They now sat on the sand on blankets, using the canoe closest to the dock as a backrest, eating something that one had unwrapped from a banana leaf. They were talking and eating, looking with great interest at the Zodiac. Robin had put down the camera and started his hidden recorder, the replacement from Ian, for the one that had been broken in the crash back in London, and maneuvered the small directional mike in their direction. He immediately recognized the phonetics and singsong nature. They were using a form of

Balaluka! He was certain, but with the waves rushing in and gulls squawking overhead, begging for a free meal, Robin could barely catch a word or phrase here and there. He focused the mike, thinking, "just get every bit you can on tape, I can refine it out later on the computer." He had a software package on it Zenoida had installed, that with time and some effort would filter out unwanted background noise, leaving him to utilize his vast knowledge of languages to pick up their dialect. What for him was mostly "gibberish" one day was familiar the next. It was the one gift he had intellectually that even he couldn't explain away as being merely "a recipient of good genes through chance breeding." Even now as he tuned in closer and closer, (and the gulls had flown away, as the young men had finished eating), Robin was putting snippets of their conversation together. "Can't wait— big game. —not scared—Topani tribe." Said one of the lolling young men, throwing a bone down the beach at a gull, who ran off, than right back to the prize, to takin flight from a half-dozen who materialized out of nowhere. "–girls like—that. If you—flying—first time—ten days enough."

Robin got up and slowly ambled down to the dock to the pontoon boat, trying to act like the two men didn't even register as he threw pebbles in the water, then bending down to pick up a shell to toss, as he got to the end of the dock closest to them, they abruptly stopped their animated dialogue, and didn't start again until Robin was out near the skiff, out of earshot. He sat down on the ramshackle wharf, his back to them, leaning against a mooring post, looking out to sea. The two started back up, this time talking about him and the boat, not having realized Robin had placed a bug on a shell on the sand right next to them, he had only pretended to pick up. "I sure hope they take the baskets back too," he thought, having deftly stuck one of the small receivers in one of the lids when they had walked back to their canoes, playing their little game of grab-ass. "—Hair—eyes—looks—great one—" the bug was picking up every sound now, and Robin had unconsciously already formed the basic algorithms that formed the foundation of their language. He could already predict what their pronunciations and variations from the Balaluka he knew were going to be. If one of the men were about to say 'blue sky' Robin had already ascertained it would be "nazcul opo" or "nathclu oko", it could go either way, depending on which branch of the older dialects that the words were derived from.

"No—not—seen him already." Robin closed his eyes, blocking out everything but the rhythms of two young toughs talking of rivals, conquests, and feats of skill that could have been taking place in dozens of languages all over the world, at the same moment. He lost himself in their world and the new words turned into more words, and words became sentences. "Not if he was on the other island," one retorted, "Listen, Tosi, for one who hasn't played against Topani, you sure know much of their ways and you've only seen the great one three or four times like me, how do you know? That could be his son, or relative, for all you know you could be facing him on the field next moon."

"Hah, he's not big enough to face me, Loka," Tosi said, albeit with a hint of uncertainty.

"White men are weak!", he finished lamely.

"Well, what if he's real fast, what if he flies right past you?" Loki goaded him, enjoying his companions attempts to maintain his original bluster, "He could be staying on the other and practicing every day! He might be sizing you up right now, planning on how he's gonna take you out!"

"Shut up, jerk!" shouted Tosi, shoving Loki over and leaping to his feet. "Just shut, alright, you shouldn't be joking about such serious matters. It's not like it's your life we're talking about anyway," Tosi muttered and stomped down the beach.

"Robin, give us a hand, will you?" Conrad yelled coming out of the general store, bags in hand. "Okay, be right there, Mr. Frye!" Robin said, and saw Conrad look at Warlock as if to say, see? He grabbed the bug off the shell as he ran by, and purposely put on a little burst of speed as he went by Loki, executing a cut like he was a running back cutting through the line. It was childish, he knew, but it felt good, none the less. Besides, he was the fastest man back at the Center; he had blown away some stiff competition at the Centers annual picnic and fitness day completion.

Robin ran or swam every day, but as he pointed out when asked how he managed to out run bigger and more experienced athletes, "You try keeping up with a chimp that has the strength of three men!" Robin took the groceries in one hand and the camcorder in the other, and as he started to tell Conrad about the two young men and his discovery, Conrad cut him off sharply.

"Yes, yes, we're ready to go, lad," he said in his TV voice, "Mustn't keep your uncle waiting. The producers always right, after all." He turned and gaily waved at the store owner who had come out behind McCoy and Warlock. "See you tomorrow!" He kept that goofy grin on his face all the way to the skiff, even waving at Tosi and Loki. "Look at these fine young specimens;" he said to Robin, "they are perfect for the documentary!" As soon as the Zodiac was pointed out of the bay, Conrad dropped the act. Robin noticed that Warlock was being very quiet and subdued, barely raising his head when Robin handed him the video-cam to pack up. "Well, that was close," Conrad said, and looked at Warlock, "I don't think he caught it." "Sorry," croaked Warlock, "It just slipped out. I'm just used to saying Colonel and it was out of my mouth before I knew it."

Conrad turned to Robin and said gravely, "Mistakes do happen, but usually because someone gets in too big a hurry." He looked back at the store, fading in the distance. "We almost got made." When they got back on board, Robin told Conrad of what he accomplished. "Fantastic!" said Conrad, upon hearing the news, but before he could say another word Robin was rushing down the stairs to his room. He was back in a flash with a pair of binoculars and a device the size of a DVD player that had a small collapsible parabolic mirror on it.

"I forgot about the bug on the basket," he explained, and went starboard up but the bow. Looking out towards the island, he told the curious colonel how if he spotted the canoe he could possibly pick up the four men talking, or at least the two in that canoe.

"Assuming they brought the baskets back with them. I don't know what they had in them, but it's an easy guess that they were there to trade." While Conrad and Robin took turns with the field glasses, Conrad filled Robin in on what had happened in the store. "First of all, its very important to remember who it is you're dealing with," he said, "Now what would a man like Mr. Whitney there be doing out here in bum-fuck Egypt, selling ropes and fishhooks to a bunch of savages, you could very well ask yourself, and it would be very well that you did because it almost goes without saying that said person is probably wanted from whence he came." He handed the glasses over to Robin, lit a cigarette, and leaned back against the stainless steel railing. "Now, having said that, it stands to reason that Mr. Whitney could possibly be involved in shady dealings out here in this lovely, but lawless, paradise he's now forced to call home. So if there's funny business going on, Whitney probably not only knows who owns the circus, he's also one of the clowns. He's got a generator and a satellite phone, he's one we have to manage very, very carefully. That's why I kept you out of there, and still we screwed up." He took a long drag, tossed his head back and exhaled slowly. "So tomorrow, he has agreed to provide us guides to show us around the islands."

"Did he talk to the two natives while you were there?" Robin asked.

"Very, very little." Conrad replied, "He's got this native woman that works there, she took them to the back and was showing them boles of cloth, other things we didn't see. I got the impression real quick that the camera wasn't welcome, so I had McCoy shut it off," Conrad smiled ruefully, "My mistake there, I should've had a recorder like you did. Why did I think a con man, hiding out from God knows what heinous crime, would be jumping up and down to get his face splashed all over national TV?" They sat and talked some more. "Of course, we could be barking up the wrong tree," observed Conrad, taking back the binoculars. "The only thing we have is that Balaluka, or at least a version is spoken by some locals, but that's a start."

"In research, you develop a mindset something along the lines of Great! We failed! Now we are one step closer to finding some solution that does succeed," Robin added, "Edison tried four thousand different objects before he got the simple light bulb to work." "Hey! There's our friends, right on time!" he cried, looking out past the jutting peninsula that blocked the "Genus' from seeing directly into the bay. Robin handed the field glasses to Conrad, and began adjusting the settings of the tracking device. He furrowed his brow, concentrating, trying to track the moving target barely discernable in the distance.

"...Widdey...tomorrow...Elo and Acho...any better...Great one know. We get home by noon...see him...other." And they faded out completely, out of sight as well. Robin translated this down on paper while Conrad went to the topside cabin and returned shortly with a coke and a Heineken. He lit another cigarette and sipped on his beer, looking on the broken translation.

"OK, me first," he tapped a scrap of paper. "Widdey is what the native woman called him, too." "May need to let the great one know, home by noon, go see him, the great one, on the other island," Conrad looked at Robin, "What do you get?"

"The same," Robin said, "but it doesn't add up." "Well, the Great One must be a chief for more than one island, the chief we saw was only head of an island or maybe just a tribe,"

Conrad said. "No, it's not that," Robin replied, producing a map of the surrounding area that he had printed out last night, courtesy of the dedicated team back at the Center, "They're heading due west, right?" He pointed to two islands. "This is Birimbi, and this I think is Topani." "So?" Conrad asked. "It's an hour an a half from noon, island time, y'know, where the sun will be at its zenith," Robin said. "They said they would be home in an hour and a half."

"And," Conrad said. Robin looked at him, and then pointed at the scaling on the map.

"That's thirty miles away," he said.

"Thirty miles?!" Conrad exclaimed.

"Thirty nautical miles," Robin continued, "We missed something somewhere."

"I wonder what," Conrad mused, looking at the map, "Perhaps their noon isn't high noon, it's later in the day."

"Maybe," said Robin, "Even then, thirty nautical miles! That's really trucking!" "Hey maybe there's a Gulf Stream situation out there, like a jet stream in the water,"

Conrad suggested–then, "You think they bought an outboard motor from Whitney?" "No, we'd have heard it when they were talking," he corrected himself, in the same breath. Robin couldn't put his finger on it but Conrad had hit a chord. "I'm going to play it back," Robin told him, "Tell me what we're missing. Words, inflections, a fart. Anything you hear. I'll double-check my translation." Robin played the recording. His wording came out the same. He looked at Conrad, who had a odd, complentative expression on his face.

"Again," he said, not moving an inch, his cigarette ash growing long in his hand. Robin played it again. Conrad looked at his cigarette ashes now down to the butt, and tossed it in his empty beer. "Well, do you hear something?" Robin asked. "Nope, didn't hear a thing," Conrad said, "Not one paddle-stroke, not a single one." That evening Colonel Conrad called a mission briefing in the top deck's stateroom. Steck, Robin, Conrad and the eight mercenaries sat around the mahogany conference table, sipping beers, smoking cigars and cigars, the tilted casement windows cracked wide open.

The ceiling fan on low so as not to send the maps, checklists, and data updates flying off the slick waxed surface. Dr. Steck remarked that if "I spent much time around you gentlemen, it would be akin to a death sentence." The entire room swiveled as one to stare at him, no one saying a word. Conrad burst out laughing and went around the room, slapping everyone on the back and shoulders, and then everyone was roaring. Fists slamming the table, high fives were exchanged- Robin looked at Dr. Steck, who started to look around uncomfortably.

"What's so funny?" he stammered. Warlock stood, with a beer in one hand and a cigar in the other.

"Well, doc, the fact is that none of us are guaranteed a ticket home. We shoot people, they shoot back, and they'll shoot you whether or not you got a gun in your hand. Yep," his Texas drawl dragging out the syllables, "Chances are real good we ain't all going home. Being around us, 'gentlemen'," he grinned, "is most definitely hazardous to your health!"

17

It's All Business Now

The alarm went off at five am, and it was all business from there. Breakfast at 5:15, showers at 5:45; top deck muster at 6:15. Conrad was checking off weapons, equipment, and men who in turn were also occupied with their own checklists. McCoy was checking one skiff, Jose Wolfe, the Spaniard, the other. Steve Koenig was packing video equipment for Wolfe's boat, Warlock the same for McCoy's. Marc Drake and Red Jones were assisting Warlock, Geissen, the German and Romanov the Russian were packing up Wolfe's Zodiac, quietly and surely calling out items to be crossed off the list. Weapons were stashed, surveillance equipment had been plastered with stickers that said "The Discovery Channel" or "PBS" to blend in with the video equipment, some of whom had been already modified to hide their true function.

All the mercs carried weapons hidden upon their body, most wearing light windbreakers with logos to aid in their concealment. Robin saw Warlock walk up to the bow away from the rest of the crew, taking a bagel from the box set out by the ship's cook. Robin, having a free moment, and having been barked at twice by crew members for being underfoot, followed him out of idle curiosity. Robin rounded the bridge and stopped short, for Warlock had his silenced pistol in his hand, munching on his bagel, and looking out to sea. He suddenly flipped the bagel in the air and quick as a cat whipped the pistol up into a classic two handed stance, firing three shots in quick succession. The sailing bagel split on the first shot, and the large piece disintegrated with the third and final shot of the long-barreled nine-millimeter automatic. He popped out the magazine, produced another from somewhere behind his back and reloaded never taking his eyes off the floating crumbs bobbing in the water below. Robin was speechless–the whole episode from start to finish was over in five seconds. Warlock turned and saw him, but registered no surprise. Walking by Robin as he safetied the weapon. "Check and double-check," he said calmly, heading back to the crew.

The "Real Genus" wasn't the only hub of activity early on this gorgeous equatorial day. Elo Acho and Acho Acho, the two natives hired by Whitney to guide the film crew, were already at Whitney's general store, for some of the things that they were loading in their small fiberglass launch weren't intended to be seen by prying eyes. Whitney had called them yesterday on their maritime radio–as luck would have it Elo had been in the brothers hut with a pretty little young thing with the big ears that was prevalent in the tribes in that area, named Ishti, and had just rounded third base when the base unit crackled to life. "Elo, Acho, pick up, it's Whitney. I've got a job for you–repeat, it's Whitney, I'm talking big bucks, close together, over," and saved Ishti's alleged virtue for at least another day, for when Elo heard Whitney's proposal he shooed her off, then went looking for his younger brother. Acho was found behind the local dive, trying to decide whether to wager his fifty dollars he had just gotten from the proprietor for some more of his homebrewed mushroom beer on the impromptu cockfight that had sprung up.

"The big yellow one is a veteran, scarred up pretty good," Acho drunkenly shouted over the din of bets being placed by the growing crowd, "But he may be blind in that one eye." He pointed at the reddish-brown opponent, smaller but feisty, straining against his handlers grasp, lunging with his beak at the other rooster opposite the ring of crates hastily thrown together.

"No, the smaller, he's my pick." Elo steered his sibling away amidst young Acho's protestations. "Forget about your cock, brother," he said, "Believe me, you're not the only one." Now Whitney handed Elo a satellite phone. "When you find out something, push menu, contacts, and select the first one, it's my phone," Whitney instructed him, "And keep it on you at all times, it's set to vibrate. I'll pass the info along and get back to you with more instructions."

"What if those instructions aren't included in our agreed upon fee?" Elo asked, ever the opportunist, even though the three thousand American dollars was the most money he had ever seen at one time in his hands. "If so, you and your brother will be compensated accordingly," Whitney said, "On a pro-rata basis, of course." Elo didn't know what pro-rata meant, but he nodded astutely. "Yes, pro-rata," he said, "of course."

By this time the two pontoon boats had been lowered into the deep blue waters and loading of personnel commenced. Robin paced back and forth on the gently rolling deck of the "Genus", chanting a little mantra to himself.

"I will not stop, don't look down. I will not stop, don't look down, just go." He knew that he was going to be weighed and measured today, starting with the climb down the ladder. The little speech by Warlock last night had etched itself in sharp relief–the implication plain to see, that he and Steck were outsiders, extra baggage that could slow them down and cost them their lives. He cinched his new backpack from Ian tighter as his turn came close.

"Ok, kid," Vlad the Russian said, "You're up." Robin strode up to the railing, grabbed it determinedly. Throwing his leg over, his foot found a rung, slipped off, and Robin felt the Russians strong grip on his shoulder.

"Easy, turbo," Romanov grinned, "You're doing fine." Robin's foot regained its purchase, and he clambered down quickly, the weight of the backpack actually helping slow the swaying of the flimsy rope ladder. He sat between Marc Drake, the beefy Englishman and Red the American. He looked straight ahead, trying to be inconspicuous as possible.

"Well, laddie, maybe you can help me and Red on a disagreement we'd be having," Drakes brogue went well with his twinkling eyes. "Rumor has it you're one of the fine benefactors financing this endeavor, but Red here doesn't want to buy into it, so we made a bet that the loser has to do his turn at next mess on the dishes." Red jumped in, "So which is it, kid?"

Robin cleared his throat. "Well, actually, I did contribute, but it was from an inheritance, you know Edie Langston is my aunt, so it wasn't like there was much of a decision to make."

"There, you have it!" Drake cried, "From the mouth of babes as it were." He slapped Robin's thigh. "You just stay between me and Red here, boy, you'll be safer than you would at home in your own bed." He winked at Red. "We'll not be letting any harm to the one who cuts the checks, now, will we?" Red just grunted and messed with his equipment bag. The two skiffs powered up and roared away from the "Genus" in a long arc around the peninsula and headed into the bay, side by side, cresting waves, crashing down and up over another. Robin thought of the scene from Apocalypse Now, with the helicopters heading to the beach landing, music blaring; he looked to the shore and thought "so this is it." He drew a sharp breath and steeled himself for the adventures ahead.

"Okay, gentlemen," Whitney cried, "Here comes Mr. Frye and his crew. Elo, try to keep Acho reasonably sober and please remind him that he is too speak in Balaluka to you as much as humanly possible." Whitney had seen Acho Acho drunk, and he tended to ramble at times. "But what did his employer expect brain surgeons?" Whitney thought, rising to his own defense. The skiff coasted up to the dock in tandem, "like trained professionals," it occurred to Whitney. The more he saw the less he liked, but the money he stood to make on this deal he was very, very fond of. To watch the film crews every move and to make sure that London Frye found nothing of interest to justify hanging around and nosing into everyone's business was not only lucrative but also in his own best interests.

He was wanted in two countries for money laundering, not to mention his ex-employer would love to eliminate any chance of him turning states evidence against them, so the last thing Whitney needed was any publicity, not to mention TV. "Ah, Mr. Frye!" Whitney turned on the charm, "May I present Elo and Acho Acho, the most experienced guides for a thousand square kilometers. They both speak most of the many different dialects n these parts, and know the locals very well."

"As well they should, being smugglers and two-bit thieves." Was Conrad's first thought, but instead flashed his toothy TV smile and said, "How wonderful! We certainly need the best and by Jove, I believe you've outdone yourself, Mr. Whitney!" Conrad pumped the two thugs hands like they were guests on a talk show. "Shall we get started?" There was a short discussion in the store to lay down an itinerary with Conrad, McCoy, Whitney, and the two brothers. At the last second, as an afterthought, Conrad pulled Robin along with them into the store, Whitney caught the gesture out of the corner of his eye but showed no expression to the effect. He spread a map out on that table in the middle of the floor, and Conrad started explaining to Elo what his strategy was for visiting tribes and islands, starting with Birimbi first. Whitney went out back and was gone for a minute, retuning to stand by Robin. Elo was explaining in broken English where the villages were on the various islands, and Robin felt a tug on his sleeve.

"Come on, young man," Whitney said jovially, "Let me buy you a coke." Robin was pulled away towards the counter further back, "Poli, get this man a soda." A native woman appeared as if on cue from the back and she beamed at Robin,

"Oh, my what a handsome young man you are! What would you like, Pepsi or Mountain Dew?" "Uh- Mountain Dew," Robin said, not wanting to seem impolite. He looked back at the table where Whitney had re-joined the group. "Here you go, dear," said the short woman pleasantly, handing Robin the drink.

"Thank you, thank you very much," he said, and noticing her expectant look, took a swallow.

"You're welcome, I'll let you get back to your friends," she said, then suddenly, "Oh, wait, could you help me just for a second? I can't reach this one box I need and Mr. Whitney looks busy," she said and before he could utter a word, she had Robin on a step stool handing her boxes down from the top shelf. She couldn't seem to make up her mind on which of two boxes she wanted down, he was trying to be nice but really wanted to get back to the table and hear Conrad's sailing plan. "The red box, it has canned tomatoes?"

Robin pulled it out, but suddenly Poli cried, "Look out!" and he moved his head just in time to keep from being brained by a big jar of pickles that crashed to the floor. "Laot duca mai?" she asked, her hands flying up to her face in surprise.

"No it didn't," Robin said, "It barely missed me." They left shortly afterwards, Poli cleaning up the mess in back, Conrad with the map rolled up and tucked under his arm. Robin fell in step behind Conrad and Whitney.

Conrad glanced back at Whitney and commented humorously that it looked like Poli had gotten her moneys worth for the soda.

"You bet'cha she did," Whitney said, "That she did."

They all boarded the skiffs the same as before, Whitney walking down the dock and wishing them good luck. He proceeded up to the V-hulled cruiser of Elo and Acho's, where he had a rather prolonged conversation with them. Robin was watching the cres' synchronized movements for launching the craft. He was on before he realized, he could have snooped in on their conversation. "Pay attention!" he chided himself, "Anytime you see a chance, you should be all over it, it's why I'm here, the only reason, to pick up on conversation, especially when there's a possibility that Balaluka could be spok..."

"Holy cow, Poli had said "Did it hit your head in Balaluka!"

Robin was dumbstruck–had she or did he just imagine that? He played the scene over in his mind. "Loa duca mai?" No, he didn't, did he? Oh, no, surely not. She tricked him! "Slow down," he told himself, "just slow down." Robin went back through the entire sequence, then again, and again. It was a slip of the tongue, Poli was genuinely frightened, she probably didn't realize that she had fallen back into her native tongue. And besides he didn't exactly answer her direcly and in the excitement he could have just answered automatically as much to the situation as to her specific language. "OK, that's more like it," Robin convinced himself, "It was an old fat lady stocking shelves, for crying out loud, not Mata Hari!" The little cruiser headed due west for Birimbi's main village at a crisp thiry-five knots, the two pontoon boats right behind, on a sea smooth as glass. Robin passed the time trying to figure out how fast those natives could make the trip from Kilakou to Birimbi, with a current, with a tailwind, heck, with a mast and sail, even the best the natives could have made it back home would be three hours. He made a mental note to ask Elo or his brother about the Birimbi's time system, "In English," he reminded himself, "Don't forget how easy it is to switch into another tongue." Look how quickly it had happened back at the store with the nice little old lady, imagine what the results would be at the hands of a trained professional.

About an hour later Robin heard shouts above the roar of the twin Mercury engines, and looked up to see McCoy at the helm, pointing directly ahead to Conrad, who was being handed field glasses by Warlock. Drake and Red stayed seated seemingly disinterested, Red chewing gum laconically, Drake toying with his windbreaker's zipper. Five minutes later, Robin got a nudge in the ribs from Red, who gestured with a nod to the front. There rising in the distant haze, were the green hills of Birimbi. As they drew closer Robin could tell that Birimbi was an ancient volcanic island, typical of the region known collectively as the "Ring of Fire." Formed over millions of years by a combination of tectonic plates shifting and magma rising up through the fissures, the Ring of Fire was a series of island chains stretching from the Atlantic throughout the equatorial regions into the Pacific and beyond. As the continents drifted, the slowly migrating plate's edges passed over so-called "hot-spots", areas of the earths crust that had split and spewed mile high mountains of magma, one after another, in daisy-chains of islands all over the world. The Hawaiian islands were a series of mountains that had passed over the same fissure over a period of hundreds of thousands of years, Oahu being the oldest and therefore the smallest of the Hawaiian group, with gravity and erosion diminishing it's proportions. Waikiki, the youngest and largest, would slowly, inexorably, erode and sink down to its older sister's size, and a million years from now slip beneath the seas, never to be seen again.

The shoreline began to take shape and now the Acho's boat veered to the right, heading north, following the coastline, cliffs and breakers giving way to sandy beaches and gentle waters. The boats suddenly took a sharp left, heading into a sheltered cove, a primitive pier jutting out into crystal clear water. Elo cut the motor as young Acho jumped onto the bamboo pier, stumbling and almost falling off the narrow structure.

"Damn it, Elo, you came in too fast!" he cried, regaining his balance as Elo tossed him the mooring line he'd dropped.

"And you're already half-drunk!" retorted his brother, "Hurry up, tie us off, before the others see your sorry ass can't even stand up straight!" He glanced over his shoulder at the skiffs, and waved as the more cumbersome craft approached the pier.

"You know what to say," Elo said, "Let me handle the Birimbis." Conrad saw Elo heading up the beach towards some small grassy dunes.

"Okay, let's lock and load," he said, "Scene one, 'Polynesia– the first Native Americans?" The younger of the tow guides straightened up as the skiff bumped against the dock behind his launch, and closed the cooler full of beer, tipping up the one he just opened. "Where did your brother go?" Conrad asked briskly, not appreciating the lackadaisical attitude, but stopping himself from saying anything more.

"He said for you to stay here," was the answer back, and Conrad inwardly bristled- that wasn't what he asked, damn it!

"Let's go ahead and start unloading, men" Conrad said, ignoring the insolent Acho. "Just don't leave the beach," retorted Acho, draining his beer and tossing it in the bottom of the boat. "You wait for Elo, he's got to get permission before we head up to the village."

"Sure likes giving orders, now, don't the little shit?" muttered Drake, "You want me to teach the young man a thing or two about respecting his elders, Colonel?" Conrad gave Acho a big "We're on the air" smile, and without taking his eyes off Acho, "No, cameraman Drake, and please feel free to call me London, no need for formalities out here in the bush, now it there?"

"Sorry, sir, uh-London," Drake said, and shot the finger to the smirking Warlock, who now felt partially vindicated for his faux pas from the day before. "Won't happen again." Drake was relieved to see Elo reappear at the top of the dune, accompanied by two natives. There was some gesturing by Elo, pointing down to the group, the two native men stoic, arms crossed.

Finally one spoke very briefly, one hand pounded into the other, and then pointed down to the assembled crew. Elo nodded vigorously, clasping his hands together, like a subject bows to a king. He backed up a couple of paces, repeating the gesture, then turned and clambered sideways down the dune. He trotted up to Conrad, "Okay, we can go," he said, a little out of breath, then pointed at Robin. "Every one but him."

"What?" Conrad exploded, "What do you mean everyone but him? What's the problem?" he demanded.

"Calm down," Elo said, "Paktu said it, not me." "Well, Elo, does h–Paktu," Conrad forced himself to remember his role and paused to wave to the chief up on the dunes, "Have a particular reason for this unusual demand?"

"Yes, yes he does," replied Elo, non-plussed, "He doesn't allow any young males of marrying age from other villages into his." He shrugged, "That goes for the other islands as well." "Now, see here, Elo, Robin is not from another village, he's barely fourteen, for Chrissake, he has no desire to court the chief's daughter or harem or whatever it is he's worried about," Conrad said, "We can't very well leave him waiting in the boats every time we stop somewhere, can we?"

"Then we must leave," Elo said, "It would be against their religion, it's basically out of his hands anyway." He looked at Conrad quizzically. "Is he not able to watch himself, perhaps one of your men could baby-sit him?"

At this young Acho burst out laughing, and took out another beer from the cooler. "I'll stay, just tell me where his diapers are?" and laughed even harder, like it was the funniest thing he'd ever heard.

"No, that's not it, I–well, it's just unexpected, that's all," he said, "We're here, and on a tight schedule. I guess we don't have a say in the matter." He turned to Robin, "Sorry, but I'll have

Warlock take you back after we visit with the chief," he said, and then, "Do me a favor and transfer those equipment bags over to the other boat." "And don't worry," he said to Robin, emphasizing that he had not forgotten why Robin was here in the first place, "I'll bring you something to chew on when we come back." The laden-down crew struggled up the dunes, Elo and Acho leading the way.

"Look, Acho, I've got to call Whitney," Elo said, "Just remember, the Birimbi don't speak English, or anything but Balaluka. The foreigners don't have anyone else that speaks Balaluka, because Frye wouldn't have bitched so much about it." He smiled at the chief, "Right, you stupid son of a bitch?" The chief smiled back, happy that the foreigners were coming, bearing gifts. "Why isn't the young boy coming up, too?" he asked Elo in Balaluka. "He's not feeling well," Elo replied, punching up Whitney's number.

18

The Mermaid

Robin couldn't believe his bad luck, but wasn't going to let it defeat him. He wasn't built like that, to just lie down and give up at the first obstacle. He merely had been presented with a temporary setback- now what was the solution to this new challenge? To take his mind off it for a moment, Robin replayed the scene in his mind from yesterday of the two young toughs lolling against the canoe, talking about the Birimbi version of Friday night football. What had that one said about him? He looked like the Great one, or maybe his son, was that it? Robin said the words aloud, "La-tan-doct-sal. Pito-boli-noca-do. Ki-ton-abi-diro-nos?"

"Well, you are, aren't you, and who taught you Balaluka, anyway, it sounds like you learned it from an old Topani woman." Robin whipped around and was stunned to see a beautiful young girl smiling at him, her eyes bright as the smile that she wore challengingly, daringly. She was simply the most gorgeous thing Robin had ever seen in his life, standing there, water dripping from her long, jet-black hair and running in little rivulets down her tanned brown skin. "Where did y-you come from?" he stammered, embarrassed at having been caught talking to himself.

"Fishing for pearls, what else?" she said, walking out of the surf with a small net that was bagged full of oyster shells. "Give me a hand, will you?" She handed the bag and bent over to untie a cord that was tied to her ankle that connected to her net. "There, that's better," then, "What's your name, little great one?"

"Robin, Robin Langston," Robin said in awe. She was so unassuming, so sure of herself, he had never met anyone so relaxed and yet confident before. He realized he had been busted and now his mind raced to develop a cover story–could he persuade her to secrecy? "Robin Robin," she asked, flipping her hair back off her shoulders and out of her eyes.

"No, just Robin," he replied, "And you are?"

"I am Tami," the young girl said, making it sound like "Tah-Mee". "Are you here about the games, I saw these two jerks, the Achos, I thought they weren't supposed to know, it being secret and all?" Robin saw his chance and went for broke.

"Uh- yeah, as a matter of fact we are–I mean, yeah it is." He fought to appear calm and in control, then, "You can't say anything, no one's supposed to know."

"Know what?" she asked, raising an eyebrow.

"Well, I can't tell you everything if the Great One found out I even talked to you about it, Tami, I wouldn't be allowed to play, so you gotta promise, if I do tell you something, it's between you and me, you can't tell anyone, OK?" Robin was getting his confidence back, he could see Tami's expression changing from dubious to a dying curiosity.

"You're going to play?" Tami was visibly impressed. "Aren't you a little small for Klaktu?"

"No, I'm fast, real fast, I mean I can really fly, right by those bigger guys," Robin said, having no idea where he was headed.

"You can fly?!" Tami gasped, and it was more like hero-worship than impressed. "So that's why you stayed down here, so you didn't have to lie if someone asked if you were a flyer for the Topani tribe and be accused of cheating on game day?"

"Yes, Tami, that's exactly right," Robin Stated solemnly, "I couldn't have said it better myself."

"That's right, the boy and one of the men are going back to Kilakou after we leave here," Elo said, "And the rest of us are going to Topani Island. What do you want us to do?" He listened intently, watching the film crew and the men of the tribe eating cooked fish and yams. He hoped that Acho wasn't getting drunk on the rice wine the Birimbi women were serving- he had work to do.

"Ok, but that's gonna cost extra," he added, "Pro-rata, of course."

"So you dive for pearls, huh?" Robin said, eager to change the subject, "That's amazing, I've never seen that before."

"Look, I know that only men are supposed to do it," Tami said, "But I'm different. When my parents died, I had to make my way, my uncle wasn't going to feed me for free forever. Besides, I like diving. Hey, you want me to show you? Wait," Tami said, her hand brushing aside his open shirt, and in the process Robin's heart skipped a beat, "Where's your beads? You need your beads, dummy!" She suddenly gave him a knowing look. "Oh, so no one would know you're a flyer, I get it. Well, you're in luck, Robin," Tami said, opening up her net, "I always carry spares. I hope you're not scared of sharks," she said, rummaging through her bag, "There's some twelve-footers out there today."

Elo sat down next to Acho and turned to Conrad. "Good food, eh! And the women aren't so bad either!" He jabbed Conrad in the ribs and turned to Acho, not waiting for a reply as the Birimbi women entertained the seated men with a tribal dance that in some parts would have received an R rating.

"Acho, sober up," Elo commanded, speaking in Balaluka, "Whitney said he wants you to..." and first looking around to make sure only Conrad was in earshot and none of the natives, continued on with the instructions from Kilakou. Conrad rocked back and forth to the music, obviously enjoying himself, looking over at the two brothers and giving a thumbs up approval of the risqué entertainment. Elo smiled, and gave Conrad the same signal back, never stopping the explicit directions to young Acho.

"There that's almost perfect," Tami said, "I can't believe that no one bothered to show you this before, I guess all you've been strapped with were the game beads," she added.

"Pretty much," Robin said, now nervously adjusting the strings of beads around his wrists as Tami's hands finished tying the strand around his neck. "Did you really mean it about the sharks?"

"Well, of course," Tami cried gaily, "but even when they chase you, just remember you can always lose them in the turns." Robin was starting to question the wisdom of his charade, but every time Tami's hands caressed his neck or her eyes met his, he went blank. "Ok, it's somewhat like what you've been doing in the lava dome, so just let me get you started," she said, "Now then, hold my hand." Tami faced him, and raised her hands to his like she was instructing Robin on how to slow-dance, "Take this hand and strike your other wrists so that the white bead strikes the black bead," she demonstrated, "Then follow me!" And she dove into the water off the pier, dragging Robin by the hand.

He opened his eyes and about fainted–he was zipping through the water at an impossible speed. He couldn't understand why every thing was co clear, almost as clear as if he were walking down the beach. But he wasn't walking; he was going much, much faster that he could even run, trailing Tami, who had his one hand in hers. She was in deeper water now, forty, fifty feet deep, speeding along the bottom, dodging rocks and coral, even a huge fish of some sort. Robin realized suddenly he should get to the surface, he must be running out of air, feeling his lungs start to burn a little. He tried to shake loose of Tami's grip, but no sooner than he did that she slammed to a stop.

Turning to Robin, she floated slowly up to him, her hair wafting all around her face in the current. She drifted closer and closer to his face, her eyes unblinking and locked on his. An inch from his her eyes closed–her lips found his and Robin felt wet air pass into his mouth, slipping down his throat and into his lungs, like liquid heat. Her hands were on each side of his face and they both floated as in a dream to the surface, a mile out to sea.

Acho was not happy. Why did he have to leave the party to do Whitney's bidding while Elo got to stay and drink wine, watching the beautiful women dance? He came over the dunes and crab-walked, half-drunk, down the steep incline.

"Oh no!" cried Tami, "They're coming back, hurry, let's go!" She clicked her wrists and disappeared under the gently rolling waves. Robin was left with little choice, he clicked his wrists and dove his head back under water, not knowing what to expect. It was clear, just as before but he wasn't moving, suspended, floating just beneath the surface. Tami appeared at his side, and she moved his right arm out in front of him and put his left hand to his breast. She shook his left forearm slightly yet vigorously–Robin shot forward, then coasted to a stop. Tami was back at his side, mimicking the motion against her breast, nodding encouragement. Robin put his arms back in position and shook his forearm as close to what he had done before, and started cutting quickly through the water, but not as lightning fast as before. He followed her, and every now and then she'd look back and smile, her eyes dancing with excitement. Tami led him to the pier and they surfaced underneath, the rocking boats on either side. "I've got to go," she whispered, "We can't let the others see us, it's forbidden." She pointed up to the top of the dock–Robin could hear Acho muttering curses coming down the pier, his footsteps coming closer. "Now I know your secret, and you, mine. We're bound together forever in secrecy!" Tami whispered in his ear. She kissed him lightly on his lips. "See you at the games, little great one!" And just like that she was gone.

19

Robin Is Sent Back

Robin came walking down the dock, whistling a tune.

"Where were you, you were supposed to stay right here!" Acho snapped angrily.

"I took a dip, so what?" Robin retorted, "What are you doing in our boat?"

"I've got to do a little work on our boat," Acho said, "and my brother forgot to pack the toolbox." He hefted the mechanics set of tools out from under the small drawer under the Zodiac's helm. "Not that it's any of your business."

"What an asshole," thought Robin. "OK, I'm just going to move the bags over to the other boat, then," Robin said.

"Knock yourself out, looks like the parties over for you, anyhow." Robin looked out to the beach and saw the net with the shells lying in the sand, left by a mermaid he'd never see again. "Yeah, the parties over, alright." Robin headed to set the oysters free. "Over before it even began."

Acho got to the brothers launch and retrieved the brickish-looking slab adorned with electronics, one of several objects Whitney had given them back in Kilakou. "If you can set your alarm clock, you can operate this," the fat man who never seemed to stop sweating said, showing how to turn it on and set it up. Both brothers were rapt with attention, not so much in admiration, but more due to the fact that they had never owned an alarm clock. Acho now took a hammer out of their boat, and with a Philips screwdriver, punched a hole in the bottom of the metal tool box. He ran a slender cable through the box and wired it to a switch on the gray brick. He then carefully placed it in the box, and picking up the small tube of super glue that came with the kit from Whitney, he headed back to the pontoon boat.

Robin was almost finished with transferring the equipment and was now taking inventory making sure he hadn't missed anything. He was standing by the helm and reached out for the tool box as Acho approached.

"Here, I'll put it back," he said brusquely, "I know where it goes."

"Acho shook his head and jumped in the skiff, elbowing his way past Robin. "No way, you just do your job and I'll do mine. I took it out, and I'm putting it back. I'm not going to be accused of being a thief if anything comes up missing."

"Yeah, like that would be a first." Robin shot back, as he grabbed the small bag that he'd overlooked, tucked under a seat next to the inflatable life-raft and other emergency supplies. Acho started to rise up and smack the little smart-ass, then thought the better of it, remembering what he held in his hands. He went back down on one knee, concentrating. Acho broke open the super glue, and carefully dabbed it's contents on the metal tab on the cables protruded out of the tool box. He kept it dangling between his thumb and forefinger as he maneuvered box, cable, and tab into the small drawer under the steering helm, pressing the tab firmly against the back of the wooden shelf, barely squeezing his finger tips into the tight nook. After a few seconds, Acho slid his fingers out and the metal box in. He heard Robin coming back from the other skiff, and Acho quickly raised the lid and flicked the power on to the unit, then snapped the box shut and secured the small drawer shut. He jumped out of the flat-bottomed boat, just as Robin walked up.

"There you go, kid," Acho said cheerfully, "Got you all fixed up!" He grinned amiably at Robin, "Hate to see you get half-way home and have anything go wrong!" He headed back to the luau. "Yessir, that'd be a damned shame, a real honest to God tragedy."

Conrad was getting nowhere with the chief, Paktu, it was tough sledding, with Elo translating, seemingly taking interminable lengths of time to relate a simple question. "Have the

Birimbi's ever had other foreigners come to their island, asking to explore?" he asked surreptitiously, "Any foreigners at all?"

Elo thought for a minute, and then fired off another long stream of gibberish to Paktu, who listened carefully, then answered with gestures and several words back. "He says No," replied Elo, and Conrad would smile like that was wonderful news but inside he was steaming.

"That's all he said, with all that waving around, was No?" he finally demanded, his temper starting to show.

"In a nutshell, yes," came back the guide, whom Conrad was beginning to take a real dislike to. Eventually Conrad gave up and took leave of the Birimbi tribe, passing out gifts of hunting knives and of all things, duct tape- Whitney's suggested items. Conrad suspicioned Whitney was taking an opportunity to dispose of excess inventory, but they were well received, with Paktu smiling broadly and walking the group back to the dunes, chattering away to Elo and Acho. Robin greeted them at the beach, and was surprised to see the chief waving at him.

"I thought I was persona non grata," he thought, and quickly dialed his little microphone he had just put back on towards the Achos and the chief Paktu. "...back anytime. My village is their friend," he was saying to Elo, "And tell the young one, we all hope he gets to feeling better soon."

Conrad walked down the dock to Robin with a purposeful stride. He seemed a little angry, jaw set; Robin thought and decided against relating his adventure or the strange comment just right at this moment. "Look, here's what's gonna happen," Conrad stated tersely, slipping a small voice recorder into Robin's hands, "Put this in your pocket, quick, before anybody sees us. You listen to it on the way back to the 'Genus', call me the second you get back, I want to know what Elo was saying to Paktu and vice-versa." He turned as the Achos and the crew approached. "Two can play this game," he said, then broke out his goofy, toothy grin, and jovially cried, "OK, men, good job! Great work! On to Topani!"

Warlock was pissed, why did he get stuck with carpool duty? Maybe Conrad knew how much he couldn't stand being around kids, any kids. Now this was his punishment for calling Conrad "Colonel" at the store yesterday. Hell, the fat old fart never so much as raised an eyebrow why did that mean he had to get cut out of all the excitement? He started the pontoon boats powerful twin motors, and then had to untie the skiff, too–little Richie Rich was off in another world, listening to his I-pod, not even lifting a finger to help. He gunned the motors, swinging away from the dock, and almost throwing Robin out of the boat. "Serve him right to take a bath," Warlock thought, "Bad enough he's putting our asses on the line, now he's not even trying to pull his own weight!" Cursing his misfortune, Warlock went to full throttle, speeding back to the 'Genus', hitting the waves with a vengeance, taking his frustrations out on the boat. Robin held on with both hands as the Zodiac violently crashed down off another wave. Jesus, what was Warlock trying to do, kill them both? He closed his eyes and listened in on the three men on the recorder, trying to make sense of the conversation. At one point it was Elo and Acho talking about Whitney, with music playing in the background. " … And the women aren't bad, either!" He heard singing and some kind of flute playing, but he discerned enough to know that Elo was sending Acho back to the boats. "…and set the timer for thirty minutes, but don't turn it on until it's back in the boat," Elo was saying, "Make sure that kid doesn't see what you're doing." "What do I use to run the cable with?" Acho slurred, obviously drunk. "Shit, I don't know, use a hammer and a screwdriver out of our tool kit," Elo said testily, "Just be sure it's glued down good and out of sight, and connected so that the timer starts with the ignition switch. If they see it they could just throw it over otherwise, and then we don't get our Pro-rata." "What's a Pro-rata?" asked Acho. "It's what you get for blowing up foreigners, stupid." said Elo.

20

The Bomb

"Stop the boat! STOP-THE-BOAT!!" Robin screamed in Warlock's ear. Warlock gave him a look that could kill, but throttled the Zodiac down.

"Look, if you had to piss, you should've taken care of that before we left," he said derisively.

"No, no, I think they're trying to kill us!" Robin cried, and reached over and turned the twin engines off.

"What the hell do you think you're doing?" Warlock barked, "I'm in charge here, not you!"

"Listen, I'm telling you there is a bomb on board, Warlock." Robin said, "It's in the tool box right by your feet!" Warlock looked at Robin like he was insane.

"And what makes you say that, Sherlock?" Warlock sneered, "You think this is just one big adventure, don't you, Pee Wee? Stop playing around, you think this is funny, wait till they start shooting real bullets at you, you're gonna get all of us killed if you don't wise up!"

"It's you who needs to wise up, jerk!" Robin yelled, and immediately regretted it. "Look, I'm sorry you got screwed over, Warlock, but Conrad gave me a voice recorder he had on him up in the village, and I just heard the Achos on it talking about Whitney paying them to kill us," Robin pleaded, "The youngest one took out our tool box and put something in it, a bomb that's wired to blow up in thirty minutes, and it's got some sort of trip wire too, so we can't just throw it overboard." He looked at Warlock, pleadingly, "Please, you got to believe me. We've got to get off this boat now!" Warlock was looking at Robin dubiously.

"I believe you're ape-shit crazy, you must've heard wrong or something," but his voice now carried a tone of indecision, then, "Are you shitting me, because if you are.." he trailed off, then looked down at his feet at the tool box drawer. "What did Acho do, exactly?" he said, quietly and with an eerie calm. "Tell me exactly what you heard," he said, and went down on one knee, pulling out a Leatherman multi-tool from a holster on his belt.

Conrad was putting another voice recorder in his pocket when the explosion came, rolling like thunder across the sea. He had McCoy shut down the skiff immediately- it sounded like it came from the direction of Birimbi Island. The Acho brothers had turned back and came alongside them. "Did you hear that?" Conrad asked, "What do you think it was?"

"Probably some natives playing with dynamite," Elo said, and then explained how Whitney sold old dynamite to the locals to kill fish with. "That stuff, you got to be careful," Elo said, "You can blow yourself up without even trying. "That's right!" laughed Acho Acho, swigging on his mushroom beer, doing a little jig, "You go to kill fishes, but instead you end up sleeping with the fishes!"

"What the hell?" Warlock jumped to his feet at the hissing sound.

"I'm not sticking around for you to blow us up," Robin said, throwing the life raft overboard. The gas canister quickly filled the three-man raft, and Robin threw his backpack in. He leaped in the little boat, paddling away with one of the plastic oars.

"If you're bound and determined to make me look like a fool, at least use the radio to call the 'Genus' and put out a 'Mayday'."

"And say what, come and get us, there's a bomb on board?" Warlock shouted, "And then when there's not, what do I say? Oh, well, see I had this panicked kid tell me how a drunk fishing guide decided to plant a bomb on board because a fat, broke-dick owner of a sorry excuse for a general store told him to?!" He yanked the drawer open exposing the tool box, unsnapping it. Warlock said, "I'm already in deep enough- SHIT, LOOK

OUT!!" and Robin was knocked out for the second time in a month, the Zodiac exploding into a huge fireball of flames.

He awoke in a different world, an Armageddon on the water. The skiff was blown to smithereens, only one pontoon remaining, pointed crazily up to the sky. There was the smell of gasoline permeating the air, and little fires scattered all around. Robin saw all sorts of bits and pieces bobbing in the water, and one piece was Warlock, maybe twenty feet away, his life jacket burnt. Robin remembered Warlock yanking it on angrily, somewhere about the time he was rummaging for the life boat. Throwing a piece of wood out of the raft, (was it part of the helm?), Robin tried to paddle across to him, the inflatable raft not wanting to go straight, making a zigzag across the water. As Robin paddled furiously on one side and then the other, taking forever to cross the short distance, he saw blood, lots of blood, pinkish in the water, drifting lazily around Warlock's singed scalp. He finally made it and grabbed on to Warlock's shredded Discovery Planet windbreaker, pulling with all his strength, to get as much of his upper torso onto the side of the boat as possible. Robin cleared his airway and started the breathing part of CPR–he couldn't press down on Warlock's chest because the craft just sank down instead. At last Robin heard a gurgling noise and here came the water out of the lungs, Warlock hacking and dry heaving.

"Wh-What's goin on, what the, where's the Colonel?" Warlock moaned, trying to get up, floundering in the water.

"Warlock, climb in the boat! It's me, Robin," Robin cried.

"What happened, wh-where's the colonel?" Warlock groggily tried to raise his head, but fell back, his eyes unfocused, gazing up at the sun.

"Warlock, you've got to get in the boat, you've got a concussion! You've got to help me, I can't do it all alone!" Robin cried, on the verge of tears, "Please try, come on, give me your other hand!" Warlock flopped his other arm over, and Robin braced his legs against the side of the raft, and pulled with all his might, pushing with his legs and finally managed to get most of Warlock in the small orange craft, with only his legs sticking out, hanging over the water. All his energy spent, Robin gave in to his fear and pain, and cried like a baby.

21

Captured

Conrad checked his sat-phone as the two boats neared the shore at Topani Island. Robin should've called by now, hadn't he made it clear enough for him? He'd really liked to have known before going up to another village if there was some shenanigan's going on. He put his voice recorder on voice activation as they floated up to a sturdy and well built dock, at least by the local standards. The Achos were waiting on the dock, and Conrad asked

"Don't you have to go up and ask permission, Elo?" "No, not this time," Elo replied, and he turned and said something in Balaluka to Acho, who snickered and replied in the same tongue, and they both laughed. "Come on," said Elo. "Let's go say hello to our little friends." The crew unloaded and assem bled on the small strip of beach that led directly to into the jungle's edge.

"Ah, Colonel, at last we meet!" came a voice from behind Conrad, who had turned back to check on any stragglers coming from the dock. Conrad spun around and was face-to-face with another white man, calmly holding a large handgun that was pointed right between his eyes. "Whitney told me so much about you, I can't tell you what a pleasure it is to meet you in person."

Robin pulled himself together, wiping the tears from his eyes with the back of his hand. He looked over at Warlock who had slipped back into unconsciousness, but was, thank God, still breathing. His chest was rising and falling rhythmically in time with the rafts bobbing up and down in the gentle rolls of the sea. "Damn it, Warlock! You should've put out that 'Mayday!" Robin said angrily, "But no, big bad trained professional killer can't listen to anyone else, what could they know?" He slammed his fist into the side of the little boat, "Professional fuck-ups more like it." He looked around getting his bearings. The raft had drifted away from the wreckage during the interim, so they were safe from the few remaining fires, and jagged debris still floating around the one pontoon which now was almost totally submerged, Robin reached across Warlock's body and finished dragging his legs out of the water and into the boat. He found a first aid kit in a built in pouch on the side of the raft along with flares, gallon of water and some kind of K-rations and survival gear, including a knife. Robin debated suturing Warlocks gash across his forehead with the fishing hook and line he found in the survival knife's handle, but decided the risk of Warlock attacking him in his incapacitated state was too risky, opting for gauze and medical tape instead. The knife had a small compass built in the end of it's handle, which gave Robin a small boost of comfort. His thoughts turned to rescue- how long would it be before they would be missed? And how long before a search party was organized, heck, for that matter who would that be? The crew of the 'Genus', what few could be spared, the Colonel and his team, maybe a few natives? Robin's predicament sank darkly home; his revised estimate went from how many hours to how many days. He idly played with the compass, pondering their fate.

"You can tell your 'film crew' they can drop the act," the man said, as Conrad heard the unmistakable sound of automatic weapons being locked and loaded, "And they can drop their weapons as well." Out of the jungle came a dozen heavily armed men- they had walked right into an ambush, no chance to mount a counter-offensive, Conrad knew, and he held up his hands.

"Surrender your weapons, men," he commanded, "It seems we have located our objective."

The commander of the small force had his men round up and thoroughly search the crew and the pile of hardware was "Impressive, very high-end liquidation equipment," the commander dryly observed. He turned to the two Achos who were obviously pleased with themselves, having delivered such high-value hostages. "Did you do everything you were instructed to do?" he asked genially.

"Oh, yessir," Elo replied, "Pro-rata all the way, no doubt about it." The lead commando looked strangely at the fishing guide, started to comment, and then changed his mind. "So you thought of everything, did you?" he continued gently. "Yep, we're trained professionals, we covered everything," said Elo, savoring the attention of such a powerful man. The commander smiled thinly, and reached over to Conrad's front pocket on his khaki shirt, and with his long, slender fingers pulled out the voice recorder. He walked up to Elo, eyes locked on his, pressing one button and then, after a few seconds, another, holding it up to Elo's ear. "..luca-no-ton-pli-po-say," Elo's voice emanated and the two Acho's laughter pealed out from the unit. The commander switched it off, and tapped it forcefully and steadily on Elo's forehead. "No, not everything," he said icily.

Robin set the compass, and started paddling towards the west. "The devil you know is better that the one you don't," he said to Warlock, still unconscious. "Wake up, you lazy bastard, I could use some help here!" he said an hour later, knowing he probably couldn't hear him, but the release it gave him was too good to pass up. "So you guys are some of the best in the world, highly trained in the ways of espionage and kung fu, huh?" he said twenty minutes later, his arms starting to ache as he water-bugged across the ocean, "Weapons, tactics, Dem-Oh-Lish-Shun," Robin mimicked Warlock's Southwestern drawl, "Couldn't just get out of the boat, Oh, no, I'm an expert, I'll just have a little peek- KA-BOOM!!" He took a swig of water from the gallon jug, "Idiot." Robin developed a system to keep up a manageable pace. Row for ten minutes, take a reading on the compass, a taste of water, tell Warlock what a dumb-ass he was, and then back to rowing–it kept his mind from the uncertainty he was facing. "So you're a natural born killer, huh?" Robin said, "Well, you almost killed me, that's for sure." He picked up the paddle, "Slick move, Ex-Lax."

"I'm Captain Kurst," the commander said, picking up a particularly nasty-looking pistol from the pile, examining its range-finding laser, night scope, and hi-tech suppressor. "And you're not 'London Frye', but a Colonel." He eyed Conrad briefly, then back to the weapon, caressing it, running his fingers down its sleek lines. "What is it you're a colonel of, Colonel?" Conrad remained silent, as expected. "We may be in the same business, you and me, eh?" Kurst tossed the gun back on the pile of weapons. "We both appreciate the value of advanced armament, for example." He barked a command to a commando, who with another grabbed Elo and Acho and started dragging them towards some palm trees that were standing alone, twenty meters away. He pulled out a pistol, a bulky-looking affair, and handed it out to Conrad, who just stood there, coldly, with his arms crossed. He stared arrogantly at Kurst, refusing to acknowledge any kind of brotherhood or kinship. Kurst kept it extended for a couple of seconds, shrugged, and continued.

"This is a prototype, my idea actually. I was hoping to get your expert opinion." He looked out at the Achos now tied with their hands behind a tree. One of the guards took out a long knife, and slammed it into the palm tree; about two feet above Elo's head, then hung the voice recorder's carrying strap over the knife. The guard stood there, waiting for Captain Kurst. "Mr. Acho, I'm going to give you an instruction. This is a test, not only of your ability to follow directions, which is now in doubt," and Kurst held up the handgun, "But also of the DK-12, my project, the first tracking handgun in the world. I have designed this weapon to strike moving objects, my personal experience being that people trying to kill me in combat have mostly been physically active, as they seek to avoid being killed by me." Kurst flipped the switch on the side of the gun, which began to give off a low hum. "Stand very still, Elo," Kurst said, motioning to the commando who lifted the recorder and let it go, swinging it back and forth. The commando backed up quickly behind a large rock near by. Kurst looked at Conrad and smiled, pointing the gun directly at Elo's forehead, and fired. The recorder exploded into a million pieces, and Elo sagged against the tree, his bound hands the only thing keeping him from falling into a heap on the ground, crying uncontrollably. "Don't cry, Mr. Acho, you should be happy," said Kurst, looking with a little amazement at the gun before holstering it. "You both passed."

22

Lost At Sea

The sun had set, and night took over in that sudden way peculiar to the equator. Robin found Warlock's mini-mag light and checked his eyes. Warlock stirred awake, but was still incoherent. Robin got him to swallow some water, and he lay back down, babbling about how horses hated lightning.

"You gotta get'em in the barn, Jimbo, in the barn!" he cried out, "They'll run right into the fence, rip'em to shreds! Get'em in the barn!"

Robin knew he was running out of options, the original plan to row back to Birimbi having failed miserably, so far. If he had another man on an oar, it might be different, but not being able to maintain a straight line, zigzagging across the water, had thrown him hopelessly off course. He was, to put it bluntly, lost at sea. Robin had stopped paddling, and lay on his side in the boat, resting his head on the flat ring of air circumventing his raft. He was wet, tired, and scared- and didn't know what to do. He lay there contemplating the two remaining courses of action left, neither offering much in the way of hope as much as a choice- of potentially slow, agonizing death from exposure and dehydration, or the other, offering a myriad of sudden painful forms of death. He could try to swim for it, and drown, or be eaten by sharks or god knows what else. Robin let the beads sift through his hands, like a strand of rosemary beads, examining the sum of all his fears- he was terrified to try and swim to safety amongst sharks and other less tangible things that lurked in the cold, black sea. Every time he convinced himself otherwise, a scenario would inevitably appear to spawn a new, paralyzing fear. "It's really only sharks that are a real danger," then remembering the crocodile hunter who was skewered through the heart by a manta ray. Oh, wait, what about those jellyfish he'd read about, people died every year for those. And on and on it went. But what about Warlock and the raft? If he abandoned him, he might go into convulsions and choke to death. Besides once he swam away, how could he ever find his way back, whether or not he found land?

Robin rolled over on his back staring at the stars, thousands of them in the dark of night, listening to Warlock's breathing, in and out, with a slight throbbing sound in between breaths. Robin nudged him with his foot. "Roll over, Warlock," then his eyes widened as the throbbing came not from where Warlock was but to his left, and getting louder. A boat, a plane, something with a motor! Robin lurched to his feet and kept falling down, and finally settled on his knees, straining to ascertain the exact direction of the steadily increasing hum of distant engines. "Wake up, Warlock, there's someone out there!" Robin cried, craning his neck this way and that. "Dude, listen, someone's coming to rescue us, we're gonna make it!" But Warlock didn't budge his head rolling side to side with the craft's violent gyrations as Robin lunged from one side to the other, looking for lights.

He remembered the flare gun, it was by Warlock, and Robin struggled to roll him over, his two hundred-plus pounds of muscle not moving in reaction to Robin's tugging and shoving. "Move, Warlock, roll your ass over, you're on the flare gun!" Robin cried, and finally got his hands on it, and yanked hard to pull it out from underneath Warlock's mass. It was snagged on something- Robin braced himself and gave it a ferocious yank- and as the gun tore loose, the unthinkable happened. It fired, Robin's hand unknowingly on the trigger, right under Warlock and through the floor of small craft, setting Warlock's life preserver briefly on fire. But the water rushing in put out the flames, as Robin threw back his head and screamed out at the pitch-black night, "Noooooo!!"

"Did you hear something?" said one commando to another, "I thought I heard something."

"You're imagining things, like last week with the mermaid," laughed the other, who was at the helm of the Zodiac, "You need to get one of those Birimbi women for a girlfriend, they' got a cure for that!"

"Hey, I didn't say I saw a mermaid, I said it just looked like one for a second." The other protested, eager to let the matter drop.

"Whatever, lover-boy," said the helmsman, cutting the engines, "Get ready to initiate field penetration procedure, we're home."

Robin was livid. How could this be happening to him? "It's not fair, God damn it, GODDAMMIT!!" he screamed. He pounded the side of the raft which was now half-submerged, having lost the buoyancy of the floor compartment. Before he'd cried when the skiff blew up, now he was just MAD, road-rage, rabid-ass dog mad, and he grabbed the beads Tami had left him and strapped them on his wrists, angrily tying the one strand around his neck. Without a moments hesitation Robin seized the mooring line, wrapped it around his left shoulder and put the end in his mouth, biting down determinedly. He leaped in the black water, and struck out towards the now diminishing sound, towing the raft and Warlock behind. He was moving swiftly through the water, just under the surface, not thinking now, just operating on animal instinct.

Robin surfaced every so often, listening, and then adjusting his course accordingly. His was a silent and furious battle, and there existed no if, only when. Breaking through into the night, Robin saw an outline on the horizon, and plunged ahead, redoubling his efforts. When he next came up bursting half way out of the water, like a marlin, twisting his head against the line, Robin spotted his prey. Gravity being gravity, it did its thing–as he fell back in the dark waters Robin dropped the mooring line and with a short burst of speed he came up out of the water at a steep angle, launching himself completely out of the water. Not more than twenty feet away was the pontoon boat, with Conrad and crew being held under armed guard by some very large and dangerous-looking men. Robin fell back into the sea, momentarily stunned. Gone now was his single-minded, gut wrenching push for the finish line, replaced with fear and trepidation. His next thought was to get back to the raft, before they were spotted. The pontoon boat was sitting dead in the water, he wasn't sure why.

Robin swam back away from the boat about forty yards, then surfaced. Warlock was just off to his left, sprawled across the partially sunken raft. If they swept a light across the back of the Zodiac, they were as good as dead. Robin towed Warlock back another twenty yards, and crawled up beside the comatose ex-marine, his heart racing. Robin was physically played out and his chest was heaving like he'd just run a marathon. For three solid minutes he went totally blank, not thinking, just listening to his pounding heartbeat, and waiting for the fire burning his lungs to extinguish. Warlock stirred and tried to sit up.

"Where's Amy?" he said, groggily, "What happened?"

"We are in the middle of the ocean, we're lost, you triggered a bomb that blew up our boat, almost killing us both," Robin said, "And we have found our rescuers, for they are us."

Captain Kurst stepped up to the conning tower. "Up periscope," he said, "Stand by for force field penetration."

"Stand by for force field penetration, "echoed the commando/ first mate. Kurst dropped the handles of the raised periscope and peered into the eyepiece, rotating around to check on the two boats following in single file. "Initiate penetration sequence duration setting to one hundred twenty seconds." The first mate punched in the settings and flipped up the double trigger safeties. "Penetration in three, two, one…Mark!" "Aye, aye, Captain, force field penetration complete." He replied, as a powerful whine filled the small subs hull, building into a throbbing crescendo. There was a new noise that shook Robin out of his exertion-induced stupor, and as he raised his head up he became aware of a faint glow from the direction of the captured vessel. Robin now noticed the Acho's boat idling in front of the skiff, and beyond, a metal pole that looked like a periscope.

My God, it is a periscope!" Robin could see the mast segments and the little hood on top, just like the movies. There was a faint reddish orange light emanating from the under the waves, like a Las Vegas fountain, a short distance in front of the mast. The glow intensified, and now arced up into the air, forming a semi-circle thirty feet wide and thirty high at its apex. The mast started moving forwards, into the light, and Robin heard the two boats motors rev up to half throttle, slowly easing forwards following the submarine. The mast passed into the light and the glowing curve shimmered casting multi-colored hues out towards the outer edges, and then returned to its original state.

Next came the "Mach Acho Beer Company" and the scene was repeated. The small launch disappearing into a color wheel of reds, greens, and blues. Robin didn't react when the mast had vanished into the curtain of light for it was a slender object easily lost in the pulsations, but when the Achos' twenty footer disappeared, he did a double take, shaking his head and rubbing his eyes in disbelief. The commando at the helm spun the wheel of the pontoon boat and surged forward- seeing the crew and Conrad heading into the unknown abyss jarred Robin back into the realization that he was moments away from being adrift and alone once again. He clicked his wrists and slipped into the murky waters, his sudden movement awakening the dazed Warlock, who said to no one in particular,

"Alice, hey, where's Alice? Anybody know where Alice went?" Robin followed the skiff, towing the raft, thinking,

"If she went through the looking glass, we're on the right track."

23

Finding The Commandos

Conrad shifted in his seat at the back of the skiff, pulling McCoy's manacled hand along with his. "Did you hear that?" he asked the younger man. "Hey! You! No talking!" growled the huge commando, jabbing Conrad in the ribs with his assault rifle. Conrad glared at the brute, who stared back, but couldn't outlast Conrad's steely gaze, and turned back to face the front. Conrad looked at McCoy, who nodded affirmatively.

"Warlock" he said, and smiled pleasantly at their guard who had wheeled around and threatened him with the upraised butt of his rifle.

"Sorry, chief," he said, "thought I heard the cavalry coming."

Robin swept in towards the glowing wall of light at an angle, staying just outside of the halo of fiery colors that lit the surface of the water. He stayed back in the shadows until the last moment, and then made a mad dash through the ring of fire. He was momentarily paralyzed, his neck and head experienced a stinging, numbing sensation like he felt when he struck his funny bone, and just as painful. Robin almost lost his grip on the rafts rope, but fortunately the painful state of limbo passed quickly. He and Warlock were close enough to touch the stern of the Zodiac just having exited the waterfall of incandescence. As soon as he regained feeling in his head and neck (right where his implants were, it hurt the most, it occurred to him), Robin veered to the left sharply swimming as hard as he could to slip back into the safety of the night.

"Move over, Warlock," he croaked, hanging onto the side of the raft, which seemed to be lower in the water than before.

Warlock moved a little and Robin was able to crawl upon the outside rim of the boat, enough to where he could flop out and rest his aching body.

"Hey, did anybody find Alice yet?" Warlock asked. Robin looked over to where the skiff of the 'Genus' was being tied up to a modern looking structure, well-lit by towers of lights, jutting out from the shore. Next to the pontoon boat was a submarine, and one slip over was another sub in a dry dock, with cranes moving pieces of equipment and flashes of sparks cascading into the water as dozen robotic arms were welding on the partially built structures hull.

"I don't see her, but I'm pretty sure we're in the right place," he managed, still sucking wind. "Welcome to Wonderland." Robin knew even as he lay there that no matter how badly his body hurt, he had to get moving before they were spotted or the raft completely sank. He had food, water, Warlock, his backpack that he needed to get to a place on the shore where they could hide out and figure out what they were going to do. He slid painfully into the water and struck out into the night, away from the brightly lit docks, trying to stay roughly parallel to the unseen shoreline, by the sound of the breaking waves. Robin had made it a mile or so down the coast when the noise from the crashing waves subsided. He swam closer to shore and found himself next to a natural breakwater, a small arcing pier of rock that climbed to a cliff by the time it made shore, forming a small, one sided cove that led up to a little spit of sand. Robin's feet scraped bottom, and he struggled to shore, collapsing unto the little beach face down and didn't even remember passing out, the raft's rope still in his hand.

"Hey! Wake up!" Robin tried to open his eyes, but the warm sand beckoned him like a soft pillow, and he borrowed his head deeper into the shore, his eyes flittering closed.

"Hey, kid, it's Warlock! Come on, we gotta find out where we are, man, get up!

Robin moved his head and tried to speak but sand crumbled around his mouth and he suddenly had to spit, his teeth gritty and his tongue feeling like it was coated in sandpaper. Robin pushed himself up on an elbow and spat, then fell back on his back, moaning. He felt like he'd been in a car wreck, it hurt to even breathe. He opened up one eye and looking at Warlock, whispered, "Water- I need water," and silently watched Warlock struggle off his knees, limping out of his line of sight, and then he returned with the half full gallon jug of water. Warlock sank back down, and raised Robin's head in his arm, pressing the jug against Robin's lips, tipping small amounts of liquid into his mouth.

"Not too much, it might make you puke," Warlock said, and put the gallon jugs cap back on.

"How's your head?" Robin asked.

"Hurts like hell," Warlock said, gingerly touching the bandaged wound, "Must have had a concussion, I don't remember how I saved your ass from drowning, much less dragging you back to dry land."

Robin looked at him, dumbfounded. "Give me a few minutes," Robin said, "I'm gonna tell you all about it, Rambo." He went back to sleep.

"Take the prisoners up to the lava dome," Kurst told Ginobi, "And no matter what no one is to be harmed. You watch those men of yours, they're just–, "the Russian searched for the diplomatic term, "a little too deadly."

Lt. Ginobi smiled a rare display of informality for him. "I most certainly will, Captain, and with your permission I'd like to use your exact words. I'm sure they will appreciate the compliment." Kurst merely nodded, and turned to greet his head engineer, who had a roll of blueprints under his arm. Another no-nonsense kind of man, Kurst thought, and wondered for the hundredth time what had brought the German, a seemingly staid and uninspired type, to Bomani Island.

"Well, Herr Gruden, I'm having a good day, didn't even have to use my AK," he half sang, "Let's not ruin it now, OK?" He clapped the slightly confused scientist on the back, heading for the dry dock, "Let's go check on our baby, shall we?"

Conrad was unshackled from McCoy by the big guard called Kindel, who had hands like catchers mitts. Lt. Ginobi addressed the crew as they massaged the blood back into their hands and wrists.

"You are on an island called Bomani, which is an unknown island between Birimbi and Topani, and is inescapable. It's undetectable by virtue of a unique security system, of which," he paused dramatically, "you soldiers of fortune are among less than one hundred civilized men that have ever laid their eyes upon." He raised his hand and pointed to the top of the small mountain, the remains of a volcano about 600 feet high. "That's were you are going. You will be treated with the respect of fellow professionals, but if you give us reason to act otherwise..." His implication was obvious, and Ginobi raised his hands in supplication. "We not only know why you're here, we're glad you came."

"Bullshit!" Warlock cried, agitated almost beyond words, and then, "Bullshit! No way!" Robin stood up, walking down to the waters edge, and dragged the deflated raft up the shore, putting it with his backpack and other salvaged items.

"Like it or not, that's how we got here." He was glad now that he'd left out the beads, the swimming, (he'd replaced that with paddling), and for the fact they were on an invisible island. The savage blow he had dealt Warlock's ego by stating he had pulled Warlock's 'sorry ass' out of the fire, literally, was making things difficult enough. "And it isn't nearly as important right now as it to get off this beach, before we're spotted. They must have patrols, even if they don't know we're here."

Warlock looked happy to change the subject, and he limped painfully off the beach into the jungle's edge, following Robin.

"You can't go far on that leg, at least for a couple days." Robin had performed a precursory examination and pronounced a mildly sprained MCL, "but that still means some torn ligaments."

"Hey Warlock, hold on, I found something," Robin cried, bursting out of the undergrowth. "Head this way, I found a good spot by the cliff, a little clearing. We can lay up there until you're ready to travel."

"I can walk, damn it, it ain't that bad," Warlock grumbled. "We still got to find water and something to eat, I'm the survival expert here, remember?"

"First of all, yes, you can walk, barely, but it will be worse if you do. Then you're down two weeks instead of two days." Robin said, firmly but politely, "And, yeah, you're the expert and I'll do every thing you say to help us get out of here and get help, for Conrad, the crew, everybody. But I'm sure it is going to require you to stay off that leg and be patient, I can't do this without you, a reasonably healthy you." Warlock said something unintelligible under his breath, but hobbled over to the little clearing by the cliff.

He wouldn't admit it, not in a million years, but Robin had stumbled on to an almost perfect spot from a military perspective. No one would know they were here, unless they walked right up on them, and the trees and undergrowth were so thick that no one could get very close without being heard. The small sandy spot backed up to a cliff that rose thirty feet straight up, with a small indentation that could serve as shelter from inclement weather.

"What do you think, am I lucky or what?" Robin exclaimed, "It's like somebody built this place on purpose, it's so perfect!"

"Water, if we don't have water, nothing else matters." Said Warlock, conducting a spontaneous lecture on survival 101. He sat on a small round boulder with a perfectly flat top. Leaning back against a banyan tree, his leg elevated on a low slung branch.

"We've got several options. One," he went on, happy to be reasserting his place as leader of the pack, "We should rig up the raft to catch rainwater into our water jug. Two, look for running water, streams, springs, and such. The easiest way to do that is with your eyes and ears. Look at the vegetation; you want bamboo, rushes, reeds, whatever looks like it grows in wet conditions. Listen for water running over rocks, waterfalls, birds calling, especially waterfowl. And if all else fails we can desalinate sea water."

This went on for part of an hour and Robin was duly impressed. His confidence got a major boost, knowing that he was truly in the presence of a survivalist. They had made a canopy out of the raft, and used banana leaves to rig a funnel through the hole conveniently made by the flare gun. Hanging it from the cliff into the banyan tree, it could serve as both a tent and rain catcher. Robin then struck out to get a feel for the lay of the land, taking the jug, the survival knife, and the compass with him, after convincing Warlock he wouldn't go far.

The first thing Robin noticed was that every thing was uphill, always, broad plateaus of jungle, followed by sharply rising hills or cliffs, heading up any where from fifteen to thirty feet, and then up to another flat terrace. The undergrowth was thick but in places Robin found remnants of old foot paths, and he explored for the better part of an hour without seeing any evidence of a stream or spring. Coming upon another sort of steep inclines, Robin's ears perked up at the sound of falling water. "Yes!" he cried, and clambered up the cliff. Upon further review it was actually a steep hill, and by grabbing vines and onto the branches of bushes that grew up out of the terrain, Robin made it to the top. He dragged himself upon the ledge- and froze.

There were natives at the edge of a large pond, filling large water bottles by the waterfall, no more than fifty feet away. Robin slid back down over the edge, and he could make out their voices, talking as the men worked.

"This will be the last trip, tomorrow the women and children come," said one, "They can carry water, we men have to get ready for the games, right?"

"Yeah," said the other, "With both Birimbi and Topani tribes here, my main worry is not having fights break out before the games, the new warriors are the always the worst."

"I know," pitched in another native called Tuco, "We work all year for the Great One and the one time a year we get to relax and have fun with our families here before doing battle and a few young ones can't wait to prove themselves on the field, oh no, they have to drink and start trouble."

"Hey, Tuco," laughed the other, "What about that old scar on your nose, I forget was that from the ball game or from the night before, when you were drinking and a Birimbi knocked over your cup of wine?"

"That was different!" protested Tuco.

"Yeah, but young and stupid, all the same," came back, and all of them laughed as they went up the path.

Robin made it back to camp and told Warlock what he'd found, with the good news first and the bad news second. "I'll go back tonight, it looks like they're camped higher," he said, "All the trails I came across were old and overgrown, and the ones they left on were well-worn and bare." Robin set down the water jug.

"I'll be right back," he assured the grumpy merc, and ten minutes later he returned with a large limb he'd hacked out of a fallen tree, the branch forming a 'Y' at one end.

"Try this on for size," and he handed the makeshift crutch to Warlock.

"Needs to be six inches shorter," Warlock said, after a few tentative steps, "Hand me the knife."

While Robin opened a can of sardines with the multi-tool, Warlock went to work. The branch was green as the tree had only recently fallen, and Warlock hacked and whittled away, finally he took the limb and placed it against the cliff wall, and went to finish lopping it off, swinging the large knife like a machete. "Thunk!" The knife went cleanly through the limb and sank an inch into the flat, vertical rock wall.

"What?" Warlock exclaimed, pulling out the knife, "Did you hear that? It sounded hollow!" Robin stood up, still munching on the sardines.

"Do it again, Warlock that definitely sounded hollow."

Warlock tapped the cliff with the flat thick blade of the knife, listening, then tapped some more. "Hand me that rock," he said to Robin, and Robin gave him the oblong cantaloupe-sized stone–he tossed it in his hand a couple of times, getting the sense of its weight, then suddenly reared back and smashed it violently into the rock face. A hole appeared magically, the size of a basketball, into a dark void back inside the cliff.

Warlock peered inside, then turned and handed the knife back to Robin, who was standing there, mouth agape, amazed. "It's a cave," he said nonchalantly, taking the sardine can out of Robin's hand. "Mind if I finish these?"

24

The Games

"You want us to what?" Conrad was incredulous. They were standing inside the collapsed dome of the volcano, having entered through a small tunnel cut into the side of the mountains wall.

"I don't fucking believe this," said McCoy, turning around in the small stadium, "this is whacked!"

"You want us to run around the track?" Conrad asked Ginobi, "What for?"

"For exercise, of course," replied Ginobi, "I know you just got here, but we can still get two workouts in today."

"Workouts?" Conrad shouted, "We didn't come here to try out for the football team, Lieutenant!"

"No, you came here to kill us, my friend," Ginobi calmly said, stripping off his fatigues, throwing them on a table in front of a bunch of shelves holding workout clothes. He pulled a jersey with the number '1' on it, tossed it into Conrad's amazed hands. "And there are no tryouts-you are the football team."

"And what if we refuse?" Conrad tossed it back, angrily.

"Why would you refuse?" Lt. Ginobi seemed confused, "You get to play against us, your enemy." He tossed a football underhanded but hard, at the unsuspecting McCoy, who caught it in his gut, uttering a "Ooomph!"

"A chance to battle," his eyes hardened for the first time and his voice chilled, "To the death."

Robin switched the knife out for the rock Warlock had first used to open the hole. He had chipped away at the orifice and with one final blow; the remaining clay and straw stucco gave way to reveal a small doorway.

"Let me see your flashlight," Robin asked Warlock and ventured inside. It took a second for his eyes to adjust to the dim light, but it was immediately obvious that the cave was once inhabited–there were artifacts, piles of small stones, strange implements and writings, hieroglyphics, covering the walls. Robin looked up, the den was tall, thirty feet tall, and there was sunlight indirectly filtering in from its peak. Now that Robin's eyes adjusted to the dusty confines he realized he could see quite well in the semi-darkness, and switched off the light.

"Hey, Warlock," he said excitedly, "You got to see this! People lived here and there are all kinds of artifacts and writings!" He stepped out. "This is an incredible find!"

Warlock stopped eating and asked, "Would there happen to be a two-way radio in there, Robin?"

"Well, no, but–,"

Warlock interrupted Robin's excited reply- "Then it ain't that incredible," and went back to his sardines.

"I think he's serious," said Conrad, as the mercenaries jogged around the field, "and even if he's kidding, we're not gonna take a chance." The crew were all strong, fit men, but some were naturally faster than the others, so they all ended up spread out, but McCoy stayed next to Conrad.

"Hey Colonel, look up there!" McCoy suddenly exclaimed, "Is that an elevator shaft?"

"Jesus Christ, I think you're right," Conrad replied, "I wonder who that big blonde guy in the suit is?"

"I don't know, but he sure looks like the head Nazi," McCoy said, "Look at the way Kurst is talking to him, all ass-kissy like."

Herman Ludwig Kochler gazed down at the captured mercenaries striding around the ancient stadium, a natural wonder, whose field had been stained with the blood of warriors and human sacrifice for untold centuries. He barely listened as Kurst relayed news of Herr Grudens latest crisis. Engineers always wanted you to empathize with their problem, before they solved it, building it up for a dramatic finish, and over what, that this flange needed six bolts to withstand the torque instead of four? "Like a bunch of old women," he thought contemptuously.

"Look at those two running together," he interrupted Kurst, "I bet the younger one will be their tight end, and the other quarterback. They're lean but the muscle tone is phenomenal! What do you think the young one goes, 220, maybe 230?" He was beaming like a racehorse owner analyzing a thorough bred bunch of yearlings cavorting in a field.

"I'm sure your guests will be in for a treat, unmatched in the history of the planet," Captain Kurst said, ever the diplomat.

"Captain, send for our two current residents, I want them to see my newest acquisition," Herr Kochler said expansively, "While they are still in one piece."

Conrad's whole crew was at the weight station, and with the two armed guards sitting nearby their faces impassive behind reflector shades, it bore an uncanny resemblance to a prison yard. The Spaniard Wolfe and Drake, the team's engineers were spotting each other on the bench press, both thick-chested and burly men, the largest of the crew. Definitely linemen, Conrad noted, doing squats with McCoy, Red Jones, and Koenig, the German. Helmund Giessen from Portugal was over with Romanov, a Greco-Roman wrestler who was on the Russian Olympic team in his younger days, alternating between curls and crunches.

Conrad was encouraged to find out most of the team had played some organized football- if you counted rugby.

"You know, I bet ole Ginobi was just messin' with us," speculated Red, an all-star running back from high school, Conrad had happily discovered. "I bet its flag football; we don't have enough guys to fill out a squad, what do they expect, Iron Man football?" Iron Man football was the way the game was originally played, Conrad knew, nine guys playing both defense and offense. As Red spoke there was a commotion on the other end of the field- it was recorded crowd noise playing over speakers that Conrad now saw were mounted on the light poles that were spread out over the small amphitheater. The mercs all dropped their weights and watched as Lt. Ginobi, in full uniform and carrying a helmet in his hand, led his commandos onto the field at full sprint. They were yelling at the top of their lungs, and now heavy metal music was blasting along with the piped-in cheers.

Lt. Ginobi's men charged to midfield, and started jumping around and chest-bumping each other in time to the head-banging sounds of Ozzy Osbourne. Ginobi ran up to Conrad, his eyes shining and flashed a ferocious smile at him and his men.

"A little like it's gonna sound on game day, never hurts to acclimate," he shouted, "I hope you don't mind a little mood music! I know its old school but somewhat appropriate, don't you think?" He tore back to his squad, screaming like a banshee.

"Christ," Drake hollered over the din, "What kind of dope's he been smoking? And what did he mean, about the music being appropriate?"

"It's old Black Sabbath," Conrad yelled back, "It's called "Iron Man."

Edie and Dr. Hollings rose up the elevator in silence, having been told nothing by the guard. Edie thought Stephan looked pale and wan–she tried to get him to stop and take breaks but he refused, staring for hours at a time at data or an equation she had helped him fabricate and edit. She had been his nurse, aide-de-camp, and research assistant, or more correctly, his liaison, to Dr. Kochler's interns. Stephan commented one evening at the quarters they shared that Edie knew him better than he knew himself.

"You are my right hand, which is my unbelievable good fortune as my own has chosen to betray me," he'd said. Edie replied with,

"I don't care about that 'smartest man in the planet' junk Newsweek stuck you with, how did they miss your world-class wit and charm?"

The elevators doors slid open, and Edie pushed Stephan's wheelchair out to a stone-paved concourse. "What a gorgeous day," she exclaimed, taking a deep breath of clean fresh air, and gazed with wonder at the scene below, looking for all the world like a primitive coliseum.

There were two teams of men, one team in football uniforms, practicing and working out on the grassy field below. Dr. Kohler strode up and as usual Edie felt a little revulsion form in the pit of her stomach. His patronizing affect had an oily, reptilian undercurrent that sent chills down her spine–"like a mouse in a boa's cage," she confided to Dr. Hollings.

"What do you think, eh?" he asked smiling with a little too much teeth, she thought.

"Well, I see a coliseum, and I suppose those are the gladiators," Edie said, "what's next, lions and tigers?"

"Oh, no lions or tigers, that would be inhumane," Herr Kochler responded, and pointed down to Conrad's men, "Not when we already have Christians."

Red Jones lined up at tailback, McCoy in the slot, with Conrad behind Drake at center. "32, 32, hut-, hut!" and on the second hut everyone surged into motion, Conrad faking a handoff to Jones, then breaking left on a zone read with Romanov the right guard pulling and clearing out an imaginary opponent.

"Not bad," Conrad shouted, and clapped his hands, his old quarterback skills from high school starting to resurrect itself from the almost forgotten past. "Alright, huddle up; we're in hurry up offense, guys."

Lt. Ginobi walked up applauding. "That's the spirit, I see some talent here!"

"Yeah, well, I don't know how long that's gonna last, "Conrad said, gesturing at Ginobi's team, which looked to have at least fifteen men dressed out. "Looks like you got us almost two to one."

"And that's precisely why I'm here," the lieutenant replied, and out of the tunnel came a half-dozen Birimbi men- Conrad recognized several. "There's the rest of your team," he said.

"And what do they know about playing ball, and how could they understand us, even if they did?" demanded Conrad.

"Oh, they're ballers, alright, I'll wager you'll be thankful sooner than later for their help," Ginobi laughed, a sly smile across his lips. "And as for as the translation problems," he snapped his fingers and Elo and Acho Acho came stumbling out of the tunnel gate, still manacled, a burly commando pushing them ahead with the barrel of his rifle, "Well, let's just all be glad Captain Kurst's 'Space Ranger' worked for a change." He looked at Elo and shook his head. "You're one lucky bastard–that pistol never worked before!"

She looked at all the men on the field, but didn't see Robin. "Where was he, with the Great One?" Tami thought, "I can't wait to see him, I wonder if he was telling me the truth about being a player?" She hoped he was, for her own sake, but she was having a major crush going either way. Tami hoped he was experiencing those same feelings and wondered, if her life got put on the line, this first year she was to be in the pageant, would he, could he save her?

"Tami, uncle wants you to go with the others for water," her aunt said.

"I'll be right there," Tami said, and left to join the others.

25

The Cave

Robin stood transfixed, staring at the wall of the cave. He was beginning to immerse himself, to sense the flow; the symbols were starting to talk to him, just tiny whispers, but talking little by little. Warlock was down at the beach, fishing with the hook and line that came in the handle of the survival knife. He had saved a couple of sardines from earlier and Robin had found him a bamboo cane, long enough to serve as a casting pole, making Warlock in his own Texas- inspired colloquialism, "happier than a three-peckered billygoat in a pussy patch!"

Robin idly toyed with the tiny hand held cross bow as he searched the etched and colored walls for connections and correlations, picking up a similarity here, or suddenly a symbol transforming into a word, very much like one big crossword puzzle. "Little black ones…bit water ones…" no, "big, water, watery ones."

"Watery ones what?" Robin said aloud, not having any luck with the middle symbols as yet. He walked outside to remove himself from the dizzying maze of hieroglyphics, and saw Warlock limping up the small path to the clearing.

Triumphantly holding up a large zebra fish, he exclaimed, "who's your daddy, I say, who's-your-daddy?" talking to the fish. He sat down on the piece of driftwood Robin had found, and placed next to the round rock table with the odd flat top. He threw the fish on the makeshift table.

"Hey, kid, give me the knife," Warlock chuckled, "Tonight we feast!" Robin absently handed him the large bladed instrument, and Warlock's eyes fell upon the little crossbow device Robin held in his other hand.

"Well, well, well, what do we have here?" he said, losing all interest in his scaly prize, "Let's take a look-see at that, youngster." Warlock took the weapon from Robin without asking–Robin realized that naturally a weapons expert would take great interest in such a thing that Robin had barely deigned to examine. To each his own, Robin thought, a little amazed at Warlocks deftness and sureness in handling the object as he flopped, tugged, and probed the workings.

"This is sweet!" he exclaimed, aiming it at a coconut in a nearby palm. "Where's the ammo?"

"Ammo?"

"Yeah, ammo, dummy, where'd you find it, there's got to be some ammo somewhere?" Warlock said, and pointed to the tube-shaped barrel that lay just in front of the string. "See this little black rock on the string here," he pointed, "You use it to strike whatever goes in the tube, this ain't no toy, go look for some arrows or darts or something." He swatted Robin in the direction of the cave, "Now! I bet I can get this to work, I bet'cha anything there's ammo in there, Go!"

"Alright, alright, hold your horses, Warlock, I'll look," Robin said, a little miffed. He wasn't liking Warlock's presumption of authority, but knew he needed him on his side, so Robin had thought it best to play along, but it was starting to get to him, all this 'kid' stuff. "Not now, not now," he said to himself, as he went back in the cave.

Robin let his eyes adjust and carefully looked among the bowls, baskets, and tools that all in one corner of the den. "See this little black rock on the string here? Look for arrows, or a..." Robin let the words go unfinished in his mind as he slowly rose and went over to the painted wall, where he had just been. His mind jostled and the symbols became words and sentences.

"The little black ones are opposite of the bigger, translucent ones!" Robin shouted and found another spot on the wall. "The paddle rocks chase the front beads," and then over a little, that symbol was obviously swimming, "the order of the beads is important..." Robin tore out of the cave, victoriously.

"I've got it, I've got it!" He danced and strutted around Warlock.

"Got what?"

"I can read it, Warlock, I can read," Robin cried, fist pumping the air.

"Great," Warlock thought, "Stranded on an island inhabited by commandos and savages, and I'm stuck here with Robin, the boy blunder, thinking he's on Sesame Street!"

"Here, check this out," Robin said, jerking the crossbow out of Warlocks shocked hand, and placed a milky white stone into the end of the bamboo tube, wedging it under the reed that held it in position, "Try this." Warlock started to reply, but Robin cut him off, his face flushed with excitement. "Just shoot the damn thing, Warlock, I swear it's gonna work, it has to, the instructions, I read them on the wall!"

Warlock eyed Robin warily, then stood and slipped the bow over his wrist and gripped the handgrip. Warlock aimed it half heartedly at a coconut that had fallen in front of the cliff where it headed down to the shore. He drew back the bow with two fingers and cocked the string, and aiming once more pulled the trigger. The air was ripped by the stone shooting out of the tube at supersonic velocity and the coconut exploded like a bomb. The stone ricocheted off the rock and tore by the stunned Warlock, ripping through vegetation back into the jungle, eventually fading away. Speechless, Warlock turned from the diminishing sound of the projectile's path and stared in a combination of fear and amazement at the little bow, then Robin.

"That's a prime example of the importance of reading the instructions," Robin smugly gloated.

Robin sat in the middle of the cave, examining the wares of the shaman who had lived and worked here. Things were falling into place, and he had banned Warlock from the cave, saying that given a little peace and quiet, he might uncover more useful information. He had handed Warlock a pile of rocks to play with, and momentarily appreciative, the merc had quietly sat down and cleaned his fish, occasionally picking up the crossbow and toying with it, still amazed by its power.

Robin now knew how the Birimbi's had traversed the ocean in such rapid fashion, and how the beads, (which were actually stones also) arrangement allowed for the incredible feats of swimming he had performed. Robin knew what no one else knew, too. That the stones, beads, and ammo were from another dimension, and he was beginning to put together how that influenced and gave them their power. Robin was in uncharted territory, a scientific state of ecstasy, the likes of which he'd never dreamed of achieving.

"I think I know what it means to be floating on sunshine," he thought, "What a high!"

26

About The Rocks

Robin had put together a basic working theory- the rocks, just like the ones in his implants, the ones from Africa, some of which he now took out of his back pack and held in his hand, were from an alternate universe, another dimension or dimensions. The stones were probably the result of a collision of particles and anti-particles, dark matter so small it only very rarely collided with miniscule particles in our universe. That's why they were magnetic to each other, but not to elements of this world; the rocks were from some other world and ended up in this one when the fabric of space was ripped asunder, probably for one billionth of a billionth of a second. The stones atomic structure wasn't based on nuclear and electronic forces; therefore even gravity had no control over them, either. Robin had at that moment, an epiphany, and some of the items at his feet now made all the sense in the world.

"No, what I mean to say is, it makes all the sense in another world," he said giddily, and broke into a hysterical laugh. He pulled on the fingerless gloves, not really gloves but more like a fish net material, and strapped the toeless socks on his feet. Robin took one of the softer, almost 'gummy' rocks and popped it into his mouth. Rolling it around in his cheeks gave him a tingling sensation in this throat where his implants were nestled, next to his nerve bundle that connected his vocal chords to his brain. Robin felt a light headed sensation, not dizzy, just a pleasant little buzzing in his head- he stumbled a little as he walked cautiously to the door of the witch doctor's cave.

Robin peered out of the den, and was relieved to see Warlock taking the fish guts down to the water for disposal. The last thing he needed right now was ridicule; he knew he must look silly, and even more so if this didn't work. Robin walked to the center of the camp and turned to face the cliff. He took a big gulp of air, cleared his mind as best he could, and taking three quick steps leaped as high as he could- and soared up into the air, landing on the top of the thirty foot cliff's precipice.

He didn't exactly stick the landing, instead falling flat on his face. Robin gazed back at the seagulls who were eyeing him from their rocky perches, no doubt wondering "What kind of bird was this?"

Robin looked out to the beach. Warlock was washing his hands in the surf, already beginning to rise. He looked down, and had a momentary panic attack. "Don't think, don't stop, just go," he repeated his mantra, and now knew it had jumped his mind- it was about the same height, same little fear tugging. "Don't think, don't stop, just go" and he stepped out into nothing but air. Warlock came up the path, wanting to ask Robin some more specific questions about what he meant when he had said that the cave may "help them off this island".

"Hey Warlock, I'll be back, I'm going for water," he heard, Robin say, as he came back into camp, and saw the ferns and bushes rustling back into the jungle. He started to say something and stopped, picking up the crossbow instead. Robin floated, a little out of control, over the canopy, his motions jerky and uncoordinated. He needed to think, make a plan, but right this moment staying airborne and out of a tree was his main priority. If his mind wandered even for a second Robin's precarious sense of balance vanished and he would suddenly find himself careening out of control. He settled down in a small grassy field just before the waterfall, and was pleased when he only fell to his knees and didn't allow his momentum to throw him sprawling like his first descent off the cliff had. Robin picked himself up and grabbed the water jug, heading for the pond. Safe on the ground, he began to work on his plan.

"Hey, look out!" yelled her young cousin, who flew by Tami and jumped into the air, balling himself up into a cannon ball and soaking anyone nearby to the skin. That set off a chain reaction of water fights among all the young children that Tami was in charge of on the water detail. She got clear of the minor riot and sat under at tree munching on some bread she had brought for a picnic. There was no hurry, let them play, she thought, and Tami relaxed looking across the pond at some yellow orchids on the far bank.

"I wonder if I can get Eroi to swim across and bring me some for my hair to wear at the festival tonight." Tami started to go ask her cousin the cannon baller when the flowers rustled. She looked again, then eased back behind the tree and took a closer look. What was that, some kind of animal? Robin peered through the bushes at the little kids splashing in the water, thinking that they were too young to be out here all alone.

"But we're two thousand miles from civilization," he mused, "and when in Rome…" It was obvious that he was either going to have to wait or come back. The picnic looked in full swing, Robin saw, and after watching them for a few minutes he turned to climb back down the steep incline. The water jug slipped out of Robin's hand and as he reached out to snatch it, the branch of the flower bush he was holding onto snapped sending him head first to wards the bottom of the slope. He threw out his hands automatically and pushed with his legs to get clear of the tangled underbrush, and he was in the air, floating slowly down. Robin set down gently five feet away from the plastic jug. He went over and bent to retrieve it- and a pair of bare, dainty brown feet stepped right next to his outstretched hand.

"Well, I guess you can fly," Tami said, with a look of astonishment on her face, "But since no one else has been able to fly outside of the lava dome for over three hundred years, would you explain what makes you so special?"

27

The Practice

Elo and Acho listened intently to what the head of the Birimbis was saying, and then turned to Conrad. "He wants to know when you will be done exercising and be ready to run some real plays," said Elo.

"Those were real–," Conrad began to shoot back, and then smiled through gritted teeth. "Well, we were just waiting for them, that's all, right boys?" Conrad said loudly as his men gathered around. "Here," he said, tossing the ball to Taro, "Ladies first, we'll take defense." The leader of the natives barked a couple of orders, and the group lined up in a loose, relaxed formation with Taro in the shotgun.

"I'm blitzing the cocky bastard," yelled McCoy, obviously not pleased with Taro's snide remark. The larger mercs towered over the natives, who weren't in pads or helmets, at least three inches shorter and a good thirty pounds lighter. As they clinked their beads and bangles that they wore to a man, Drake yelled,

"Let's give'em one back for the Colonel, lads!" and the native in the middle hiked the ball.

The defensive line of Drake, Wolfe, Geissen clashed violently against the largest of the natives opposite, and McCoy charged past from his linebacker position, straight for Taro, who was casually rolling out to his right, avoiding the main rush, his eyes downfield. Wolfe executed a perfect swim move on his blocker and was in the backfield, forcing the smaller tailback to pick him up. That gave McCoy a clear path, and he intended to make the most of it. He lowered his shoulder and catapulted himself at the quarterback, who now saw him, a half-second before impact. McCoy closed his eyes just before delivering the crunching hit– and found nothing but thin air, his arms closing futilely as he crashed hard to the ground.

He rolled to his feet, thinking "No way! How did I miss him, I had him right in my sights!", and looked downfield as he rose. There was Conrad in coverage on their wide receiver, who was running a fly pattern, but the ball McCoy could see had been hopelessly overthrown, a good fifteen over the heads of the two streaking men. Conrad pulled up as he saw the un-catchable pass go by, but his opponent soared into the air, catching the ball at its zenith, and then glided to the ground. The slightly built native dashed into the end-zone, and did a little chicken dance before spiking the ball.

Conrad walked back over to his new teammates, gasping for air, and asked Elo, "What in the hell was that?!" Elo spoke to Taro, who replied in short, terse sentences, and then walked back to his native tribesmen, who all stood there, looking at the mercs rather dismissively. "Well, what did he say?" Conrad demanded, as the crew gathered round.

He said that's his cousin, Maro Tokupalamoku," Elo replied, "But the guards just call him Super Mario." Elo looked at the entire group. "He also said you have much to learn, you guys really suck."

"Did you see that, Stephan?" Edie asked excitedly, "That man just flew through the air! Or jumped and glided or something," she corrected.

"You like football?" asked Kochler, smiling, his eyes bright. "I was a cheerleader in England," said Edie, "for our rugby team, but I love college football, hook'em horns!" She cried the University of Texas' battle cry.

"A cheerleader," Kochler praised, "Looks and beauty, yes?" And Edie blushed in embarrassment. Kochler gave her a big grin. "I'm sure you'll enjoy being in the beauty pageant at the big game, then," he said, "But I'm warning you, the competitions murder!" and he walked off to speak to the hovering Kurst, laughing like he'd said something incredibly funny.

28

Tami's Story

"And that's how I ended up here," Robin told her as they both sat by the waterfall, watching the children play. They were up on the cliff where Tami could get up and see the young ones, but out of sight when she sat down with Robin, thereby keeping him out of sight. "Now you tell me all about this 'Great One', and the big game, and all the other strange things going on around here."

So Tami talked of how the Birimbis and the Topanis had lived on the two islands for countless generations, always in harmony.

"Always?" Robin was doubtful, knowing more than a little about world history, "You realize that would be an anthropological miracle, every one goes to war against their neighboring countries, sooner or later."

"Oh, we go to war, alright," she replied simply, "Every year, here on Bonami. That's what we call the big game." She went on. "Legend tells of many wars back in the dark days, always over one thing. Can you guess what that was? The answer is closer than you think."

"Bonami, that's what most wars are fought over, right?"

"Yes, but not just any land." She paused, reflectively. "Bonami is the source of all things sacred. It's just strange to you, but to us, it's hallowed ground. For many, many years, Bonami was inhabited by whichever tribe was larger and more powerful. The legends tell of constant war and bloodshed, the island was a thousand year old battle field. Then one day one tribe captured the other chief's only daughter."

"Which tribe captured which other chief's daughter?" Robin asked.

"Depends on which legend wall you look at," Tami said, "The walls on ours say Birimbis captured Topani chief's daughter, and," she smiled wryly, "The Topani walls say the opposite, of course."

"Revisionist history," Robin thought, but instead said, "Legend walls? Like painted pictures on rock walls, maybe in caves?" Tami looked mildly surprised.

"They do that where you come from too, huh?" She toyed with the yellow orchid in her hair as she told of how the Birimbis (her story, her version, she stressed), had intended to ransom the Topani chief's daughter, but as negotiations dragged on how the son of the Birimbi chief fell in love with her and she with him. The son begged his father for him to let them marry, but this was unheard of, and the chief refused to even though he loved his son very much. So the son devised a plan- he and her would run off together and hide on the uninhabited part of Bonami, which the Topani currently held.

When the two disappeared, the chief cried, "The lovesick fool, he's gone to Bonami Island to ask the girl's father for her hand, he's going to be killed!" He organized a huge war party and they headed in their canoes for Bonami, to try and stop the son before it was too late.

The single canoe of the two lovers, however, had been spotted as it made land by a Topani sentry who ran to the chief and cried, "The Birimbis are invading the other side of the island! That chief also put together a war party and proceeded to where the canoe had landed. The two war parties landed on the same beach at the same time, and were advancing on each other, screaming war cries and brandishing their weapons. There were over three hundred warriors, and a bloodbath like never before was inevitable. The two lovers had flown up to the top of the huge cliffs, (for every body could fly on Bonami, if they had been given beads by the shaman back then), and seeing their fathers and fellow tribesmen about to decimate each other, the lovers took off their beads and jumped hand in hand off the cliffs to their deaths, right at the feet of the two tribes. The two chiefs, grief-stricken, ran to their dead children, weapons dropped to the ground and on that day Bonami became sacred, belonging to everyone and no one.

"This sacred day, this blood sacrifice that was made by both tribes, is celebrated every year. And on that day the two tribes have a one day war." She smiled wistfully at Robin. "A few die so that many will live."

Robin was absolutely floored.

"That's one of the saddest stories I ever heard," his voice breaking, "That men have to die in the game to keep the tribes at peace."

"It's not just men," Tami said sadly, "Women die, too, just like the lovers did."

"What do you think he meant by that?" Edie asked Dr. Hollings, as Kochler and Kurst left the stadium.

"It seems that he thinks you are attractive."

Stephan hadn't been paying much attention watching the men on the field instead. Kochler had him working on some unfinished equations that were now starting to make more sense–that's why he'd had them brought up here, of course.

Every thing Kochler did was for a reason, no matter how inane or trivial, Stephan had begun to realize early in the game. For instance, why kidnap him, when the problem and promise of a new unified theory would have been all the bait Dr. Hollings could have needed to drop everything and join him in pursuit of the ultimate prize, the secret of the universe? Because Kochler had no intention of sharing this knowledge with the rest of the world, but meant to profit from it instead. But he'd be the most famous man on earth, and rich beyond his wildest dreams with the successful creation of that discovery, what more could he want? Power, immense power, enough to bring nations to their knees. An endless supply of clean energy, the secrets of the universe–Kochler didn't want to be given the world, he meant to take it. Stephan watched the men flying around on the field below, and knew then that Pandora's Box was on the verge of being opened.

"He says you're all trying too hard, not to force it, to feel it, like a lover in the dark," Elo said, and shrugged apologetically at Conrad and his men as they glared at him in unison.

"Hey, that's better than when 'Super Mario' said you all looked like eight monkeys trying to fuck the same coconut," young Acho helpfully added. The men had strapped on strings of beaded stones and were finding out that coordinating running, jumping, and gliding together into a skillful and graceful motion was not as easy as it looked. They had run around the track twice now, jumping hurdles, but the hurdles were bamboo poles spaced thirty feet apart so that you ran about five normal strides then long-jumped over the space between the poles. The mercs had flown off in all directions, crashing and colliding with the ground and each other, with little improvement.

"All right, men, stop fighting it, let's try it again," Conrad said and they went around again–then McCoy suddenly had it down, running with smooth, long strides and seeming to effortlessly take to the air and glide back to the track, barely missing a beat. He quickly left the others behind, and soon he lapped them, whooping and hollering like a big kid, which in all reality was what he was. He ignored the hurdles now and was just taking big jumping leaps, landing on one leg and taking back off on the next step- he turned a 360 degree flip right over the heads of Conrad, Drake, and Red Jones as they struggled to get their timing and balance right.

"Asshole showoff," Conrad said over his shoulder to his equally frustrated comrades, but to the flying McCoy he cried, "Way to go, Turbo, way to go!" as he flew by, lapping them again.

Later that day all the men could maneuver around the track, Elo and Acho brought out a basket and under the direction of Taro started passing out short ropes studded with stones, about two feet long. The Achos tied these ropes to the right wrist of each man with a pair of leather strings.

"Taro wants you to now get used to running and jumping with these," Elo said, "Full contact drills start tomorrow."

"What are they for?" asked Wolfe, flopping his around a little like nun-chucks, in a figure-eight pattern in front of his body. Taro tied one on as he answered the posed question, and then faced Wolfe as if he was on the field, in a three-point stance.

"He says to try and tackle him, or go around him to get the quarterback," Elo translated, and that was all the burly Spaniard had to hear–he'd had enough of the snooty son of a bitch, anyway. He smashed into Taro, and tried to sweep around him in another swim move, flailing his arms to get around the smaller native. He felt something strike his lower leg, wrapping painfully around it, and he went sprawling to the ground. Taro whipped the short lasso off his ankle as they went down and slipped on top of the bigger man. He sat on Wolfe's broad chest, one knee pinning his right arm to the ground, his left hand on Wolfe's throat. Taro's right arm was raised above his head, the embedded stone lasso swinging in an arc- then he slammed the hefty weapon into the ground right by Wolfe's ear, swooshing through the air like a medieval mace. He grunted something to Elo, never taking his hand off the others throat or his eyes off his prostrate opponents.

"He said to kill you, that's what it's for."

"So no one can fly like they used to except at the top of Bonami's volcano?" Robin asked.

"Yes, the old ways were lost when the two tribes shaman got into an argument with a greedy chief, many years ago, and left the tribes, taking all his potions and spells with him," Tami replied, and before Robin could ask, she answered, "Yes, the Topani legends say it was a Birimbi chief, and us them."

She continued. "But even in the lava dome where the magic of Bonami is most strong, men cannot fly as you, they can just glide for short distances. What you did that I saw was lost long ago."

"Hey Tami," cried a young voice, "We're ready to go, where are you?"

"Up here," Tami answered standing and waving her hand.

"How did you get up there?" asked Eloi, looking up at the pot of the waterfall.

"I flew on the back of a bird," she cried out, gaily.

"I guess that bird brought you that flower in you hair, too," Eloi teased his older cousin.

"No, that came from a prince, just like in a fairy tale," came back the reply.

29

Back To The Cave

Robin flew home, and having mastered some basic techniques he could now afford the luxury of thought. Tami was to meet him at the feast tonight and show him the back ways of the stadium to avoid being spotted when he tried to contact Conrad. She seemed only to glad to help, when Robin pointed this out, she very coyly said a girl was entitled to a few secrets of her own, wasn't she?

Robin had kept a few, too, like the fact that he knew where the shaman had run off to all those hundreds of years ago. And how Bonami wasn't a volcano, at least in the strictest of definitions. It was the product of a collision in mid earth; between anti-matter and matter perhaps the matter was in a tiny black hole. The infinitely dense striking the incredibly fast, other universe fast, gravitons or neutrinos, most likely. These things that passed through the earth usually unimpeded, materialized for that brief nano-second. It ripped into of the center of the world like a microscopic bullet that mushroomed into an exit wound the size of an island, spurting hot magma like blood. The small pieces of another universe were trapped in that micro billionth of a billionth of a second state of flux, ending up here on this side, trapped as in a head wound, like tiny bone fragments of a skull. All those beads that he now wore were just like the stones from Africa and not subject to any of the laws of this universe.

Robin also knew that was the reason the 'Great One' was here, and why he had kidnapped the greatest quantum physics theoretician on the planet–because he couldn't do the math, not being able to fit the final pieces of the puzzle together without him. Until he did, he couldn't, couldn't do what? It dawned on Robin, slowly, powerfully, almost causing him to crash into a stand of coco-bolo trees–he was just able to stop in time, hovering and realizing the massive implications of the absolute power one would have in such a situation.

He resumed his flight back to the shaman's magical little world, intent on finding a way to save his own planet from disaster.

Warlock heard him coming through the bush.

"What took you so long?" he asked, mildly irritated. He was getting cabin fever already, his leg was coming along nicely and another day should do it. He wanted to get a plan of action put together, but he needed Robin to explain how the things he had found in the cave could help.

"Had a hot date," Robin said, setting the jug of water on the rock turned table-top.

"Must've been interesting the way you're dressed up, who's the lucky guy?" Warlock snapped, "Or is it Halloween already?"

Robin realized he still had on the fishnet gloves and socks on–no matter Warlock was getting ready to get an earful anyway.

"Warlock, you may want to sit down for this, I'm going to tell you a story that is literally out of this world."

"And you expect me to believe this shit?!" Warlock snickered, "What do I look like, some kind of idiot?"

Robin had expected this and thus was prepared for rejection and scorn.

"Now, I know you're skeptical, and I wouldn't dream of asking you to accept this without proof of some kind." Robin was going for dramatic effect, "Now, you must admit that the cross bow is a little strange and not truly explainable with conventional scientific reasoning, correct?"

"Look, kid, I ain't got all day, you're telling me this big story about black holes and asteroids and how these savages here used to be able to fly, when we need to be figuring out how to get help."

He stood up and pointed towards the beach with his crutch.

"We build a raft, and the ripped-up one we can use as a sail, maybe..."

"Yeah, like that movie, 'Lost'," Robin jumped in , sounding like he was further away than he was before, Warlock thought, but at least the kid was getting the picture.

"Now at night, we've got the stars, I figure due east must be our best bet," Warlock continued, "When we see birds, we're close to land. That means ships, planes, whatever, got it?"

"Look, is it a bird, a plane, could it be…" Robin cried, and Warlock wheeled angrily around.

"Look, kid, you can shut up with the comic book shit, I'm trying to get us out of here and you're making jokes like you're superman or something- what the fu-?" Warlock was talking to thin air, the kid had disappeared.

"Not Superman, Warlock," Robin said, and Warlock looked up and saw him hovering twenty feet off the ground, "And my names not 'kid', its Robin."

Robin flew through the air swooping down to grab the jug of water, then settle on the big rock table.

"And its Batman that's gonna get us out of here."

"So you, and only you, can do- that?" Warlock couldn't bring himself to acknowledge Robin's new skill.

"So it would appear, Mr. Warlock," Robin said insouciantly, "You see this?" he held out some of the discs from Africa. "I have these in my neck, and the legend wall says that in the old days the shaman put pieces of the flying stones in the necks, arms, and heads of natives and then they could fly. So the natives of today only have half the equation, because the shaman left the tribes and his knowledge with him.

"I got lucky," Robin said, thinking of Tami, "Maybe real lucky."

"So what are we waiting for?" Warlock said, taking his shirt off and handing Robin the survival knife.

"What do you mean?" Robin was puzzled.

"Well, I thought that's what all this long-ass story was all about," Warlock said, sitting down on the piece of driftwood.

"Go ahead, doctor, let's get'em in, you can use the fishing line to stitch me up."

"You expect me to slice you open, stick some rocks in your neck, and sew you back up without anesthesia or antiseptic, using a bowie knife as a scalpel?" Robin said, incredulously, "Are you crazy?"

"Look, kid, you're talking to a soldier of fortune, a man who puts himself in harms way on a daily basis, who jumps out of perfectly good airplanes for fun." Warlock noted. "Hell, yeah, I'm nuts." He tilted his head sideways, exposing his neck.

"Now are you gonna start cutting, or am I?"

30

Robin Flies

The sun disappeared over the top of the island's crater, a big orange scoop of ice cream topping the cone of the lava dome. Robin waited for one more hour before he set off, just like Tami said. Checking on Warlock one more time, Robin was amazed to find him snoring in the cave, lying on the mat of palmetto leaves.

"Sleeping like a baby," he mused, and after he'd endured a twenty minute surgery, shaking at times, but never uttering a word. Robin now knew what tough was, and it was with new found respect he left Warlock, flying off into the darkness.

Robin gazed upwards at the star blown sky- it never ceased to amaze him how the millions of dots of light that one never saw in the light-polluted skies of civilization extended undiluted to the very edge of the horizon. As he flew up to the lava dome he became aware of a faint brightness towards the coast off his right side- it grew even as he veered off the route laid down earlier by Tami to examine this new mystery. Robin knew he was getting near the docks- he could now see the blue flashes of the robot welders falling to the sea like fireworks over a waterfront. Out in the bay, the semi-circle of colors was beginning to materialize, throbbing in and out at first, and now firming up into a concrete object, breathing life into light.

Robin stayed up at about two hundred feet; this force field still a puzzlement. He hadn't quite figured it out yet, but the thought of its huge military potential was bone-chilling. The arc of light shimmered–and the bow of a ship's beam began to emerge from the undulating surface. The bow gave way to a bridge, then another flying bridge–it was a large yacht, richly adorned in brass and mahogany accents, liberally appointed, with well-dress olive-skinned body guards toting automatic weapons.

"Well, well," Robin thought, "It would appear we have some very important visitors, that yacht's over seventy feet long, and state of the art- it must be worth a couple million dollars if it's worth a dime."

It was a floating palace, fit for a sheik or a king, whoever owned it was very definitely rich and powerful. Robin made note of the fact that the vessel was of Liberian registration, which was a popular choice of maritime ventures of questionable nature, and resumed his journey to the top of Bonami.

"You and your team are cordially invited to a pre-game dinner," Kurst said to Conrad, oozing eloquence and false formality,

"What if we refuse?" Conrad asked–he was exhausted, sore, and nursing a blister.

"But Herr Kochler insists, he wants to introduce the teams to his guests of honor. Besides, who could turn down Beluga caviar, Don Perignon- have your men ever had a chance to dine on Kobe beef?"

"Maybe some other time," Conrad replied, "We'll just have to take our chances, eh, men?"

"Oh, Colonel," sighed Kurst, "Why must you insist on spoiling things? You know you have no choice in making your dinner plans–just imagine you're married."

"And really," he continued, "It's a mortal sin to pass up a good meal, especially when it could be your last."

At that Captain Kurst left their quarters, a small dormitory of stone walls and steel roof design, with one door and two guards outside. The small open windows with iron rebar allowed the single fan overhead to circulate the double bunked tank into a very small degree of comfort–now that he thought about it, that evening of fine food and drink started sounding better and better. McCoy was the one to break the uncomfortable silence, with the furtive looks exchanged among the men only serving to embolden him.

"Come on, Colonel, it's just a meal, for Chrissake. I wouldn't mind being served some damned perignon by some pretty island girls in grass skirts; I guess I could tolerate it for a spell."

"Yeah, Colonel," chipped in Wolfe, "No reason not to be sociable is there?"

Conrad grinned, thankful for the bailout, "Okay, Judas, it's your last supper."

Herman Kochler was nervous, spitting cobra nervous, his eyes never leaving their prey as the humvee approached. He stood under the porch of his island mansion, an ancient stone temple turned into a modern palace, out of sight, back in the shadows. The humvee came to a ponderous, stiff stop, the armored limo's huge tires scrunching on the crushed pumice drive. First out were the three body guards, followed by an impeccably dressed man in dark shades of Latin descent.

"Senor Orpeza, Welcome, Welcome!" Kochler boomed, jauntily stepping down the stairs, much like a politician heading down the courthouse steps to a news conference.

"Welcome to Bonami Island, welcome to the future!"

The cool look he received back as the don removed his Oakley's suggested Kochler tone it down a bit from the corny-sounding intro.

"Come, let me offer you a drink," Kochler motioned to the ancient abode with contemporary windows and a leaded glassed entry door. "Tell me about how things are in the real world."

"We have much to discuss," the wealthy Colombian spoke. "My associates are not the most–"he searched for a word, "accommodating when it comes to schedules and delivery dates."

"Of course, Don Orpeza, let me assure you, we're on schedule, but come, we have all the data and timetables ready for you." Kochler beamed, relieved that was all the Don and Company wanted to meet about. He was a meticulous planner and fanatic when it came to scheduling–no engineer or dock worker was ever allowed to leave until a day's stated goal was achieved. And no one complained at all, at least not after Kurst had tested that stupid pistol on a junior-level engineer from

America who had balked at staying at the dock until the days assignment was reached.

"I'm going back to my hut and no ones going to stop me," he'd exclaimed, after a particularly trying day had stretched deep into the night. Kurst calmly had him tied to a mooring pole and had a crane operator swing a melon in a net over the young miscreants head, swaying it slightly in the breeze.

Kurst bragged to the assembled workers of the weapon's capabilities, "And when it needed work we didn't say, "Oh, gotta go, I need a cold beer and a hot Topani girl", no sir, we worked some more!" He pointed the gun at the hapless American and pulled the trigger, blowing his brains out, the melon still swinging like a pendulum above the decapitated body.

"Hmm," Kurst said, looking at the still spurting corpse, then at the strange-looking pistol, "I guess it still needs some more work."

Robin crept up the stones cautiously, his head itching from the root dye Tami had shown him how to prepare and apply. It didn't bother his skin so much, diluted down with the aloe and mud to achieve a nice bronze tone, but the pure extract of Poloca root in his hair was driving him mad.

"Look, the Bonami people don't know who you are, they'll think you're Topani, and Topani will think you are Bonami. If someone gets a good look at your face, tell them you're the bastard son of the 'Great One' and a girl of the other tribe."

Robin waited at the top of the landing just outside of the pavilion, next to the lava dome's upper edge, close to where it overlooked the arena below.

"Hey, handsome," a voice cried, and Robin turned around. When he did, Tami's hands flew up to her face in shock.

"What's wrong?" Robin demanded, a little put off, "This was the best I could do on short notice, okay?"

"Oh, it's not that, you look positively so-so manly!" she said, then laughing, "Go look in the fountain," and she took him by the hand and led him over to a stone pool decorated with a native warrior, swinging a small knotted rope over his head at another warrior that was lunging for his knees.

"Wow!" Robin managed. The person he saw was like a Bonami version of him, very tanned and muscular. Had he had all that muscle tone before? It must be the oily tanning lotion he had smeared all over his body, but damn if he didn't look like a little Tarzan!

"This is so weird," Tami said, and Robin asked

"What?" still mesmerized by the transformation. "This is what your son would look like if you married a native," she said, looking into the mirrored eyes of the reflection.

The Colonel led his men up the stadium steps to the pavilion which jutted outwards on one end like a stone runway overlooking the arena's end zone, hanging out twenty-five or thirty feet past the sheer cliff face of that end of the lava dome. The rest of the lava dome was of a more moderate gradient, the result being a horse-shoe shaped seating area, with a tunnel cut in the other end zone leading to the team's quarters, and eventually down to the small bay. The pavilion was lit with torches flaming in the warm breeze. Even though the place had electricity, it was as much to honor the ancient traditional dinner as it was to lend a tropic flavor.

The native women were working alongside gourmet chefs and helpers, and were preparing tapir, chickens, and peacocks, next to white coated Europeans basting and brazing away at some of the Western world's most exotic dishes. Tami handed Robin a large basket of fruit, "Just keep moving, like you're stressing and angry- keep your head tilted forward so your hair is in your face- yes, like that, as long as no one gets a good solid look, you'll be fine." She was called away by a large woman, who was in panic mode.

"Tami, over here, hurry! Take the sliced pineapples and molasses out, before the molasses cools, Go!" And Tami was back to work, but not before a quick peck on the cheek.

"Wish me luck," she said, and Robin was momentarily puzzled. Then he remembered that part of the age-old traditional feast was the beauty pageant selection, and he frowned, recalling her telling of not wanting to be chosen. "Oh, not just men," he remembered, shuddering, "Women die, too."

31

The Dinner

Don Orpeza, Kochler, and Kurst sat at the table with the Colonel and Ginobi, the talk deliberately light–amazing hotels, great wine, favorite places to eat in Paris or Rio, with Conrad and Ginobi mainly smiling and nodding, a little out of their element. Orpeza was getting a little drunk–he was having a fine time now that he knew that the fifty million dollars the cartel had invested was paying off, with more opportunities on the way.

"So tell me," Orpeza said at one point. "This special entertainment tomorrow you've been so secretive about, Herr Kochler. Does it have any practical applications in the context of our business dealings?"

"Do you and your friends still have enemies that would do you harm?" asked Kochler. "And would these enemies have gangs of men, armies even- that you would squash like the dung beetles they are if given the chance?" Kochler motioned for cigars all around, clearly enjoying enigmatic moment.

"More now than ever," replied Orpeza, leaning forward, arms on the table. He and this Kochler could be brothers, they thought so much alike. Orpeza took another drink of brandy, enjoying his evening very much. He wondered what the women were like in this tropical paradise, perhaps he could ask his new best friend to arrange something.

"Well, then I think you're in for a treat–you'll find tomorrow's demonstration very interesting. Its tactical advantages could turn a few men into a special unit that would vanquish a force ten times as large. I'm this close to creating the ultimate weapon, and the ultimate fighter isn't far behind. And you and yours get first offer of refusal, a chance to bid on this opportunity of a lifetime!" He grinned wickedly, and took a long, slow pull on his cigar.

"Those submarines you're buying will be powered by a revolutionary power source, propelled silently through the oceans and invulnerable to radar detection. It will have an impenetrable shield against any conventional weaponry or bombs, but the beauty is that the ship will be invisible behind its force field. You arm it with my equipment for your men, and your enemies will be useless. You can ship all the product you want to the U.S., undetected, right into her major cities. You and your associates could easily become the most powerful organization of all time on the planet!"

He pulled again on the expensive Cuban, and leaned back, exhaling luxuriously.

"Are you ready for some football?" he sang merrily, with a hokey country accent.

Robin almost dropped the box of cigars he'd been holding for the waiter. He'd stepped up silently as he had seen the white-suited man looking for another member of the staff to assist him. Robin had jumped in at the right moment, hoping to get Conrad's attention. He hung on the periphery, listening to every chilling word. He was stunned, and then even more so as Stephan and Edie approached the table.

"Ah, Dr. Hollings, and the beautiful Miss Langston," Kochler rose, as did everyone. Robin had never noticed how pretty she was–the dress she wore was expensive looking and chic, showing lots of skin in all the right places. Don Orpeza was quick to pull out her chair, smiling like a well-dressed weasel.

"This brings us to another item on the entertainment, but only I'm afraid for pleasure," Kochler said, and turned to Robin, "Boy, go sound the horn!" Robin was caught off guard, trying to signal Dr. Hollings by using his implants and looked blankly at Kochler, not sure what was said. Kochler looked at him coldly, and then said it in Balaluka, which threw Robin again, hearing him speak in the native tongue.

"Hey, somebody go blow the fucking horn, this idiot doesn't have a clue what I just said!" he cried in English.

"That dumb son of a bitch couldn't manage an ant farm!" the half-drunk Orpeza yelled, having just one hell of a good time. "Hell, he's just as lost as I am, and I live four thousand kilometers away, what's his excuse," and with that Kochler, Kurst, and Ginobi burst out laughing, as Robin beat a hasty retreat, looking for someone to blow that goddamned horn.

Robin sprinted up to a native that looked to be in charge. "Sound the horn! The Great One says, sound the horn!"

"Sure," said the older native, "Hey, you're not..."

"I'm with the Great One," Robin replied, with a wink, "Kind of a secret."

"Yes, yes, of course," the native said, eying him curiously, "We often thought he had, uh, exotic tastes. Not that's any of my business," he added hastily.

"Thanks, sweetheart," Robin gushed, and simpered away to find the Colonel's crew.

He found them off to the side as the horn sounded, and all eating and serving stopped. The entire gathering headed towards the runway looking finger of the cliff. Robin took the cigars and eased up to McCoy.

"Cigar, sir?" he said in English.

"Why, don't mind if I do," McCoy said, reaching in the box, "Got a li–Hey, where'd you learn English?" He peered at Robin, and then slowly the realization spread across his face.

"Hey look! It's the kid! How the hell–," Robin shoved the cigar in his mouth. Lighting it, he said, "Warlock's alive. I think we can spring you loose. Now tell me everything you know."

"The nominees from the Topani tribe are," Elo Acho intoned from the dais by the cliff, as Acho Acho executed a surprisingly passable drum roll on a bongo-like drum, "Nopi, daughter of Aslo!" A young girl of maybe sixteen that was gathered in a throng of Topani youth stepped out of the crowd in a daze, amidst raucous applause.

"Look, Stephan," Edie cried, "The beauty pageant–Dr. Kochler told me it goes back thousands of years! We're in a time warp of civilization!" She was aglow with excitement, her eyes shining bright.

"I feel like Margaret Meade, I wonder if Dr. Kochler would let me take photo's of the contestants for Princess of the games, oh, this is priceless!" she exclaimed, craning her neck to watch the nubile young girl walk out to the runway to it's edge, turn and walk back as the music played from speakers hidden somewhere. Dr. Kochler was telling Orpeza something about how the game and the pageant were connected, but with all the noise she only caught a snippet here and there.

"And every time a team scores...down the runway..." Orpeza was smiling broadly now, and the two men started offering up opinions on the growing group of contestants as Elo, gaudily dressed in cutoff shorts, a tuxedo jacket over his bare chest, and a top hat perched on his head, continued adding to the list. Now the Birimbi girls were being called, and they formed a line next to the assembled Topani girls, on a line of stairs by the cliff, as if posing for a high school class photo.

"Excuse me, Dr. Kochler," Edie interrupted, and noticed Orpeza's eyes riveted on her, taking in the low-cut, slinky red dress that Kurst had presented her earlier. "On behalf of all civilized men on this island where time has stopped, long before the birth of Christ," he'd so eloquently said. "Would there be any way I could get a photo of these lucky contestants to put on my computer? I've been keeping a journal and this, this incredible tradition–I would love to share this with the world when we get back!"

"Why that would be a grand idea! Yes, yes, of course!" Kochler exclaimed, as the Black-Eyed Peas "Tonite's gonna be a good night," came over the speaker system. He said something to Kindle, the huge bodyguard, who took the camera out of Edie's hands.

"And Tami, niece of Blamo, is the final native contestant," cried Elo, reading from a piece of paper he'd drawn from the skull of a horned animal. A pretty young girl almost fell to the ground in a faint, but recovered and did her walk, the strange juxtaposition of the ancient walk against the hip hop of the Black-Eyed Peas lending a surrealistic aura to the proceedings.

"How do I work the focus?" asked Kindle, pointing it at the bevy of beauties now joined by the last girl, who had moved into her spot in a zombie-like trance.

"Why don't I just take the picture?" Edie replied, but as she reached for the camera, Elo Acho's voice boomed over the music, "And as a token of thanks for her selfless dedication to the Great One's g-g-great little buddy, Dr. Stephan Hollings, and for her natural grace and unsurpassed beauty–for a white chick," he added with a tinge of sympathy like one would give a mongoloid child, "The final selection, Miss E-E-E-die Langston!!" and Kochler leapt to his feet, as now did the others, applauding and shouting praise. Edie was stunned in amazement, and Kindle led her gently to the runway- "Tooo-niiitess gonna be a good, good, nite, oh yeah," the natives were singing, while Edie walked as if in a dream to the end and back, to thunderous cheering. She dumbly took her place center of the two lines of beauties, and Elo pranced up with his microphone. Kindle was fighting for position amongst the native thronging the stage, as was Kurst and another body guard of Orpeza's–all were taking photos and the flashes were blinding her. As the crowd cheered, Elo asked, "How does it feel to be the first foreign woman to be selected to participate in the longest running beauty pageant in the world?" Edie's face was flushed with excitement and she was crying tears of joy.

"I just feel like the luckiest girl whoever lived!"

"And we wish you luck back, and hope you do!" Elo cried, and the cameras flashed some more.

Robin stood there, God-struck, as Edie took her place next to Tami.

"Oh, my God," he thought, "What am I going to do now?"

"Get the hell back out of the light before someone sees you" came the answer, from somewhere in his mind.

"Oh shit," Robin realized he'd wandered right up nearer to the crowd and a couple of natives were now looking at him and whispering.

"I better get out of here!" he thought, and as he turned a voice in his head said, "Not before we figure out a plan." Robin was thunderstruck and looked around for the source as he slipped into the bushes.

"Over here, to your left," came the voice stronger, clearer.

"What in the world..," Robin began, but was cut off, "Listen, young Jedi, I don't know how you pulled off finding us, but Obi-Wan mightily impressed is," the voice n his head said, "It's me, Batman, and we've got a world to save, Robin."

Robin flew back to camp, lost in thought. Edie, Tami, Conrad and his men were all in imminent danger, and he, an invalid, and a busted-up merc to rescue them, not to mention manage an escape through that ancient field of energy surrounding them. He swept down to a deserted campground and a trip to the beach revealed no Warlock either.

"That's good, he went for water," Robin thought, pleased at Warlock's recuperative powers. Yep, the water jug was gone, that would give him time to think, the game was tomorrow night,

"Oh dark hundred," was the phrase McCoy had used. The main problem was coordinating and communication. Somehow the two of them, he and Warlock needed to free the other mercenaries, free Dr. Hollings and Edie, hold off a counterattack while laying siege to the laboratory deep underground while figuring out how to alert Steck on the 'Real Genus' to their whereabouts. And disable the force field. It didn't seem possible but Robin was determined to see it through. Where was Warlock? It didn't take that long to walk to the lake and back.

32

Planning The Rescue

"Warlock!" Robin cried, "Where are you?" He got up and started to fly out and check- "Well, hey, little buddy, I been here all the time," said Warlock and Robin looked up in time to see Warlock launch himself off the cliff above and somersault down to a perfect landing. He grinned at Robin, "What say we go kick a little mad scientist ass?"

"First of all, your plan has flaws, fatal flaws, probably," Warlock lectured. "You don't have to do all that complicated shit–rescue this, seize that, break into underground labs." He looked at Robin, the tactics and weapons specialist in him swelling with pride, enjoying the chance to make Robin look like the dumb-assed idiot student for a change. "Do you?"

"Ok," Robin started slowly, methodically trying to follow him, "I thought that by rescuing Conrad and the men first–"

"Wrong, Grasshopper!" Warlock shouted, then with a flourish he pulled out the little crossbow and aimed it right between Robin's eyes.

"You don't rescue them, dummy, all you gotta do is arm them," he twanged the bow string and laughed as Robin flinched, "For they are the meanest son of a bitches in that valley!" He spat. "Rescue, my ass!"

"What are we going to arm them with?" Robin asked, giving in to Warlock's new and extremely annoying habit of being right about something for a change.

"With the weapons we're gonna take away from the guard-house!" Warlock said, jumping up and performing an obscene gyration of sexual intercourse from behind, grinding his hips and slapping imaginary ass. "Damn, I'm good, how do you like me now, huh, how you like me now?"

"What guardhouse?" Robin asked, "I didn't see a guardhouse."

"Looky here, son," Warlock drawled like an old country hick, ("and having way too much fun making me look like am imbecile," Robin thought) "You done tole me that most of the guards are gonna be in the game, right? Sooo, their guns are somewhere close, probably where they dress out. So just go find the stash, which will be guarded, so when we find armed guards, we're there." He smiled benignly at Robin.

"How do we get by the guards, the armed guards?" Robin pointedly asked, "We don't have any guns."

"We got this," Warlock retorted, waving the bow, "And these," flexing his biceps, posing like he was Mr. Universe.

"Okay, you're gonna knock out two or more armed guards with that little crossbow and your bare hands." Robin said dubiously, "Just like Chuck Norris, huh?"

"Screw Chuck Norris," Warlock executed a blazing quick series of steps and suddenly the survival knife was at Robin's throat, his hair gripped and head pulled back–it happened before he could move, in a blurry half-second.

"I'm not gonna knock'em out, Robin," and frozen as he was, Robin realized it was the first time Warlock had used his real name. "This time tomorrow, people will die."

Robin swam out towards the bay, and he was surprised to see no welding taking place, just white-coated engineers standing on the dock with Captain Kurst. He had been sent by Warlock to reconnoiter the escape route and find where the natives had their canoes.

"Look, Robin, those natives have been coming and going through that thing for thousand of years, there's a hole or something, you find it, we're in business."

"But those canoes are never gonna be able to outrun a sub or a boat." Robin said, "You and the mercs would be sitting ducks, we'll all get killed."

"See, that's your problem, Robin," said Warlock soberly, "The mercs ain't leaving in them canoes, you, the doc, and Edie are."

"But what about you guys, how are you gonna escape?"

"We ain't, we were hired to do a job, the successful execution of the mission doesn't depend on us, it depends on you three getting out," he bluntly stated, "We're expendable."

He had found the native's canoes not too far from the docks-he had briefly entertained taking one out to the shield, but they were too close to the workers to chance it, so Robin decided to slink up and see who he could spy out.

"This is most opportune, Herr Kochler and his guest are coming right now," Kurst was bouncing on his feet, "You're sure, right?"

"Oh, we're sure," said Gruden, "It's ready to launch, except for one thing."

"One thing?" shrieked Kurst, "They're on their way, what one thing?!" His eyes were wide with fear.

"We need a bottle of champagne," Gruden laughed, "For the christening."

"Oh, no," Robin thought, "Not now!" He heard a vehicle approach, and stop by the dock. He levered himself up by a mooring post and saw Kochler, Orpeza, and his entourage coming down the dock. They were laughing and singing. "Tonite's gonna be a good, good, nite," a little drunk.

"I pride myself on staying on schedule," Kochler said, "And here, my valued friend, is the ultimate smuggling machine."

"And killing machine," chimed in Kurst, "You and your friends can stop all your competitors from ever getting a boat out of the harbor, now."

"Oh, this is going to be so exciting, let me see it in action!" cried Orpeza, and said SOMETHING IN SPANISH I HAVEN'T WRITTEN YET.

"Here you go," Kochler handed Gruden a bottle of champagne and climbed the gangplank to the bridge.

"Captain Orpeza, would you care to join me on your vessel's maiden voyage?"

"Yes sir, Captain Great One!" Orpeza clambered up. Kochler called down the hatch to the pilot below, "Prepare to launch!" and a small hum emanated from the sub.

"I christen thee, - wait, we need a name!" cried Gruden. Kochler looked at the drunken cocaine king, who shrugged and then brightened, "How about the U.S. Muerta Blanca, eh?" and laughed harder, his cigar's red end bobbing around in the night. "U.S. White Death!"

Robin watched the vessel slip into the bay, silently heading for the sea. "Bring up the shield" said Kurst, and Gruden walked over to a guard shack and pushed a red lever forward. The field began its rhythmic transformation, and the sub eased through the arc of light, out to open waters.

"Leave it up," Kurst smiled at the head engineer, "meanwhile, perhaps we can discuss my latest idea." He put his arm around Gruden's sloped shoulders and they started back to the lab. "It's a grenade you throw straight up in the air, and it blasts shrapnel in all directions around you, everywhere except straight down. First we'll need some volunteers…" he said, as they walked back to the lab.

"Why are you so nervous, Senora?" the Colombian said to the rather frumpy lab technician, a junior engineer.

"I don't like leaving the shield up, this technology has not been thoroughly tested," she replied. "It could be unstable- we just haven't had it go down yet."

"You worry too much for such a beautiful woman." The large dark man said smoothly, and he gently pushed her glasses up off the end of her nose. "Come, show Sergio how it works, we worry together, eh?" The mussy engineer nervously adjusted her eyeglasses.

"Well, Sergio," she smiled hesitantly, "What we have here is a chain reaction of sorts, but of a powerful force that doesn't conform to standard laws of nature."

"Go on, chica, I once thought of becoming a lawyer, these laws interest me very much" Sergio said, pulling her eyeglasses off and tucking them in the front pocket of her lab coat, "There now I see you have beautiful eyes, tell me more of this powerful, potent force."

"Uh, well," she fumbled, unused to the attentions of such a big, strong, exotic man, "We've basically created a form of energy that converts our world's atoms into another sort of charged particle, with various, rather incredible characteristics." She was starting to warm up now, her confidence building and she flipped her hair a little as she pointed out the mechanics of the engine that powered the force field 's gate.

"This contains two special types of magnets, well, other world magnets you might say, and they are incredibly dense, not like our world's atoms" she said, "They continually push and pull at each other at a speed vibrating just over and back under the speed of light, creating vast amounts of energy that can't be seen normally in this dimension. So this energy would be akin to a constant flip-flopping of attracting and repelling forces. Once we had figured out what we had, we developed the technology to grab one element and have it drag another forward, and then to quickly, like nano-second quick, release and grab the other so fast that it held its position relative to the other, which we then re-grabbed using just a fraction of the energy that was being generated. This is not how the basic building blocks of our elements work. Ours are made up largely of space–look, try to imagine this."

She took his hand, gently stroking it. "If the nucleus of an atom was an ant you were holding in your hand here, the nearest electron would be over by those palm trees," she said, pointing to the shore, "In between is space, and this material we've discovered exists in that space, vibrating rapidly, very rapidly. We've harnessed it to propel your sub, to control the force field on this ancient island, and we're on the verge of even greater discoveries that will change a man into the ultimate weapon."

"Can I go first?" said Sergio seductively and put his lips to hers, going in for the kill.

Things are starting to make sense now, Robin thought, paddling softly away from the two paramours. The elements of the other dimension, in certain states of excitement start to exist simultaneously in the space-time, vibrating over and under the speed of light, therefore at times unobservable in the three dimensional world! "At least not directly," he mused, "Controlling the speed they vibrate changes their physical properties, you can fly at such and such conditions, a canoe gets pushed through the water at another speed of vibration, why, I'd bet I could make things disappear at…" Robin had to stop dead in the water, the ramifications sinking in, growing in significance, until at last he shouted "Eureka!" and then realizing where he was, clicked his wrists and dove beneath the murky safe.

"Did you hear something?" The engineer said, pushing Sergio away, not noticing her blouse was unbuttoned down to her navel.

"The only thing I hear is your heart beat calling my name," Sergio said, pulling her back into his big arms, his longish curly hair falling across his eyes. "Just like Antonio Banderas," the aroused scientist from MIT dreamily thought, and she fell back into his embrace, wondering which one of the million stars strewn across the equatorial sky had become her lucky one.

Robin swam to shore with the pilfered items from the dock, the sun just beginning to rise on the calm, still waters of the hidden cove.

"What's all this?" Warlock said, as he helped Robin drag the large black tarpaulin loaded with contraband up to the cave.

"I can't explain now, I'm not even sure myself," was the reply.

"But tell me, Warlock, master of weapons and tactics," Robin spread out all the various tools and articles on the sand, "How good are you at fabrication?" He picked up the little crossbow and aimed it between Warlock's eyes and pulled back the string, and released- it twanged, making even the steely-eyed ex-seal flinch, then grin.

"All right, we're even, no more games, that thing ain't no toy."

"Not too shabby, little buddy," Warlock said, after looking over the equipment with the gleam of a kid on Christmas Day filling his eyes, "Not too bad at all."

33

Confrontation

"Dr. Hollings, you take me for a fool," Kochler cried, and swept his arm across the table, test tubes and lab equipment crashing to the floor of the lab, two hundred feet below ground. He strode over to the black board that covered an entire wall.

"You lead me on, teasing me with little pieces of the puzzle, but give me nothing that I can put to practical use!" He gestured at a finished equation here and down further at another. Kochler spun around and glared at the implacable theorist.

"Oh, I know, I know you too well, Dr.," he glared at the physicist; "You have the answers already, don't you, all in that magnificent mind of yours, hidden away, safe and sound. And why? Because you don't like me selling this great discovery of mine to the highest bidder?!" Kochler sat down on the edge of the vacated table. "But you, Mr. 'Greatest Mind on the Planet', haven't figured out the rest of that equation, have you?" He held out a hand and gestured across the room, "All this was bought, was financed by drug lords, the big cartels. That you know–but that's not the reason you're here. We have a bigger prize than a measly few billion dollars, and yes, I mean us, you and I, a team." Kochler went to his knees, placing his hand on Stephan's.

"My friend, I have no intention for letting those jackals leave here with my ship. That ship is ours, the two greatest minds in the world, and for once in the history of the world shall the natural evolution of mankind transcend from the survival of the fittest to survival of the smartest!" He looked into Stephan's eyes, "I'm creating a new world order, with reason and intelligence- that ship is our political platform, not a drug mule. With what you hold in your mind, we can put force fields over

Washington, Moscow, Beijing- any military installation in the world, we'll control it all!" Kochler leapt to his feet, extending his arms to Dr. Hollings, begging. "You and I are a few equations away from being Supreme Commanders of the World!" The German's face was flushed red with the passion of a Baptist preacher at revival time. He regained his composure, and as he started for the door, leaving Dr. Hollings to ponder his offer, said, "Now you know the rest of the story."

Edie had retreated to a neutral corner when Kochler started breaking things, and now went to pick up the pieces. She started to say what she thought of him, making a mess like that, no matter if it was his things, but Dr. Hollings said, "Quiet! Please just stand very still, Edie!" and closed his eyes.

"You think he bought it?" said Kurst, pushing the button for the elevator.

"Too close to call, could go either way. These geniuses spend all that time in an ivory tower, and then they get a little fame and start thinking about how they could fix all the world's problems by tackling something 'simple', like politics and statesmanship. I was trying to appeal to his intellectual stupidity." Kochler said, as they waited outside the lab. "Did you know that Einstein spent two years, right before World War II, trying to convince every one that there would be no war because he had gotten petitions signed all over Europe from factory workers who said they'd never work for a company in the business of manufacturing, shipping, or supplying the ammunitions factories? He was absolutely certain that he'd stopped a World War by getting the common man to promise to not participate!"

"What a fucking idiot," said Kurst, "What makes some people so stupid, so gullible?"

"I don't know," observed Kochler, "Some geniuses are just eaten up with the dumbass, I guess."

Dr. Hollings opened his eyes. "Thank you, Edie; I just needed a minute to get something through my thick skull."

"That's quite alright, Stephan, that was very rude of Dr. Kochler. I'm going to remind him not to be so childish, it's not acceptable behavior."

"Edie, can I ask you a question?" Dr. Hollings asked. "Do I ever seem simple-minded, you know, like when I'm all caught up in a particularly difficult problem? Do I ever, I don't know, look like I'm eaten up with the dumbass?"

"I'm gonna sneak on to the field, let every one know where the weapons are, then when to be ready to charge the guard shack," Warlock said, trying on the stolen uniform that Robin had dragged back in the tarp.

"Yeah, like at the half, or after a score, something like that," said Robin, working on the black tarp, "Damn, I don't have enough to cover both sides," he exclaimed, tilting the bowl to let the rest of the syrupy solution drip out. He laid the fabric carefully over some bushes to dry, next to the masks he'd had the foresight to prepare first.

Robin afforded himself a small smile, remembering the day in London when searching for clues in the kidnapping, he'd ran across a costume shop that had the Batman mannequin displayed in the window. On an impulse Robin had gone inside, and bought the surprisingly well-made Robin and Batman masks and capes not just as an inside joke, but to convince himself that by buying gifts he was still sure that he, Edie and Dr. Hollings were destined to be reunited.

Now the two costumes were serendipitously part of the rescue plan. For while Conrad and the mercs were holding down the front tunnel heading down to the bay, Robin had Edie and Stephan to sneak down the back side. Edie would be light enough and physically able to hold on to Robin so that he could fly her down on his back, but Stephan was heavier and dead weight, it would require another approach. It would be easier to leave him in his chair for transport, by far. That's where the hooded masks came in. Robin's epiphany at the docks had led him to many conclusions, one of which was a clarification of one passage on the legend walls that talked of creating a special pulpy solution from the 'gummy bears'. The rocks that slowly jellied in his mouth were what gave him the boost to fly, that's what the tribes didn't possess, and the implants in his neck were the controlling force that connected the brain to the almost imperceptible steering sense. He had finally figured out what that big, flat tabletop rock was for, and that's what the 'gummy bears' were mashed and kneaded on, it's magnetized top. They became a solution that could be used to saturate a material that in turn could be used on an object to levitate it. Robin was actually starting to get that nervous feeling a person gets when something too good to be true is about to happen, like looking at lotto numbers and not believing it could be possible to win against all the odds.

"Warlock, you ever get that feeling, like a lottery winner must…"

"Shut up, kid," Warlock interjected, "Yes I do, and things like that are better left unsaid." Warlock was down in a three-point stance, then lunged forward, striking a palm tree he had made into a tackling dummy, "What're you trying to do, make me jump off sides, or something?"

Conrad sat at his bunk, taping his ankles slowly and methodically. There was little talk as each man went through their mostly silent rituals, much the same as before any mission. Conrad, like most, kept the challenge at hand at the front and foremost of his thoughts- no use thinking about what would happen afterwards.

"That will be a problem for the lucky ones to have to deal with" he reasoned, philosophically. Now was a time to focus, review plays and assignments, to play out game time scenarios.

"On a blitz, look for the hot read on a slant, don't trust the tailback to pick up the extra rusher," he went over again, that and a dozen other potentially catastrophic misreads by his teammates. He felt confident in each ones individual talent, but with so little practice, and the speed of this hyperkinetic, souped-up version of football that made the NFL seem tame and civilized as a croquet match–well, fear of death was the great equalizer, nobody on the other side was escaping the pre-game, or pre-war jitters, either, he grimly consoled himself.

"Hey, Colonel," McCoy had walked up with the rest of the mercs, "We were all talking over strategies and Wolfe here, he brought up something that maybe we all thought of but probably needs to be agreed upon as a team."

"Yeah, what's that Wolfe?" Conrad asked, curious.

"Well, uh, I don't know if I'm speaking out of turn here, but as for me personally, if I'm in a death grip, or if some asshole is getting ready to crack my skull with one of these," he said, whipping his deadly stone studded lasso around, smashing it into the side of a nearby bunk bed, crushing the thick wooden post, "Take him out, and I mean by all means necessary, even if the hit takes me out, too." He looked around the room. "That way me and him can finish it in hell!" and with that he shouted, "Chinga las pinche putos, weys!" With that the team yelled as one, and charged the field.

Kochler met Edie and Stephan up by the elevator, with the ever present Kindle by their side.

"Oh, what a perfect night for football," he cried, and was right, Edie thought, the crisp air and clear skies reminding her of a late summer evening back home. Kochler snapped his fingers and another bodyguard appeared–together they lifted Dr. Hollings chair and carried him down the stadium steps to a regally outfitted, boxed-in area at midfield.

"Owners box?" Edie asked.

"Great Chief box," he replied, "You wouldn't believe what I had to pay for these seats–man did I get scalped!"

Here came Orpeza, over-dressed in what had to be the most garish outfit Edie had ever seen–sequin-studded electric-blue silk shirt, red flared jeans with gold piping down the sides, and crocodile boots with spurs, actual spurs, jingling down to meet them.

"Snazzy," Kochler said.

"It's called Tejano, Mexican-Texas cowboy, it's the rage in my country," Orpeza said, imitating a dance move with one arm extended in front of him, crooked around an imaginary partner, the other rubbing his belly, swiveling his hips suggestively.

"Well, I'll see if I can't get one of the natives to cook up some armadillo enchiladas while you're here," Kochler said, ever the gracious host. "Look, here come the combatants!"

The crowd, Birimbi filling one side of the stadium, and Topani the other, cheered wildly, as the two teams took the field. Kochler made a motion to Kindle, who took Edie's arm and said, "Let's go, you're sitting with all the other finalists," and before she could even say a word, was led, almost dragged, over to where the other young girls sat.

It was a beautifully decorated, tiered seating area close to the end zone. The seating was curved with a little stage in the center, and off to her right Edie saw a pit with flames rising up into the night sky. She couldn't figure out its function, for it was a large hole in the ground, maybe twenty feet in diameter, with two native men tending it, constantly throwing wood on the bonfire. She didn't see any meat or a spit crossing it, and it couldn't be for lighting, they had lights on poles all around the stadium. The fire was just outside of the end zone, in the center, underneath the finger of the jutting runway seventy feet above. She soon forgot about it as Elo Acho and Captain Kurst, dressed in striped uniforms, trotted to midfield. Elo called out over a megaphone for silence, "for the playing of the national anthem."

Everyone rose, and the music blared from the speakers surrounding the stadium, and every native knew the words. "For those about to rock, we salute you, for those about to rock, we salute you, yes we do" and fireworks went shooting into the night sky as Acho Acho lit off Roman candle after Roman candle down by the fire pit. Elo Acho was air guitaring like he was auditioning for an MTV video, his long mangy hair lending credibility to the effect. Edie looked over to see if she could make eye contact with Stephan, but her view was blocked by Kochler, bent over a mirror with a short silver straw up one of his nostrils. He raised up his head and seeing Edie looking his way, waved broadly to her, "Good luck, my beauty, I'm pulling for you to be the next Great Chieftess!" and then went back to his coke.

Conrad looked at Acho, "Only two refs?"

"Only two rules," Elo said, "Off sides, and decapitating the receiver."

"What about out of bounds?" asked McCoy, out with Conrad for the coin toss.

"Uh, Okay, three rules," Elo said, obviously high or drunk.

"What time periods or quarters, I don't see a scoreboard," said Conrad, "How do we know when the games over?" Elo looked at Kurst, who shrugged like he could care less. Elo pointed to the beauty contestants, "When only one's left, that's when the game is over."

The Topanis won the toss and elected to receive. Drake, the rugby player drop kicked the ball to the roar of the crowd, accentuated by microphones strategically placed in the stadium and fed through the speakers. The Topanis formed a loose wedge, and galloped down the field in huge strides, trying to pick off the first defenders downfield, which were primarily the quicker Birimbis. The strategy was either attack on the downward slope of a leaping glide, thereby using momentum to deliver a crushing over head blow, or to catch an opponent on his upward flight from underneath, striking his exposed underbelly like a shark slamming into a seal. But since most jumps were executed at slightly obtuse or oblique angles, most were glancing blows, the players lassos swinging like passing knights in a joust. Geissen got caught in a double team and received a nasty gash across his neck; a Birimbi woman ran out and with duct tape and gauze taped him up right where he lay. McCoy and one of the trailing Birimbis made the tackle, with the native taking a swipe at the ball carriers leg with his lasso, slowing him down for the half-second McCoy needed to deliver a crushing hit on a gliding descent, knocking the ball carrier unconscious. The mercs huddled up on defense with Acho Acho translating, while Topani women drug the injured Topani off the field. The Birimbis were chattering excitedly, nodding appreciatively at McCoy. Acho listened, and then he turned to the mercs.

"Well, what's the deal?" asked Conrad, huffing. "They said that was a good tackle, but McCoy missed an excellent opportunity, why did he pull up?"

Acho replied. "What do you mean, that dude's unconscious, they had to drag him off the field!" McCoy retorted. "Yeah, but still breathing," said Acho.

Robin and Warlock were in awe. "What the hell," Warlock said, watching the Topani dragged off the field. "McCoy almost killed that guy!" "Shh!" Robin whispered underneath the tarp, "Just because we're invisible doesn't mean they can't hear us!" They duck-walked, staying low, down the steps to the field, trying to avoid the cheering crowds. There they sat in a corner off the field, waiting for a play to come their way. The Topanis had the ball, and were in the red zone, threatening to score. The ball was hiked and Ginobi, the quarterback, handed off to the tailback, Tuco, who attempted to go over the top in an exaggerated goal line leap, fifteen feet off the ground- he was met by Romanov, surging up on a collision course from below, and joined in mid-air by Conrad, who punched the ball, trying to force it loose. A tackle that had missed his block tried to drag Romanov down by lashing out his "roso", as it was called in Balaluka, but Drake came flying in and with his 'roso' chopped the tackle across his extended arm, and the resounding crack was heard fifty feet away as both ulna and humerus shattered on contact. Coming out of the pile, the Birimbis were patting him on the head, and shouting "Luka lumu talamu!" Back in the huddle they could hear the Birimbi side of the stadium cheering the same cry.

"Ok, Acho, what's that mean, good hit?" asked Conrad, bleeding from his lip. "The closest I can come is necessary roughness," Acho replied and damned if he didn't have a beer in his hand! The next play was a Topani version of play action and McCoy tried knocking the ball out of the air, but the commando named Sergio made a circus catch, landing in the end zone for the score. He spiked the ball amidst the deafening roars from the Topani side, and then a hush fell over the entire stadium as Elo walked over to the tiers where the beauty contestants were sitting. All the Birimbi girls got up, and Kindle told Edie. "Get up, you're entered on both sides, Kochler's orders." Kurst had Elo's top hat from the night before in his hand, and Elo closed his eyes and withdrew a slip of paper, microphone in hand. "Bolaca, daughter of Pacon!" he cried out and the Topanis cheered riotously. Now a brightly dressed native from the Topani sprinted across the field. Conrad had seen him and another on the Birimbi side, with tall horned headdresses, bodies painted in wild stripes and vivid colors. He did a dance like a school mascot in the middle of the field, as the girl whose name was called walked in a trance to the stage. The mascot for the Topanis loped in huge stylized strides across the field to Bolaca, who looked as if she might faint. Now all the girls were standing and applauding, as was both sides of the stadium. Edie joined in, looking at her new friends and smiled along, noticing a pronounced look of relief from the Birimbi girls. The Topani man with the gaudy dress leaped to the dais, swept Bolaca off her feet and with powerful leaps ascended the steps that led to the top of the surrounding stadium to the pavilion. With one giant final glide the muscular native deposited the beautiful young girl at the foot of the runway with practiced flourish. She left his hand gliding slowly down the runway to the very edge as the music blared the theme from Miss America, the crowd singing along. "There she goes, Miss Bo-o-o-na-a-a-mi Girl…" and she lifted her arms to the sky as she looked out over the crowd. Edie thought it was one of the most beautiful, powerfully moving things she'd ever seen. The girl then stepped out into nothingness, wordlessly falling to her death into the now raging fire pit below to thunderous applause. "Six to nothing, Topani Tribe!" Elo boomed, into the mike, "Good play, guys!"

The crowd settled back in their seats as the Topanis lined up for the kickoff. The field had only one end zone, so the teams had to switch sides after every score. The mercenaries passed by the commandos and McCoy was the first to respond to their taunts. "You and me, big boy," he yelled at Sergio, "Leave the women out of it!"

"Too late for that, better worry about what you can do to save your own ass, punk!" Sergio retorted, in McCoy's face, and the two went at each other with a vengeance. They were separated by a struggling Conrad, who received a gash across his helmet-less head for his trouble from another commandos 'roso', just barely avoiding having his skull crushed in.

"Hey, ref, what about unsportsmanlike conduct, throw the flag for Chrissake!" yelled Red Jones at Elo.

"Uh, unsportsmanlike conduct is a compliment, not a penalty, from my basic understanding of the rule book," Elo said, then turning to Kurst, "I don't think I was ever given a flag to throw, could you maybe tear yours in half and we could share?"

The kickoff was filled with high flying collisions, but surprisingly not one player was hurt enough to go out of the game. The Birimbi team huddled up.

"There's no time period, so we can't stall. Besides, we'd lose the ball eventually. We'd probably only succeed in pissing Kochler off, which would put our client in more danger, if Kochler snaps to what we're up to," Conrad said, "We gotta figure out something, but right now we'd better just play the game, and try to take out every commando we can."

"Yeah, that's simple enough, it ain't like they're hard to find," noted Wolfe, and the overwhelming consensus was to play to win, and to stay alive.

"Ready, set hut!" Conrad hollered, and took the snap, handing off to Beli, the fullback. Beli sidled down the line of scrimmage, patiently waiting for a hole to form, then shot through a gap in the line gaining six yards, all on the ground. McCoy and Sergio were squared off near the out of bounds, circling each other like gladiators, with their rosos cutting through the air. Elo walked past them,

"Hey, Acho, bring me a beer, they're not all yours!" then as an afterthought blew his whistle at the two.

"No death matches until after the game, section 2-A, Rule eleven," he announced, looking at a little blue book he pulled out of his cutoff jeans. While the commotion was going on between McCoy and Sergio, Robin and Warlock took advantage of the distraction and sneaked onto the field. Warlock magically appeared at Conrad's shoulder, and shoved Geissen, who was sporting a broken nose to go with his gashed neck, under the invisible tarp.

"Shhh!" said Robin, "Let's get off the field before someone runs into us." Geissen nodded numbly- he probably had a concussion too, Robin thought. They made it to the sidelines just in time, the play veering right at them as they slipped out of bounds.

Where did you guys come from?" Geissen asked, then, "What's for dinner, Cookie?"

Steak and baked potatoes, Geissen," Robin said, "Try to be quiet, ok?"

"Okay, sugar," Geissen replied, but fell silent.

"Dr. Hollings, have you thought anymore about my offer?" said Kochler, after the beautiful Boloca fell to her death. "You see those men out there for the Birimbi tribe? You know they came to rescue you. It's a shame that now some of them will die because you choose not to answer." He made a motion and the guard produced a cigar box. Kochler selected one, had his aide trim it, and then light him up. Kochler sucked and puffed at the big Cuban, a gift from Orpeza. "Just let me known when you make your mind up, we can pull them out of the game, maybe before it's too late." He leaned over conspiratorially, "Personally, I hope you take your time, they're really quite good. Some of them should last for a good while, I would think." Kochler leaned back to watch the game his arms over the back of Stephan' wheelchair. "Now the woman, well, that's a different matter entirely. I guess we'll just have to cross our fingers and hope her luck doesn't run out, won't we?"

Stephan felt a tug at his sleeve. He rolled his head over–but no one was there.

"Hey doc, it's me, Robin," and Robin lifted a corner of the tarp, briefly exposing his still bronzed face and black hair. "Whaddya say we blow this joint before somebody gets killed?" and launched his new plan.

"Hey, that number sixty-one," Dolph said to Serge, "Isn't that the one that that Topani dude with the long ponytail almost killed on the on the touchdown?" "Yeah, number sixty one, plays guard," said Serge, breaking the huddle,

"So what?"

"Well, he's a fast healer," Dolph replied, "He damn near took my head off on that screen you just called, don't run it to the left anymore, Ok?"

Conrad told Acho, "Go get a beer, if we need you we'll holler."

"Holla, ya'll," Acho imitated Conrad's Texas drawl in a high feminine voice, as he ambled toward the cooler on the sidelines. Conrad looked over at the rejuvenated number sixty-one.

"Ok, Warlock, let's hear it." "The guard house is being watched by two guards, just inside the tunnel," Warlock said, wiping some blood, someone else's off his forearm. "They keep taking turns sneaking out to watch the game, and as soon as Robin gets the Doc clear he's coming back for Edie. Then he'll give us a sign, like maybe after a score, to charge the guard house, and get our hands on some weapons."

"How's that little guy gonna pull that off, what is he, Superman?" asked McCoy, incredulously.

"Damn near," said Warlock, and broke the huddle, only too pleased to be lining up against the swarthy German called Dolph. He grinned at Conrad, his fellow Texan, "Now this here is what we call real smash mouth football back home, huh?"

"I-think-I-can-give-you-what-you-want," Stephan told Kochler in his metallic voice, "Just-please-don't-hurt-my-nurse-O-K?"

"What, you don't care about the men who came to rescue you?" Kochler asked, playing hard to get.

"They-are-expendable," Dr. Hollings replied. Another guard appeared and helped drag Stephan to the top of the stadium, the two arguing about who was to escort Dr. Hollings back down to the lab. Stephan had told Kochler he wanted to look at the last set of unfinished equations to be sure he gave the right answer, as he was fond of his nurse and didn't look forward to training a new one. Kochler had nodded in agreement. Like the sociopath he was, he expected everyone to possess the same base values as he did.

Good help is so hard to find these days," he acknowledged.

34

The Rescue Begins

The two flipped a coin, and the winner laughed, saying with a smirk, "See ya, wouldn't wanna be ya!" and headed back down to the game. He had a side bet going with one of Orpeza's bodyguards, a big ladies man. "Better start digging in your pockets, Sergio," he thought, as the Topanis scored again. "Perlu, daughter of Somoka!" cried Elo, and the weeping girl was flown to the top, leaving only Tami and Edie as the remaining contestant on the Birimbi tribe. Edie still stood, as all the others, but had long ceased to applaud, as she dumbly realized there was only one other contestant left besides her.

Even if she survived to become the crowned Chieftess, Kindle had dashed even that small consolation with the observation, "He gave me his last Princess for employee of the month. I think this year the prize will go to Orpeza, though." The guard pushed the button for the elevator, cursing his misfortune. "Thanks a lot, asshole," he said to Stephan, kicking the wheelchair savagely as he went to grab the handles.

"I just can't believe my luck, it couldn't get any worse!" He froze in amazement as a young native boy with blue eyes magically appeared in front of him and his charge, dressed in some vaguely familiar mask and multi-colored blouse, pointing a small toy crossbow at his head. "It just did, jerk," spoke the apparition, and the lights went out. Robin picked up the arrow bolt with the padded end and checked the guard's pulse. He was alive, but from the size of the welt starting to rise on the center of his forehead, he'd be out for a while.

"Actually, it was his lucky day," Robin commented to Dr. Hollings, as he slipped the 'gummy bear' saturated mask over the doctor's head, underneath the invisible tarp. "I thought I had one of the arrow headed bolts loaded instead." The game was becoming steadily more violent- at times the forward progression of the ball was becoming an after thought, as blocking schemes were abandoned in favor of hand to hand combat. Elo was spending more time at the cooler than he was on the field, and Kurst often could be seen flirting with one of the more attractive of the medic's on the sidelines, leaning nonchalantly on the little barrier wall that separated the fans from the field, twirling his whistle around on its string. The Topanis had scored again, and now Conrad saw that there was only Edie and two native girls remaining, one from each tribe.

"Okay, men, let's give'em one they haven't seen- double eagle, dirty dog left, student body right," Conrad called. It was a secret play never practiced on the field, when it became obvious the Acho's were spying out their plays earlier in the week. McCoy had caught Acho Acho scribbling something down on a piece of paper by the omni-present beer cooler. "And just what do you think you're doing?" he'd cried, grabbing at the notes, but Acho had the presence of mind to cram the notes down his board shorts.

"It's a letter to your mama," Acho laughed, and McCoy yelled,

"Don't think you're getting off that easy!"

Acho yelled back over his shoulder, "That's what she said last night, but boy was she wrong!" and ran like hell for the safety of the other end of the stadium. The play was a misdirection scheme. Conrad was to lateral out to Topulu, the Birimbi receiver, with Wolfe pulling to block the cornerback. As soon as the defense shifted, following the ball's flight or the pulling guard, Topulu would throw the ball back to Conrad, who would then hopefully have the other side of the field wide open, following his teammates in a sweep around the defensive line. It was a dicey play, but Conrad was betting on fatigue and the now murderous rage of the commandos to cloud their thinking enough to pull it off. The ball was snapped and the mercs clashed with a vicious fury into the commandos, screams of rage interspersed with those of agony as men were stomped and trampled underfoot. Conrad saw Warlock administer what had to be a killing blow on the big guard Dolph–he heard the crush of helmet and skull, the German falling to the ground face first with his arms hanging loosely by his side. McCoy was tied up with a pony tailed Topani warrior, and was trying to snap kick his knee, like a UFC fighter, using the Brazilian jujitsu he held a black belt in. The pass was perfect and the cornerback, a smaller commando named Baldo who Conrad had noticed was playing off Topulu, increasing the distance between them to compensate for the natives blazing speed, played right into their hands. This gave enough time for Wolfe to come up and blindside him with a flying double kick, descending from an angle ten feet above, that terminated in his back and shoulder blades.

Conrad saw the cornerback's head snap back, almost touching Wolfe's planted feet in a way that necks don't normally rotate, dead before he hit the grass. As soon as Wolfe landed he was beset upon by a berserk Topani named Epu, beating the Spaniard mercilessly down with his roso. Conrad could only hope that Topulu would get to Epu before it was too late as the native joined in the fray.

"Reverse, reverse!" screamed Serge, playing middle linebacker, but it was too little, too late. McCoy kicked the Topani's knee one more time and the native dropped to the ground with a broken leg. McCoy never lost a beat, hooking up with the tide of teammates that were out flanking the defense to the right, blockers picking off tacklers, as Conrad wove his way through the throng of thrashing enemies, finally getting that little opening he'd been looking for. He leapt into the air, somersaulting over the hurtling Serge twenty feet in the air, so close he could feel the German's hot breath brush across his neck in a near miss. Conrad came out of the somersault into a perfect landing in the middle of the end zone. The crowd went wild, throwing flowers and beads on the field as Conrad struck his best imitation of a Hussein Bolt 'lightning bolt' pose, before jumping into the arms of his cheering team.

Orpeza was yelling deliriously, shouting praise at the top of his lungs. "This is awesome, much better than dog fighting, any day!" he cried, and pulling out his pistol shot it in the air, "Go, Birimbi, Go!"

"You're rooting for the mercenaries?" asked Kochler, wiping the white powder from his nose. "I thought you'd want the Topanis to win."

"I do?" asked Orpeza, worried he didn't know some arcane rule.

"Oh, maybe I forgot to mention it, Don Orpeza, but I customarily give the Princess Chieftess away as a gift to any visiting guest."

"Oh, really," said Orpeza, putting away his handgun.

"Yes, really," Kochler replied, "Now if the Birimbis win, that makes that cute little fifteen year old girl there the Chieftess," he winked at the Colombian, "Which is fine, if that's your thing. Or, on the other hand…" and Kochler pointed to Edie, stunningly outfitted in the expensive low-cut mini-skirt. It fully displayed the fullness of her breasts, accentuating the perkiness possessed only by the lucky few, "Well, she's okay, too, I guess." Orpeza pulled out his pistol again and emptied it into the night,

"Get in the damned game, Topani! Go, Topani, Go!" Robin glided down the mountain, gripping the handlebars, steering the levitated Dr. Hollings in front of him.

"The mercenaries are going to cover our rear flank and give us time to get out to open water," he said, "Their only chance is we get to the 'Genus' and get Steck to call Dafoe and get some major backup."

"Why are we taking canoes," Dr. Hollings asked, as they came into view of the bay, "When there's a perfectly good ship right over there?" Robin sat Stephan down on the yacht, taking care to leave him under the tarp.

"I'll be back with Warlock and Edie," he said, glad that Dr. Hollings had the presence of mind to spot his oversight that Warlock was ex-navy seal and knew how to pilot the ship.

"Here, chew on this, it'll give you energy," Robin said, taking a couple of 'gummy bears' from a small bag. He placed the bag on Stephan's lap and then he put a couple in the doctor's mouth. "They made me feel like a new man." There was more than just a little truth to that statement, Robin thought, checking to make sure that the single guard had his back turned as he slipped out from under the tarp, crossbow in hand.

The Topanis had the ball, but the mercenaries were holding their own. Both sides were fighting to impose their will on the other, neither team gaining or losing much ground. Edie and Tami sat together, holding hands that lay on the same armrest of their plush seats. Each had tears flowing down their cheeks, and Edie felt a sudden motherly urge to hug Tami, as Kindle had translated her name, fighting the impulse to get up and run from this macabre, surrealistic world she was in, where touch downs were celebrated by virgin sacrifice. Robin appeared in the middle to the huddle, throwing off the tarp. The Birimbi natives jumped back, but the mercenaries grabbed and pulled them back into the huddle, placing their fingers on their lips and shushing them.

None the less, when Robin spoke to them in Balaluka several fell to their knees, shouting "Orakapo! Digi Orakapo siso!"

Robin spoke harshly to them and the awestruck natives leaped to their feet like they were on fire. "Change of plans, guys," he said, "Dr. Hollings wants to rescue you instead."

The Topanis now moved the ball down the field, the Birimbi seemingly having momentarily lost their focus.

"Look," said one Topani to another as the Birimbi natives were prostrating themselves on the ground, "Listen to what they're saying."

"What are they doing over there?" Kurst asked the now totally ripped Acho Acho.

"They're saying all hail the New King, the Legend has come true," slurred Acho, peeing on the field.

"What legend?" asked Kurst.

"How the hell should I know, what do I look, like a fucking heathen?" Acho said as he stumbled forwards, trying to zip up his shorts- then fell, penis in hand, flat on his face. Ginobi, the Topanis quarterback, dropped back, surveying downfield receivers, pump faking the linebackers into falling back into pass coverage. He suddenly sprinted right up the middle on a delayed draw. Geissen, now back in the game, lunged but Ginobi hurdled over him, landing between the recovering linebackers and the entangled line, and then took to the air.

Conrad threw himself towards Ginobi in a desperation move, but the lieutenant twisted his body as if he was competing in the Winter X games, barely eluding Conrad's superhuman effort. He landed just short of the goal line, and with the strength of a maddened bull, carried two defenders with him into the end zone. He was swarmed by his teammates, Elo set off fireworks, the crowd roared and the music blared. The Topani mascot came cart running and did a break dance at midfield, then went straight for the stage where the two remaining contestants were standing, holding each others hands.

Warlock and Robin crept towards the commandos guarding the weapons cache. As predicted, one was peering out of the tunnel, watching the game and relaying the action back to his comrade. "Topanis got the ball on the eighteen yard line, Ginobis back to pass…" and silence, save for the deafening roar of the crowd.

"Alphonso, what happened? Alphonso," called the other guard, "What's going on, man?" He left his post and went up the tunnel cautiously, "What happened, did we win?"

Yeah, but you lose," came a voice from nowhere, just like the big fist that met his jaw a split second later.

"Give me his gun, Robin," Warlock said, after seeing the padlock. "What about the noise?" Robin asked, taking the automatic pistol from the comatose commando. "Don't worry, it's getting ready to be a lot noisier, real soon," Warlock replied, and shot off the lock.

Captain Kurst was watching the Birimbi girl walk down the runway, explaining the irony to Elo- he'd made sure that the two remaining slips of paper in the hat had her name on them, as Kochler had instructed. "Even in death she commands attention." When he heard the shot fired. Kurst looked around,

"Could your brother have shot off the fireworks?"

"That wasn't fireworks, that was a gunshot," Elo said, "Hell, he's so drunk he couldn't find his ass with both hands, much less a match." Robin folded up the tarp and placed it in the backpack under his cape. The Topanis had lined up for the extra point which would officially end the game. Tami was bravely dismounting from her rider, and she walked trembling slowly to the precipice.

"The kick is up, it's good!" cried Elo, and the entire stadium shook with ovations. All eyes were on the beautiful young girl and as she fell, gracefully swan diving to her death, Robin screamed "Now!" and set off the home-made flash bang grenade that Warlock had fashioned the night before right into the middle of the pileup at the scrimmage line. The mercs had their eyes closed and their ears covered, yet still felt the concussion from the blast as it washed over them.

To a man they charged the tunnel, forty yards away. Robin was airborne even as he had thrown the grenade, and he swooped around the white flash cloud, over the stands of the stunned tribes, then plunged towards the cliff in a steep dive, plucking the unconscious Tami out of mid-air mere inches from the flames. He regained altitude just over the Topani chief's head, struggling to maintain control as he shot up the stadium walls over the cheering crowd, headed for the bay.

"Bravo! Bravo!" cried Orpeza, clearly impressed. "You didn't tell me you had flying warriors, Kochler, but your flair for the dramatic is–is magnifico!"

"Kurst!" screamed Kochler, "Ginobi!" He tore on the field. "Get that–that crazy son of a bitch!" Kurst came running up, as gunfire erupted from the other end of the field. The commandos were putting their low gravity beads to good use as they ran across the field in huge leaps and bounds from the attacking mercenaries. Kochler ducked down and peeked up long enough to see number sixty-one swooping down on the remaining beauty contestant, emulating the same flight pattern as the crazy costumed boy.

"Kurst, if your men value their lives, you get me those flying–assholes–alive!" He jumped to the field, pulling out a pistol and firing indiscriminately at the end where the mercs were advancing in a standard two by two pattern.

"That damned cripple has figured it out–Get those flying sons of bitches!"

"Get my woman, too!" cried Orpeza, firing back at the mercs, "I won her fair and square!" Edie was in a state of shock, she pounded on Warlocks shoulders, "Let me down, you jerk!" "Shut up, lady, you're being rescued, damn it!" shouted Warlock back, "And I ain't that good at this flying shit yet, so unless you want to kill us both, be still!" Warlock was off balance and had lost his flight-sense, and they zigzagged down the outer edge of the mountain towards the harbor. "Well at least take your hand off my ass!" Edie cried, pulling down her skimpy skirt,

"And don't look!" "Ma'am, if I looked right now, I would kill us both!" Warlock yelled, as he went to move his hand, and then thought the better of it as he careened off to the left. "It's not my fault; you're the one that decided to wear a mini-skirt to a rescue mission!"

"Look!" Robin cried, "There's Warlock, and he's got Aunt Edie!" "Why's he flying so crazy, like a drunk pelican?" asked Tami.

"And why does he have his hand on her ass?" exclaimed a not entirely pleased Dr. Hollings.

35

Rescued

The commandos that had been guarding the stadium laid down suppressing fire on the advancing mercenaries. It was about equal numbers, but that was changing rapidly as the football team re-armed and was now reinforcing their comrades. There was mass confusion as the two tribes cleared the area–with one notable exception–Acho Acho was propped up by his favorite piece of furniture, the white cooler, fumbling with the top of a new bottle of mushroom beer, trying to get it open.

Conrad ran in a zigzag pattern from one covered position to another. He belly-flopped behind an equipment locker on the sidelines and looked over at Acho, who was ignoring the bullets ripping into the grassy field just a few feet away. "Get down, Acho!" Conrad yelled, returning fire.

"Help, I've fallen and can't get up!" Acho said, and got his beer open, giggling to himself. Elo walked up to Acho, wearing the top hat.

"Come on, let's go," he said to his brother, "We better leave, this might get ugly."

"Might get ugly?" Conrad hollered, then sprinted over to an over turned bench, leaping through the air, firing the SKS, a Chinese version of the AK-47, as he landed. "Elo, get down, you idiot, take cover before you get killed!"

"They won't shoot us," Elo calmly replied, dragging Acho to his feet, and together they started towards the tunnel that led to the bay, the white container of beer suspended between them.

"What makes you so sure?" Conrad retorted, as a grenade went off somewhere to his left.

"Cuz we're in the spirit world, asshole," said the young Acho, and waved his arm, tracing the path that Robin had taken over the stadium, "did you see the size of that chicken?"

"Goddamn it! That bastards escaped–and with my equations!" roared Kochler, standing over the guard at the top of the elevator, "How did you let a cripple in a wheelchair get the jump on you?"

"He had help," the guard said, massaging the welt on his forehead. "And how was that?" demanded Kochler.

"I dunno, some little kid dressed up like a superhero or something, and he shot me with this little toy crossbow," the guard rambled, "Hurts like hell, too." He was still groggy, and didn't realize how badly the words were coming out.

"Oh, did snookums get a boo-boo?" Kochler feigned concern, "Here, let mommy kiss it and make it better," as he shot the guard between the eyes.

Warlock directed Edie and Tami to cast off the mooring lines while Robin tried to activate the gate opening device.

"It's been powered down; I've got to let it warm up." He flew back to the deck of the yacht, "What do you think we ought to do?"

"Get this ship moving," said Warlock, "We may have to run down the coast if things start to heat up?"

"But then what?" cried Edie.

"We'll just have to improvise," interjected Dr. Hollings, "Let's do as he said, and get moving. Robin check the radio, see if you can figure out a way to get through to Steck. Take her with you," he said pointing at Tami, "Ask her about old stories or any tricks the Birimbi have, ask her if she thinks we could take some canoes and make a hole big enough for the ship. Now move, we don't have much time!" He turned to Edie, "You keep a lookout, and everyone remember, that we've made it this far, we're not giving up now!" Everyone ran to their assigned positions, and the floating palace's engines revved to life.

"They're trying to break through the tunnel!" Captain Kurst cried, "The bay, they're after a ship!" He grabbed his radio, "Come, Herr Kochler, come in!"

"Don't bother me, you fool!" screamed the mad scientist, "Stop them, you idiot, they're after a ship!" The mercenaries were fighting their way into the tunnel, retreating from the lava dome in a tightly scripted maneuver designed to minimize exposure to the pursuing commandos. Romanov had had the foresight to grab an RPG launcher and was putting it to good use–a few well-placed rounds gave Conrad and the rest of the team the time they needed to dash down the tunnel to the end that opened up on the bay. They spread out on the wooded slope.

Outgunned and outmanned, they tried to hold off the guards, some still in helmets and pads, from the shoreline below. Just as it looked like they had half a chance of succeeding an armored humvee came hurtling out of the tunnel amidst the gunfire and explosions, going airborne as it cleared the opening and slalomed down the crooked path to the docks. Small arms fire pinged off it's steel-plated sides. Conrad caught a glimpse of Kochler behind the wheel, his face barely visible from underneath the combat helmet he had on his head.

"Look, they've taken my boat!" cried Orpeza, "I paid six million dollars for it and those pendejo's are stealing it!"

"Fuck that boat!" yelled Kochler, "That damn kid is worth billions!" He slid around a hairpin in the road, almost lost control of the immense vehicle, then lurched back on the steep path, "I said billions, with a B!"

"Stop them, they're stealing our boy!" screamed Orpeza, not missing a beat, then as an afterthought, "And my woman, I won her, they didn't!"

"They're heading for that sub!" yelled McCoy, pulling out an automatic pistol out of his waistband and firing point-blank at a charging commando as he spoke. "All we can do is keep the main force pinned down up here," Conrad hollered back, "They'll have to handle Kochler and his bodyguards on their own!" He picked off a football player, number thirteen, as he retreated down the hill, "You picked the wrong day to be wearing that jersey, sweetheart!"

He grinned at McCoy's questioning glance, "Thirteen's always been my lucky number." "We've got company! Edie hollered, as the yacht was slipping away from the dock. Warlock looked over his shoulder to see the black hummer, pock-marked with bullet holes, slide to a stop at the docks. Robin came rushing back to where Edie and Dr. Hollings were on the sundeck. They saw Kochler, Orpeza, Kurst, and two of Orpeza's men loaded down with weapons run down the dock and start up the gangplank to the sub.

Oh, boy," Robin said, "Looks like we got ourselves a fight on our hands." "Where's the native girl?" asked Dr. Hollings, and just then Tami climbed up the rope ladder that was dangling off the side of the drug lord's palace. "Here," she said handing several lengths of beaded cord to Robin.

"I got these off a couple canoes, it's their power source."

"Did you see any guns," Robin cried, as he looked at the beads hopelessly. "Ammo grenades?"

"Listen, to what the legends have said," Tami said, "You're a bright boy, you can figure it out."

Kochler spied the Acho brothers walking down the dock, cooler in hand, heading towards their boat. "You two get over here!" Kochler screamed, and the Acho's stopped, debating. Kochler, with his camouflaged helmet adorned with three stars, grabbed an assault rifle and loosed a volley of bullets down the boardwalk, putting any idea of escape to rest.

"Aye, Aye, Captain," Elo said. "I'll take that hill, General!" Acho Acho exclaimed with a drunken salute that almost threw him off balance and into the water.

"What's the matter with that imbecile?" roared Kochler.

"He drank too much mushroom beer," said Elo. They went up the gangplank, bring their precious cooler, and managed to get on the deck of the sub as Kurst, piloting down below, pulled away from the dock. Young Acho looked at the gaudily dressed Orpeza, looking like a Latin version of John Travolta in Saturday Night Fever.

"How long you been gay?" he asked, cracking open another beer.

"Where are those gummy bears I had?" Robin exclaimed, then spotting the bag on Stephan's lap. He snatched it up- it was empty! "What the–? I thought I had more in here than that," he said. Dr. Hollings said nothing, the Batman mask hiding all expression on his face.

"Leave it on," he'd told Edie earlier, when she went to take off the ridiculous looking costume, "We may have to fly out of here as a last resort," as he chewed away, his mouth full, looking like a kid at Halloween in his mask and cape.

"Here, there's plenty of those on the cords," Tami said, and Robin dug the survival knife out of his backpack just as the ship's motor's shuddered. Robin looked back and saw the two bodyguards at the front of the sub, pointing a large mounted gun-like device at them. It was making a sound like high-tension wires, giving off an eerie hum, and the smell of ozone permeated the air.

Warlock re-started the motors to the yacht as Stephan told Edie, "Go tell him to turn the ship, they have some kind of ray gun that's shorting out the engines electrical system. Hurry!" The motors quivered, but kept running, having only received a glancing dose of the invisible beam's burst.

"Stephan said you need to zigzag, they're shooting a ray gun at us! Turn left, did you here me, turn left!" Edie screamed as she burst into the bridge. "Its starboard, lady, its starboard!" he yelled back, throwing the wheel.

"They're getting away!" cried Orpeza, who hadn't been the same since hearing "Billions, with a B!" "No, they're not, they still can't get past the force field," Kochler said, handing Elo a scooped rifle.

"See if you can hit the pilot, just don't hit that boy!"

"Yes, please, we need the boy, don't hit the boy!" Orpeza shouted.

"No problem, swishy britches," Elo replied, moving away a little awkwardly from the panicking Colombian, "Just give me a little room, huh?"

"Yeah," cried Acho, waving a limp wrist at the Orpeza, "Just go back in the closet for a while, Ok?"

A bullet ripped into the bridge, glass shattering. "They're shooting at us, everybody get down!" Warlock yelled, and saw he'd been hit by flying glass- his arm started spurting blood. "Hey, lady, get in here!" he cried, and Edie ran back into the pilot's bridge. "Get me a tourniquet or something; I got hit in an artery!" and threw the wheel hard to port.

"Can't this thing go any faster?" Kochler shouted down to Kurst.

"A lot faster, in a straight line," Kurst called back, "We're losing them every time they turn!"

"Well, we've got to figure out something!" the madman cried, watching the yacht change directions once again.

"How about shooting out their steering with one of these?" asked Acho Acho, holding up a box labeled "RPG - Grenade Launcher"

"Yes! That's perfect!" exclaimed Kochler, "Safe but effective! "Hey, how did you come up with that idea, anyway?" he asked the stoned Acho.

"Hey, I'm drunk, not stupid," said Acho, "What's your excuse?"

Robin and Tami threw Dr. Hollings wheelchair on its side, taking refuge behind the waist high wall enclosing the sundeck. Robin's mind was racing, trying to come up with the right combinations to produce what the legends said could be done.

"What did she say?" said Stephan, lying on his side.

"She asked me had it occurred to me that if the could be used to swim, fly and power canoes through the water, why couldn't they be used to stop that damned submarine?" Robin said angry at himself, "I'm just stuck, I can't seem to find an answer."

"Maybe you need to find the problem first," Dr. Hollings replied calmly. "I'd think that there would be a way to short out their ray gun, to put it in layman's terms," he said, "and since that gun is probably powered off the engines that propel the sub- well, you do the math."

"Don't tell me, I know, I'm a bright boy, figure it out," Robin replied, then, "Hey Tami! Get over here, let's try a little experiment!" He grinned at her as she returned from ripping bandages up for Edie from Warlock's tattered shirt. "Now tell me if I'm wrong, but didn't you say that the tribes used to knock each other out of the sky, back in the legend wall days?"

"Well, yeah, but it was always thought that they ripped off each others beads in sky battle, even though the symbol wasn't one for grabbing it was one for stick…" Tami looked at Robin holding the tiny crossbow mounted on his wrist. "Oh, you are a bright boy, aren't you?" she said and on an impulse grabbed his face, kissing him in excitement.

Wow!" Robin exclaimed, "What was that for?" "I've always wanted to kiss a prince, Orakapo," she said, and not entirely in jest.

"Ok, now place the firing tube on your right shoulder, and place the desired target in the cross hairs." Acho Acho read the instructions aloud to Elo.

"Check," said Elo.

"With your right thumb, flick the safety to the fire position."

"Check," Elo replied, and suddenly the rocket launcher fired, the grenade whooshing through the air, striking the yacht in the middle, exploding and destroying half the bridge.

While making sure your finger is not on the trigger, as this could result in premature detonation," continued young Acho, intent on not losing his place in the manual.

"Oh, my God, what have you done?" cried Orpeza, "You've killed the boy!" He looked close to tears.

"There, there," Acho consoled him, "There's still plenty of fish in the sea," as Elo opened up another grenade, reloading.

"Shit! Did you see that?" exclaimed Red Jones to Wolfe, "They're trying to sink the yacht from that sub with rocket launchers!"

"Look out!" cried Wolfe, firing over Red's shoulder at a commando who had breached their perimeter. "If I could help them I would, but at least we're keeping it mano-a-mano. That kid's already pulled off more miracles than Saint Peter and Saint Patrick combined, let's hope he's good for one more."

Conrad's men were slowly being pushed down the side of the mountain. Before too much longer they would run out of real estate, and the choices weren't pretty. One, they could try to commandeer the Zodiac and the Acho's boat and try to escape to out to sea, but crossing the open sand and trying launch watercraft under withering fire was sure to be a bloody affair. Two, mount a counteroffensive, but that would expose their flanks as they penetrated into enemy territory back up the mountain, and the chances of success were slim to none. Three, stand their ground on the strip of palm trees and palmetto bushes at the edge of the beach where it leveled off, and take the commandos on in a hand-to-hand battle to the death. This he pondered as another wave of commandos charged down the hill, screaming curses, streams of tracers streaking all around.

Robin and Tami worked feverishly, rolling the pulpy mass of pounded 'gummy bear' rocks into cigar shaped forms, flecks of the smashed quartzy stone glinting in the moonlight. They rolled around on the wildly yawing deck as Warlock fought to keep the ray gun from making a direct hit on the struggling engines. "Okay," Robin said, "I'm gonna start firing, you've got to load the arrows and hand them to me. If you can, make some more–if we only had one more set of hands," he said, wishing Edie wasn't stuck with Warlock and the makeshift tourniquet. "It's gonna take quite a few to disable that sub," and then, "Assuming this works, of course." He took the first arrow baited with a cigar and peered over the railing. Tami went back to rolling some more but the others she'd already made kept rolling around on the violently heaving deck.

"Hey," said Stephan to the native girl, and he opened his mouth. Tami looked at him quizzically, and Stephan rolled his eyes at the cigars, and then opened his mouth.

Ohhh!" She realized he could help in his own little way. Tami placed four or five cigars into his mouth, now stabilized and ready to load.

"What was that?" said Sergio, as an arrow bolt struck the armor plating of the hull, just below the gun he was operating.

"Looks like an arrow," said the other one.

"No, that music," Sergio said, and looked over at Acho Acho who had a small boom box sitting on top of that cooler he always seemed to be lugging around.

"It's the Rolling Stones," said Hans, taking aim as the yacht cut across their bow. Acho was dancing to the music,

"Some call me… Lucifer," he sang as Elo was fiddling with a SAM missile he'd found in the pile of weaponry the bodyguards had loaded on the deck of the sub. Another arrow struck the armored shield of the ray gun, and it momentarily changed tone, its hum dropping half an octave, then regaining its former whine.

"What are you doing, help your brother," yelled the ridiculous looking Kochler, in his Armani pinstripes and combat helmet.

"Yessir, General Nuisance," Acho said, saluting with his beer, "I don't care how big that chicken is, you can count on me!" and chuckled as he went to join Elo.

"Do you have to drink that vile concoction night and day, this is serious!" shouted Kochler at Acho.

"Hey, it's not just for breakfast anymore," said the unperturbed Acho, as Elo aimed the missile at the yacht.

* * * *

"I can't tell if it's working," yelled Robin, then "Duck!" as the missile rocketed through the air, striking the rear of the big ship, sending debris splintering and skittering across the deck. Tami was bleeding, a three-inch gash in her arm. "Oh no, you're hurt!" Robin dropped the bow and belly-crawled to her side.

"Don't worry about me, stop that gun!" Tami said, clutching her bicep as it bled.

I'll be fine, Robin, please, the sub, we've got to stop it!" she pleaded, and Robin picked up the crossbow. "Let's finish this," he said grimly, and went back to the rail.

"What happened?" Kochler cried, "Why did you stop firing?"

"It's jammed or something," Sergio said, checking the mechanism, and then, "Ouch! Is it supposed to be this hot?" Kochler spotted the arrow bolts, stuck to the hull and armored shield of the gun, a play-dough looking substance on their tips. He pulled at one and the slender reed easily broke off from the putty, which remained stuck to the hull of the vessel.

"Shit!" he cried, in frustration, "The bastard's are overloading the anti-gravitational balance!" He threw the arrow down and crushed it with his foot, as the engines stopped their whining, the submarine slowing to a stop.

"We got'em, we got'em!" Robin cried, and rushed to Tami's side She was starting to pale a little from loss of blood. Robin tore up to the decimated cabin, the door hanging by a hinge, swinging crazily back and forth. Edie was putting the finishing touches on Warlock, who now had a lacerated shoulder to go with his bandaged arm.

"I need help with Tami, she's hit!" he yelled and Edie threw him some remnants of Warlock's shirt.

"I've got to stay up here, he can't steer this ship with one arm," she shouted, half supporting the merc, whose wounds were beginning to take their toll. Robin ran back to Tami,

"Hang in there, Tami, we got'em!" A low rumbling came rolling across the water. Robin looked at Dr. Hollings, the cigars of anti-gravitons still in the his mouth.

"Diesel motor," Dr. Hollings said through clenched teeth, "The sub has a back up diesel motor."

Elo took careful aim as the sub regained its pursuit of the yacht, which was now taking on water, listing to port.

"Elo, listen to me carefully," said Kochler, measuring his words carefully, "I will give you and this brain-dead motherfucker of a brother money, drugs, and many other fine things if you-just-stop-that-boat."

"Pro rata?" Elo asked, taking matters much more seriously now. Kochler gave him a pained smile.

"Yes, pro rata, or course."

The mercenaries were lying in the palmettos, the fighting momentarily halted, save for sporadic sniper fire.

"They're regrouping," Conrad ran down the irregular perimeter line they had quickly formed, "Dig in, reload, call out if you need ammo." He had grabbed as many ammo boxes as he could at the guard house, and then had risked his life three times coming down the mountain, charging back into enemy fire to retrieve weapons and ammo from downed commandos. The mercs had lost Geissen to a grenade, and then Romanov, who when his gun jammed grabbed his 'roso' in one hand and a bayonet in the other, taking on two of the commandos, stopped only by a point-blank burst of automatic rifle fire. Conrad took a second to look out at the battle in the bay, the yacht limping away from the sub in a zigzag pattern. The submarine was belching black exhaust as it slowly accelerated from where it had earlier been sitting dead in the water. Somehow the kid and Warlock were fighting back if it was down to backup power. If the mercs could just hold off the commandos for just a little longer, maybe that would be enough time to trigger another miracle. He jumped into the hastily prepared foxhole as the commandos began launching grenades in preparation for the final assault, praying to his hastily prepared newfound faith.

Robin tied the bandage around Tami's arm and re-evaluated the situation. "We knocked out the power to their ray gun and sub, but their backup has them moving again. We're taking on water and soon we're gonna lose the edge in speed and quickness," he said, "That's a big problem." He looked towards the shore. "The mercs are getting ready to be overrun; they're almost at the end of their rope." He surveyed the shattered yacht, blood covering the deck. He could see Warlock, Edie holding him up as he doggedly fought to stay upright and in control of the ship. "I'm out of ideas," he said turning to the physicist, who was standing there listening, with his arms crossed, looking like he was on his way to a Halloween party, cape flowing in the moonlit breeze.

"You know, like the girl said, it seems we've seen these Robin's eggs do everything- power ray guns, turn people into birds, propel submarines," he said, "But there's one thing I haven't seen it do." He bent over and picked up one of the arrow bolts he'd loaded while Tami was tending to her arm. "Now, young Robin, is anything occurring to you?" Robin stared at Dr. Hollings, in absolute amazement.

"Yeah," he said, breaking into a huge smile, "We haven't seen it explode! And," he still couldn't believe his eyes, "You can walk!"

The U.S. Muerta Blanca chugged up to the floating palace, laying low in the calm waters of the bay. "Remember do not harm that boy!" Kochler had warned everyone again, and Orpeza chimed in,

"And don't harm the woman, either!"

"Fuck the woman," roared Kochler, losing his patience with the man.

"Do you think there's time?" asked Acho, using the fire suppressor on the end of his AK to open up another beer. The neck of the bottle broke off and a piece of glass fell down the barrel. Acho picked up the assault rifle and peered down the barrel.

"Do you think that'll hurt anything?" Elo gently removed Acho's outstretched hand's thumb off the trigger,

"You're probably okay, just as long as you keep it on safety."

"A safety, that's two points, right?" Acho asked, carefully sipping the beer with its jagged top.

The sub circled around to the other side of the ship, not a soul in sight, until the boy in the funny-looking costume came out of the cratered cabin. He wordlessly started throwing little handfuls of silly putty against the hull of the sub, the wads of dough sticking with a plop right below the bridge where Kochler and Orpeza were standing. Even as Kochler spoke, the masked kid kept methodically slamming the now useless play dough at the same spot- it was really quite touching, Kochler thought, like Tom Hanks firing his pistol at the oncoming tank in 'Saving Private Ryan.'

"What is your name, boy?" asked Kochler, signaling for all the men to lower their weapons.

"My-Name-Is-Robin!" the boy cried, taking the last of his anti-gravitation matter, a huge double-hand full and heaving it at the sub. The mad scientist looked sardonically down at the gooey clump that stuck right below his feet.

"Funny, I was expecting Superman, or perhaps Captain America," he sarcastically said. A dark piece of tarp materialized out of nowhere, and it flew off into the sea, exposing a masked man in a flowing black cape, holding a small crossbow in his hand. The arrow bolt glowed brightly with a red and blue and green incandescence, looking very much like the force field's gate.

"No, not Superman," said the apparition, "I'm...Batman!" and the bolt flew through the air, striking the center of the pulpy mass of play dough. Kochler looked down, stunned beyond belief, at the anti-neutrino's boiling and roiling in the critical mass of the anti-gravitons.

"Jump!" he yelled and flung himself in the water. Exactly two seconds later there was a deafening explosion as the threshold was reached- and then there was nothing, the sub vanishing into thin air.

Robin surfaced with Dr. Hollings in his grasp. Edie, Tami, and Warlock bobbed in the water fifty yards away, floating in the life raft they'd slipped off the opposite side of the yacht while Robin had distracted their attackers.

"Those poor men, I know they were no good, but..." Edie trailed off, "Where did they go, I mean the ship and sub exploded, but where are the pieces, it..."

"It went into another dimension," finished Stephan, "But right now we've got to help out our boys on the beach! Any ideas, Robin?" Robin looked over at the shoreline where a full scale assault by the commandos was underway, and saw that he wasn't the only one watching the battle, as the top of the mountain was rimmed with both Birimbi and Topani tribes.

"Yes, I do," he said, and turned to Tami, "Are you up for a little ride? I need a princess to join me on a distant cliff." "Why, yes I am, Prince Orakapo." Tami replied, as they flew to meet the thousand rightful inhabitants of Bonami Island.

Conrad was operating on pure animal instinct as the assault built to a crescendo. He fired at anything that moved, his rage taking control of his actions. He was aware he'd been shot, but felt no pain, just the red-hot anger of a trapped animal. He saw an arm rise out of the palmetto bushes, fifteen feet away, lobbing a grenade at his position. He leaped sideways, flushed out of his foxhole, firing into the brush indiscriminately, and was rewarded by the sweet sound of an agonized man's screams. He screamed with him as the grenade exploded and lifted him into the air- the last thing he saw were the two angels in the sky as he fell into the darkness below.

"Hold your fire, you are surrounded, Ginobi!" Ginobi looked up at hearing his name, seeing the flying boy hovering a hundred feet overhead, with a native girl in his arms, holding the megaphone that Elo had been using at the games. "Hold your fire, men!" cried Ginobi, fully aware of the explosion and subsequent disappearance of the two ships in the bay.

"Where's Kochler and the sub?" demanded the lieutenant. "They're gone, and they're not coming back," Robin said, "And if you surrender now, I promise you no harm."

"Yeah, you and what army?" Ginobi sneered, not buying into what could be a trick, an amazing trick, but a trick still the same.

"The one right behind you, Lieutenant," and the sound of a hundred AK-47's being locked and loaded on the mountainside above was one of the most convincing sounds Ginobi had ever heard, as he turned to face the loyal subjects of Orakapo.

Tami and Robin were walking down the beach, the sun rising over the still, calm waters.

"Look, Robin," Tami cried, spotting the white box. They walked up to the tree that shaded the two old men listening to a small boom box.

"How did you guys get away from the blast?" Robin asked.

"We didn't," said the white-haired Elo Acho, "We've been gone thirty-six years."

"What happened?" asked Tami incredulously in Balaluka.

"We got kicked out for illegal trafficking," Acho Acho said, taking a pull on his long neck, "for selling mushroom beer."

www.ingramcontent.com/pod-product-compliance
Lightning Source LLC
Chambersburg PA
CBHW070634310726
48982CB00001B/278
* 9 7 8 1 9 4 4 0 7 1 8 3 7 *